$2-

THE BROKEN RECORD TECHNIQUE

LEE HENDERSON

Penguin Books

PENGUIN

Published by the Penguin Group

Penguin Books Canada Ltd, 10 Alcorn Avenue, Toronto, Ontario,
Canada M4V 3B2

Penguin Books Ltd, 80 Strand, London WC2R ORL, England

Penguin Putnam Inc., 375 Hudson Street, New York, New York 10014, U.S.A.

Penguin Books Australia Ltd, 250 Camberwell Road, Camberwell,
Victoria 3124, Australia

Penguin Books (NZ) Ltd, cnr Rosedale and Airborne Roads, Albany,
Auckland 1310, New Zealand

Penguin Books Ltd, Registered Offices: Harmondsworth, Middlesex, England

First published 2002

1 3 5 7 9 10 8 6 4 2

Manufactured in Canada

NATIONAL LIBRARY OF CANADA CATALOGUING IN PUBLICATION DATA

Henderson, Lee, 1974–
The broken record technique

ISBN 0-14-100568-8

I. Title.

PS8565.E56165B76 2002   C813'.6   C2002-900191-9
PR9199.4.H45B76 2002

Visit Penguin Canada's website at **www.penguin.ca**

For my family—Alexandra, Byron & Lise, Bob & Rona, Tillie & George, all aunts, uncles, & cousins . . .

The broken record technique consists of stating repeatedly what you want in a calm, direct manner with the persistence of a broken record. You can use this technique in situations where you're unwilling to do what the other person suggests, but find yourself somewhat captive to the other person's persistence. Using the technique, you stay focused on what you want and don't give in to the other person's will. You simply state what you want as many times as you need to, without change or embellishment. Start with "I want . . ." or "I would like . . ."

Please note that the broken record technique is *not* designed to foster developing a relationship but rather to obtain what you want with a minimum of communication. It is generally *not* an appropriate technique in relationships with your spouse, partner, or close friends, although, on occasion, it can be useful with children.

—Edmond J. Bourne, *The Anxiety & Phobia Workbook*

CONTENTS

THE BROKEN RECORD TECHNIQUE

ATTEMPTS AT A GREAT RELATIONSHIP

B UT IT DIDN'T QUITE HAPPEN LIKE THAT. His name was Dave, no, it was Eaton. He was in love with June, and ditto her with him, but after a few months they realized they weren't. He met Angie through an acquaintance or through the personals or through sheer luck, and they went for corndogs and soon they were a couple. He spent the nights at her tight little bachelorette where they kissed and hugged, and she wore a gritty concoction on her face when she slept. Her hair was short and green like summer grass. Her big dream, which she'd never told anybody— and never would—was to own an electric guitar. She said, We can save money if we both use the same toothbrush. Yeah, he said. One day they went to rent a movie and she stopped at the Cult section and picked one out, but when they sat down on her hide-a-bed and watched it she pressed the stop button after the first act and turned to him and said, This isn't about cults at all.

HE MET REONE. OVER DINNER SHE SAID, Is this a diatribe, because if it is, I'd rather not, okay? He'd moved into her place and he could sense the arrangement wasn't satisfying the demands of a loving conjunction. In their apartment, she paced between the couch and the stationary bicycle and chose objects that were worthy of throwing and she threw them. These are my things you're chucking, he said. Don't do that, he said. He cried a lot during this relationship.

DANIELLE, SAMANTHA, NELLY, ROSE, Heather (glorious Heather), Eve, Mary, Twyla, Liz, Wilma (he almost married Wilma!), Jennifer, and, inexplicably, another two Twylas, etc., etc., etc. Sometimes his relationships lasted one splendid month, or a single hungry evening, or a whole year, replete with a parabola of intensities and lassitudes. The breakups were all the same or all completely different, but the result, obviously, remained a constant. He clumsily spilled pasta all over Anne's face and she slapped him and he asked her to go to hell. With Andrea it was more a problem of communication: he talked on the phone every night with his ex-girlfriend and, surprisingly, she didn't like that. He came home and found Susan dissecting his pet cat and decided that was it. Lori said, I'm so sorry, Eaton, I'm just not good enough for you, and went on to win gold in the Winter Olympics.

THEN MOLLY. GOOD GOLLY, how he loved Molly.

Awake, in bed, he swaddled and disguised himself with the floral-print cotton sheet. She touched him with one of her extravagantly long fingers. Molly: her hair was long, curly, and red; she wore it down. She wore garter-belts and fluffy jackets at the same time, and nothing else, while in bed. With the attention span of a nine-year-old and eyes like jawbreakers, Molly was hyperactive, and sometimes she gave Eaton headaches. But he loved her. He absolutely one hundred percent loved her. Dropping onto his sofa with a box of pre-wrapped yellow snack cakes under one arm, she had suddenly moved in with him. He found her hairs in the sink, they folded laundry together, she was meeting his parents. Funny thing about parents, she told his parents one day—but the joke fell on deaf ears, or, as she put it, ears that think jokes are like Q-Tips covered in tiny poisonous snakes.

(PERSONAL ACCOUNT) Well, when I heard what happened at the pool I didn't think she was so funny any more. No, that's true, I didn't think she was funny before. These are jokes? These little mean things she says? I don't know. It's hard, you raise a boy, you think, okay, he's not the sharpest tack, but you have hopes. Marrying his mother, best decision I ever made, that's right. Bull's eye! I'll tell you. So I was, understand? I was dismayed to hear about the pool, what with— When he was a kid, pools scared him. She should have known that much. Don't they talk? I wonder. My fault, really. We lived in the prairies. For miles and miles, no water. We didn't even have a bathtub. Not even a bathtub. We had a hose you put over the faucet, hang it over your head like this. Wash yourself that way.

HE TURNED IN THE SHEETS and came up beside her on the bed.
He loved her, he loved to touch her, and watch her, and listen to
her, and everything. He worked from home; so did she. At night
she performed acts of comedy and ventriloquism in the type of
local club where the majority of the audience is underage, the
owner's a former strip club proprietor in debt to someone in
another city, and the sign on the door says Laffs Galore, in brackets. The act's funny, she said, but it's not funny enough. It's funny,
he said. I know that, she said, but it's not, it isn't funny enough, is
what I'm explaining. Sometimes he felt as if his mouth opened
unaccountably like an oiled hinge and words she'd scripted came
from him in an effortless flow of set-ups for her punchlines.

He got out of bed and paced the kitchen looking for a clean
rag, and when he found one he roped it under the cold water tap
and squeezed out most of the water and brought the rag to her,
damp, cold, and laid it across her forehead. She whispered, I
think we should break up. On a table beside the bed a pale-blue
ceramic monkey with a creamy nose sat smiling at them. Break
up? he said, confused. Was this new material? he wondered, but
said nothing. On a wall in their living room there was a framed
photograph of their wedding, Eaton in a heavy black borrowed
suit, and Molly in a crinkly white dress that trailed out behind her
like unrolled toilet paper. We're married, he stressed.

Outside, rain fell and then stopped, and then more rain
splashed to earth, and then stopped. And this went on and on.

NO, IT WAS THAT SHE HAD LARYNGITIS and spoke to him only in
freaky *hasping* sounds; no, it was depression. She felt depressed, in
that hollow way, like a cave without any spelunkers. Molly asked

for a glass of water. He brought her a damp rag for her forehead and a ginger ale.

I thought I asked for water, she *hasped*. This isn't a case of semantics, there's bubbles in this.

Oh hell, he said. He gave her the glass.

She cranked her head forward off the pillows and drank some. The drink—water, ginger ale, whatever—was lukewarm, as though he'd left it sitting on the counter for half the day, or had put it in the microwave for thirty seconds, or had been holding it between his legs for half an hour. I'm sorry but really, she backed away from it. There'd been nights when she'd sit up, awake while he slept, imagining she was married to someone else. Sex with other men, what it might be like, she imagined this too. She examined the muscles around her mouth for tautness. Proceeded up her face towards the creases beside her eyes, the hatchwork of a million squints, where she tenderly ran the whorl of her finger-prints over the seven wrinkles that were breeding as she aged. She was getting older by the second and could feel its itching creep, and suddenly she felt very inconsequential and alone.

SHE WAS SEEING AN ANALYST, the source of more arguments than inner reckonings. I pay him to hear me talk, she said. He's being paid to fix your problems, he replied. No, he's being paid to listen to me. He's being paid to listen to you and figure out where the problem is and then solve it. No, that's not true, he's being paid to let me talk and get it off my chest. Get what off your chest? Things. What things? Anything. You're paying him to help you get over your problems, to fix them. You can't fix somebody. Of course you can, that's what he's paid to do. That they returned over and over to this topic matched the elliptical sway of the dialogue, like a wheel turning inside a wheel. He often broke the cycle by asking her if she'd like to see a movie. Oh no, she always said, but thanks anyway. Instead they'd settle down on the couch—not speaking but not apart—to watch reruns.

HE CAME TO HER WITH A SWEATING GLASS, ice cubes bobbling and twingling, and watched her drink. She gulped it down in near-choking swigs—it made his own throat constrict just to watch her—and put the glass back in his hand.

I'm talking concepts, she said. The concept of being single again, she said.

He smiled, grabbed her nose, and tugged it. She wasn't serious, he figured, how could she be? It was a joke, for sure. She was a comedian, after all.

DON'T YOU THINK WE SHOULD BREAK UP? she asked. We're married, he said, and looked at the floor their money had rented. I know, but it isn't working. I'm rowdy and you're something else. What am I? he asked. She stared at the ceiling. She said, You're condensed. She said, You're sweetened and condensed. He smiled, he didn't take her seriously any more.

We either have to break up or, you know, we have to get out the hammers and nails and fix this thing. She yawned.

I was thinking we could have a kid, he said.

She put a hand to her face and dragged her fingers over her eyes. No, no, that's not right, that's just crazy talk.

His eyes spun through the room and he saw objects fly through his vision. He picked up something he'd been working on and gave it to her to examine. She turned it over in her hands with a perfunctory glance.

There has to be humour, he said. I don't like to take my art too seriously, he said.

Well that's good, she said.

What does that mean?

It's just that—well, they're mementoes. They're not really art.

What do you mean? Of course they're art. He took the memento from her and put it carefully in his lap. He looked at the memento. Mementoes don't have to be art, he said. But these're different. They're pessimistic mementoes. You could be a bit more supportive.

(PERSONAL ACCOUNT) Eaton? I've known Eaton since high school. At the time I didn't actually hang out with him because of his acne, but we were, yeah, in the same Home Ec class. Spiro, the teacher'd say to me, Spiro Chete, see Eaton over there? Why don't you try and be a bit more like him? But no, no one wanted to be like Eaton. You don't know it from looking at him, you think when you see him that he's had a few kicks in the head. Not much going on up there, but no— I've seen some of his mementoes and they're, no, I think it's an interesting idea. He's very insecure. Loyal though, no grudges, I respect that. Because him and Molly were married and I thought, oh here's this guy who never had a friend in high school and then a few girlfriends that cheated on him, I blame myself, and, and anyway this knockout comes along with fingers as long as my arms, no kidding, and personally, I think it's one of those— Those kinds of moves. Don't mistake me, Eaton is fine, and Molly's just super, really fantastic Molly is, but no one was expecting them to go on forever, so no, it doesn't surprise me to hear they're

*having some troubles. I'd like to know what kind of troubles. My secret
to keeping a relationship fresh? I'd have to say drugs.*

WERE THERE ANY MEN who wore football armour and feather
chaps, Molly wondered, men with feet like rubber boots, capped
teeth, eyes as slick and black as vinyl pants, men drunk with
hubris who'd take her to clubs where the women pocked the floor
with stilettos and the mustachioed bartenders carried guns?
Sometimes she wanted a crazy man who'd throw money at her
and drive a car with vanity plates. Wild men. Other times,
though, she wanted a man like Eaton, with his bizarre prism of
anxiety, his peculiar misanthropy, and on those days she enjoyed
being married to him. Was it a comedy to expect someone to
fulfill all your needs, or was that what friends and pornography
were for?

Not for the first time, lately, she was feeling the weight of all
her past performances, the misjudgments and fatigue of humour,
the fleeting and capricious chances she'd turned down or missed
at a more glamorous life than this; and yet here she was with
Eaton, in a small rented house in a cold part of the city.

She peeled back the bed coverings and made her way down the
hall towards the bathroom, losing her balance at the staircase.
For a moment it could have been a dance, but then it was obvious
she was about to fall down the stairs. Oh shit. She screwed around
at the edge of the stairway, arms paddling the air to keep herself
from falling, swinging haphazardly towards the banister, Help,
reaching out and grabbing along the wall and finding the frame
of a clown painting, Help! pulling it off its nail; reeling backwards, she tossed the clown art and began to stumble down the

stairs facing the wrong way. Her head thocked against the banister as she skipped and rolled down the staircase; the wood
cracked and splintered and the support beam wobbled and split.
Finding the floor, she lay on her back and felt a low throb send
ripple after ripple over her skull.

I'm okay, she groaned. Her hands checked her body. Small
orbs of pain and ache revealed themselves.

Oh golly, he said, diving down the stairs towards her, I'll get
you some painkillers. She saw him almost run into a wall trying
to find the kitchen.

THERE WERE OTHER OPTIONS, they didn't have to break up. She
lay in bed and laughed in a faint and parabolic way as he dabbed
her stomach with the rag.

Basically, do you love me? Molly asked.

You betcha, he croaked. They kissed each other like seals do,
nipping and rubbing lips and cheeks, staying in bed all day, never
going out. Piles of laundry to do, a sink full of dishes to be
cleaned. A bathroom full of toothpaste smears and lonely hairs.
Dust. They ignored all their marital duties for a long furry day of
sickness and health, of tending and being tended to, and their
only company was the sound of the street outside their window,
the rain. The End.

HOT FUCKING SHIT, SHE SCREAMED, and pinwheeled dizzily,
suddenly, to tip over the stairs, backwards-stepping down the
flight. As she fell—or rather, stepped crazily—she thought of
Eaton in their room concentrating on his sketches for new
mementoes and wondered how long she would lie unconscious

before he noticed. But when suddenly there were no more stairs, she understood that somehow she'd never actually lost her footing. She was still alive. Eaton came running and looked down at her from the top of the stairs.

I thought you were ripping the carpet up, he said. You okay? he said. I could have died, she said and gagged on a laugh. She examined herself standing there like it was an unbelievable truth. But you didn't die, he said. You're okay, he said. Sure, she said. I'm fine, but you didn't see me—what I was doing just now? It felt like I was breakdancing down a cliff. Ha ha, he said. No, she said, I'm serious.

When he came down and held her she realized she was trembling against him and almost gave in to it and slipped down faintly between his arms. He rubbed her head, whispered into the twist of her ear, This is freaking me out.

HOLD ON, EATON SAID INTO THE TELEPHONE and depressed the star button. Hello?

It was his high school friend Spiro Chete, or it was Spiro Chete's newest girlfriend, Petra.

Nothing, Eaton said into the phone. Playing video games, he said.

Spiro Chete raised cooking bullfrogs in his basement in five seventy-two-gallon fish tanks full of viscid water. Some of the bullfrogs were mottled emerald green and deep algae-coloured, and others were dark and carbuncled, skin percolating with knobs. They were indifferent creatures, with no misguided prospects for a good life. They'd kick and stretch over one another, patiently blinking. The dankest, most fleshy basement imaginable.

I think we'd like to do that, Eaton said. Molly's been talking about divorce, so— Hold on, he said. He put his hand over the bottom joint of the phone and said to Molly, You want to go swimming?

She looked at him. No. Look at me, she said. I can barely speak, she *hasped*, stretching out her raw throat to remind him of her illness. I'm not joking here.

Whatever, he said to her. Swim'd do you some good.

I don't want to go swimming, see, this, this is the problem. What problem? he said, still holding his hand over the phone, there's no problem. She said, The problem is that, you know, you think only of yourself. Besides, she continued, public pools are like half-submerged food courts, and we need to talk. You need to listen to me.

This is a wave pool, he said. Water's good for the muscles. The things, the glands. He removed his hand from the receiver. She waved her arms in the air, a pillow gripped in her fingers like a pudgy semaphore flag. Sure, he said. We'll go swimming.

SHE TOLD HIM SHE THOUGHT A SWIM would help her throat, no, her fever, or her bruises from the fall. Her depression. He was terrified of swimming, the crowds, the nakedness. Especially the nakedness. He was scared of the exposure, he told her. The senseless humiliation of standing in water with nothing on but a pair of shiny underwear. The irreparable damage to one's modesty. And on top of that, the possibility of drowning. When she put the receiver back in its cradle after speaking with Spiro, he was silent. He folded up on the bottom steps of the stairway and hugged the banister, and his eyes were dead pools, bloodless voids. Oh come on, don't be scared, she said. He thought about his ex-girlfriends, and where they might be, and what they looked like, and he thought about his future, and his future was a million nights and a million more, and he wondered if he'd ever be successful, or happy. I think we should break up, he said. There was a pause. She stepped back from him. Huh? she said. He took a long breath through his nostrils, raked his hands through his hair. I don't know, he said, it's just an idea. A pretty damn new and weird idea I'd have to say, she said. She leaned back and picked up a glass and stared at its bottom. Out of the blue you say this, she yipped.

THEIR FRIENDS, SPIRO CHETE AND PETRA—illegally parked out front of their house—came up the walk, sat down on their couch. Spiro Chete had on a severe glove that immobilized his hand from the wrist to the thumb. There was no mistaking Spiro's odour, which was inexorably perfumed by the hundreds of *Rana catesbiana* he'd raised over the years, a vulgar marshy funk that steadied on him like a low blue fog over wet grass. Petra sat down, pressed back a few stray tendrils of her cropped black hair, crossed one long leg over the other, protracted a razor, and asked if she could remove some pictures she'd eyed in the newspapers on their coffee table.

The sexual impulse is heightened by the fluid motion of a wave parabola, Petra said, turning the razor around the antlers of a moose. As she cut away the moose from the paper, her shoulders twisted back and forth and her torso followed; she seemed to be uncorking the sofa.

Are you telling me that a wave pool is going to, going to give me an orgasm? Because if that's what you're telling me—

No, I meant, that's not what I meant, Petra said, looking at Eaton. We're all sexual beings, I just meant that—

Because I can take a dildo into the tub and—

You have a dildo? Spiro said.

No, Molly said, and turned to leave the room. Where do you keep your sense of humour, Spiro, she asked, in a what? in the corpse of a dog?

I, no, I have a sense of humour.

Eaton watched Petra remove her wallet from her totebag and unzip it and slip the moose between two bills. Once the moose was in its place, from another segment of her wallet out came warty little mushrooms.

Those, Spiro Chete said, referring to the mushrooms, are super fantastic.

UNINVITED FRIENDS CAME OVER, kicked their heels up, cut their papers up, had an idea about what they should do for the day. Go swimming at the wave pool.

I don't want to go swimming, Molly said. I've got enough wrinkles already.

My broken leg needs the warmth, their friend Spiro Chete said. He lifted his leg in both hands and attended to its crooked-ness; it cambered at the knee something fierce. The doctor set it wrong, he said, and I need physio to keep the muscles from decaying along the shin.

A wave is very sexual, said Petra. The wet force against your belly and whatnot.

I don't swim, Molly said from the kitchen, where she was filtering tap water.

IT MIGHT HAVE BEEN RAINING, although it might have been sunny. Alone, past a newly constructed highway and a coil of overpasses, in the community centre's parking lot, they got out of their hatchback and Eaton slammed the door and winced and said he was sorry.

I didn't want to go swimming, she said—or it was he who said, I don't want to go swimming. One of them said it.

SHE PARKED THE CAR AND THEY SAT in the car and neither one made any move to get out, and what was there to say? She gestured for the radio and then pulled back quickly and found a place for her hands between her legs. Are we going to break up? they both wondered. He was staring out the windshield, across the parking lot, to the scalp-coloured brick walls of the community centre. Finally Molly got out of the car, unlatched the trunk, and lugged out their duffle bag.

Bending to look him in the face through the window, she said, Sometimes you make me so uncomfortable I think I might puke.

Well I'm sorry, but that's your problem.

Don't get all defensive.

Don't get all defensive. You tell me I make you puke and I'm supposed to what?

I'm sorry, I didn't mean it that way.

What way did you mean it? It's a pretty oblique compliment.

They had driven for an hour and a half, no, twenty minutes, to spend an afternoon in the new tropical-themed wave pool.

THERE WERE LONG ARTERIAL FLUMES in semi-opaque aqua-green that coiled in and out of the ceiling and walls of the wave pool like

stitching around the building's exterior. The slides seemed
designed for some purpose other than fun, like pneumatic
message tubes dispatching endless tributaries of water and children at regular intervals into frothing pools. There were laminated vinyl palm trees rooted in ossified yellow jelly in the shape
of rocks along the tiled beaches. A bellicose lifeguard in tight
swim trunks sat atop a great chair. Mosaics of tropical scenes on
the walls, sky and mountain scenes with more palm trees as
frames. A giant sun with a face. A play pool for infants, where the
water came up only so high. Turbulent chemical-blue Jacuzzis
with rubberized spines along their rims for heads and necks to fit
into. Tire swings attached to polymer ropes. Waves autonomous
of the moon every twelve minutes, swooning and seemingly
depthful. At the pool floor, renditions of the sea's multitude.
Killer whales, orange cephalopods, shellfish, the grey nougat of
bathyspheres.

THEY HAD YET TO LEAVE THEIR CAR. Rain clubbed the roof and
the humidity of their own breathing had fogged up the windows
and little kids came running by soaking wet, either from the
awesome rain or the awesome wave pool.

He held the steering wheel in both hands and sniffed. She was
frustrated; he rubbed his nose. She got out. From the trunk she
removed the duffle bag. She opened his door and he stood and
took the bag. As he prodded the effects in the duffle bag, Molly
stretched the muscles in her hands, flicking her fingers anxiously
in the air. She said she wasn't comfortable putting on some
bathing suit in front of thousands of people, especially if he was
going to just wear his jeans and a T-shirt.

I'M ALL ANXIOUS, HE SAID. I wish I'd brought some sedatives. Do you have any on you? he asked. No, sorry, can I do anything to help? she asked. Just let me get through this, just let me focus, don't touch me.

I'm worried about you, she said.

THEY STOOD BESIDE THEIR CAR, Eaton near to having either a mental breakthrough or breakdown, he wouldn't know for sure until it hit. She took him by the arm and nudged him forward but his feet didn't follow. He thought of a turtle, the tiled carapace so utterly impenetrable and yet when you turn it over—you find another shell underneath, another turtle clenched below, and so where is that soft underbelly when two turtles join? What a beautiful thought. He was about to describe it to her when she said:

I'm trying to help our relationship, bucko. See me helping.

Sure, yes. Think about—

Lend a hand.

No, yes, I'm trying.

No you're not. Yes I am. No, you're just standing there. I'm trying. No you're not. Yes I am. This isn't funny, I can see you're not trying. You're not looking hard enough, because I'm trying very hard actually. Do you care about us at all? What's that supposed to mean? You know perfectly well. Of course I care. Then start lifting those feet off the ground like in a walking motion before I bitch-slap you, Eaton. I'm trying. No you're not. Yes I am.

THE SKY WAS WOUNDED AND SWOLLEN with cloud and it rained dark heavy pellets.

You won't let me help you, she said. This nervous thing of yours is scaring me. She looked at him and could see tinselly wet rings around his eyes. She withdrew the keys from the ignition, shut the car door with him still sitting there with his seat belt on, went swimming.

(PERSONAL ACCOUNT) Oh yeah. I was there with my kids. I've got three kids, two boys and a girl. Oh, and my nephew. He's not one of my kids in a technical way, but I'm his legal guardian. He's not one of my personal kids, thank the lord, but he was with us so there was the five of us, not including my husband, Bertie, because he didn't go swimming. Six of us in the car. All Bertie did was sit at one of them picnic tables they got set up and drink amaretto coffee. We were meeting some friends there who had some kids. It was a sunny enough day to melt your makeup off. I'd say in total I'd say twenty kids. Twenty to thirty. Hot enough to fry an egg on your ass. Well, no, wait a minute, that doesn't sound right at all. Closer to maybe twelve kids. It felt like fifty by the end of the afternoon—especially after my nephew's little fiasco.

I saw her, when? In the change room I first saw her. I don't normally, you know, snoop when people get changed. It's not a private place a change room and I'm no snooper normally. But anyways that's right, I did notice this woman because she was, how do you put it? She was giving herself an examination in the mirror? You know, the way a doctor will do, lift up the arm and press around and look for lumps? She was doing that. So it was hard not to watch her. My sister, god bless, died of that cancer and so I was thinking about that. And I got to admit that I'm always forgetting to give myself those self-examinations. I got in a bit of a panic. I started thinking, oh jeepers, when was the last time I'd given myself a checkup, when was the last time I'd seen the doctor, and

I started to feel tingly and a bit sore there? All I could think about was my breasts and what might be in them. I tell you, now I was nervous. This is serious business, them checkups, I know, and I'm always forget-ting. I'm like, what do you say? Like an elephant, what? How's it go? So when we got to the pool I let the kids go off and muck around and I crouched down in the water when the waves started and no one was looking and put my hand under my bathing suit there and gave myself an examination. Remember like an elephant, is that right? Anyways, that's when I noticed that this woman, the one I'd seen in the change room who'd sparked all this up in me, was talking with this man who was wearing, get this: jeans and a T-shirt—in the pool. Like, no bathing suit no nothing. Jeans and a T-shirt like. And here I am doing this and here's this man just sitting in the shallow part, looking cross-eyed queer in a pair of wet jeans. I can tell you he looked mentally unfit to be at a wave pool. He looked psycho, like TV psycho. I felt so stupid getting in a big tizzy and feeling myself up in public and all because of some woman whose boyfriend or whatever was mentally unfit to be at a wave pool. It's a family-oriented place. It's for enjoyment.

SPIRO LIMPED OVER TO A LOCKER and climbed out of his pants, no undershorts on underneath, just his bare genitals dangling like a creepy surprise. Eaton drew down his jeans and pulled them over his feet and put them on a bench. The locker room showcased all the different stages of the male anatomy—the bendy little-boy bodies, the crooked fucked-over teen bodies, the obesity of middle age—and steam came in raggedy milty webs from the shower room. He could perceive the effects of the mushrooms now. In a mirror stood Eaton's reflection, and that body in front of him—his own example of the male form—he saw as being slick like paint and funny like a cartoon.

Reflected in the mirror was the body he had forgotten was his own, the skin and hair that was his and not Molly's. He touched his hinder parts. He squished a testicle up into his abdomen and watched it gradually pull itself out again. Followed that tender spine below his scrotum that met his anus; he kneaded his penis like a roll of flatbread dough.

Good gravy, he said.

SPIRO CHETE AND EATON went to the men's change room while Petra and Molly went to the women's, and all Spiro had to do was pull off his pants and shirt and he was ready. He had his bathing suit on underneath his denim trousers. He said, What? I like to be prepared, I don't like changing in the locker room, big deal. His bathing suit was a tiny spandex number that made his legs appear distended like drools of caramel rolled in hair.

I'm super fucked, Spiro said, or he said, What do you think of Petra? He unsnapped his wrist protector and the skin underneath was colourless and veiny.

I think I'll just wear this to swim, Eaton answered.

What, Spiro said, just your outside clothes?

Yeah. Eaton glanced over his shoulder. He saw his face in a mirror and he saw his face covered with children. Over the other shoulder he saw dozens of boys in various states of undress.

Well, what do you think of Petra?

Don't like that razor of hers.

Oh, and Molly's just perfect I guess.

That's not what I said.

Better believe it, Spiro said. But, you know what, hey? When

Petra and I are having sex? Are you listening?

Don't try and give me sex advice because that's just perverted.

No. No. I'm saying that when Petra and I are having sex, okay, no, it's like her face goes like all ugly. She's great-looking and smart and etcetera etcetera, and I'm not complaining about the sex itself. It's good. Infrequent, but good. Hey, tell me how many times a month you guys have sex.

No.

Don't give me that face. Come on. Hey look, here we are in a locker room: how many times are we going to get to have genuine locker-room talk in a locker room?

I don't know. Eaton thought about it. Well, lately maybe twice a month.

Really. Oh. Sorry to hear that. I guess I shouldn't complain. But it's just that when we're having sex it's like these whole new muscles start working in her face. Really. It's horrendous. But twice a month. Okay.

They cranked on their showers and stood beneath them and soaked in the hot water. Spiro in his little bathing suit and Eaton in his black jeans and T-shirt. While a spray of water kneaded his neck and arms, he thought about a massage Molly had once given him, which had led to delightful sex. Spiro fussed with his lips.

Are my lips super fat right now?

AS EATON AND SPIRO WENT to the men's locker room, Molly and Petra pushed through the doors of the women's. They stepped up to a bench and began stripping off clothes, and as more bare skin became unprotected they respectfully turned away from one another. But Molly had to reach back to her locker door to get her bathing suit and she found herself taking a peek at Petra—she couldn't help but be curious, having had no sisters. Or possibly concealing her interest in Petra's body was not even an issue for Molly, who, as they undressed, stood and faced Petra and stared at her body like she was a final exam.

Is that a swastika?

Oh, god, Petra said and covered the tattoo on her arm. Don't look at that.

She also saw that Petra shaved her pubes into a faultless isosceles triangle.

Petra said, You look bad.

I have a fever. She said, I'm tripping. She said, I think I want a divorce.

All around them little girls with round stomachs and the first pinchings of breasts were chasing each other through the locker room, and their harried mothers sat on the benches and slipped rubber sandals over their heels and tried to persuade their bums back inside the elastic of their bikini bottoms.

THEY DID NOT LOOK AT EACH OTHER while undressing for the pool. When Molly finally circled around she saw that Petra was wearing a peculiar bathing suit: a purple bikini, only the top was like a tiny spandex short-sleeved shirt.

That's a curious bathing suit, I've never seen one like that, Molly said.

Petra said, I bought this from a catalogue, do you like it?

It's got sleeves.

That's why I liked it. I've got a thing for sleeves. Are you feeling okay, you sick?

Molly discovered she was sitting down. I slipped and bonked my head, I'm fine.

Is it hard being a comedienne? Petra asked.

The hardest part is making people laugh, Molly said, and Petra nodded, and didn't laugh.

THEY HEADED FOR THE SHOWERS and had to stand in line on the cool sweating tiles outside the shower room while a group of young girls took theirs. Molly felt the mushrooms breaming the walls of her face.

How many men have you had sex with? Molly suddenly asked.

Don't even ask me that. My dad booked musical acts.

Oh.

Now, Spiro Chete. A fine lay. I'd say on a scale of ten with ten being unrestrained totally gaga orgasm, I'd give Spiro about a seven. But Molly, I mean, I'm the first to admit that Spiro is not good-looking. It's almost too easy to call him homely. I've described him to people as grainy. Which is why I think this gives you an advantage, sexually, with Eaton. He's, you know, he's better-looking, he's good-looking. Anyway, when we're having sex—and hey, by the way, just out of curiosity. If it's not too, you know, private. How often are you guys doing it?

Oh no, geez, I'd say maybe twice a month max. Maximum.

Really. Well. I was going to say Spiro and I had infrequent sex but I guess— The point is, when we're having sex, it's like you don't even know the meaning of ugly. Spiro is like something swept off the killing floor of a slaughterhouse. He's a borderline emetic at his climax.

Too bad, Molly said and rinsed her hair. I think the worst for me is that Eaton sometimes looks like he's about to cry.

Oh give me a break. About to cry. Spiro sobs. Like his whole body is convulsing and he can't find his breath.

A KID BLEW OUT THE END OF A FLUME and kicked Eaton in the head. He fell backwards into the water. He stood up, drenched, and butted the heel of his hand against the kid's face. The kid just laughed at him. What kind of bathing trunks is jeans! the kid honked. Another kid came down the slide and kicked him in the kidney. He walked slump-shouldered over to the shallow end and sat on a ledge and let water lap over his calves. Every twenty seconds a child swung over the pool on a tire swing and landed with a crack of water. He saw a lifeguard in tight red shorts sitting on a great chair over the pool and watched as the lids to his eyes drew shut and his jaw clacked open and he shook himself awake again—over and over. Eaton looked out the wall of windows and saw the rain slashing against the glass and began to shiver.

Why'd you do that to my brother!? a girl said to him.

Fuck you, he told her. The waves started.

AN OLD LADY WITH A PINK RUBBER SHOWER CAP wigged over her skull surfaced with a splash and blinked her eyes behind a pair of green-tinted goggles. She opened her mouth and there were a few teeth in there, and suddenly she sneezed wetly all over Molly's legs.

Oh, so sorry, the old lady said, and splashed some water on Molly to rinse away the sneeze.

HE SAT WITH PETRA IN THE HOT TUB, just the two of them and the frizz of bubbles, and Eaton put the crook of his neck in the moulded leatherette dent and watched the kids fall from the tire swing into the giant apocryphal surf. He could feel Petra beside him, looking him up and down.

Why don't you do that? she said, nodding to the tire swing.

What? Oh, no. His motorcycle shirt bloomed around him in the gurgling water and he kept having to force it under. I'm afraid of oscillation, he said.

She laughed. A chain of bubbles brought her closer to him, her feet and calves swimming to the surface and descending again, toes last. There was a hand on his knee. I think I'm high, she said.

He kept staring up at the kids; he was smiling, and things started to take on a flat look. The kids swung back and forth and then let go, fell with wild gesticulation.

He said, I've heard that at this heat semen curdles instantly.

She laughed again. Ha ha, she said, ha.

SHE BENT HER HEAD BACK and concentrated on the bubbles wiggling up her body, and the heat exhaling from her ears, and the little boys on the tire swing screaming like apes as they fell into combers and breakers. She sat with Petra's boyfriend Spiro. She'd watched him climb in with his one wonky leg bending funny as he did it.

Why don't you do that? Spiro said, nodding to the kids on the tire swing.

Oh no, she said. Pendulous movement gives me panic attacks.

He laughed. He put a hand very casually on her knee and for a while they sat like that without talking, just heating up and frothing over. Bubbles emerged and drove across the surface of the water and then disappeared. Delicate gurgling water lapped against her neck and she considered herself a single woman for a moment, god, single, what did it even mean, like a finger disconnecting from the muscles of the hand.

I think I might be high, she said.

He looked at her, and without laughing or even turning a smile he leaned over her and gave her thigh a good squeeze and said, Do you, I mean, is that an advance or— Because I find you very— He was working fast, the hand on her leg was somehow, without losing any of its grip, finding its way towards her groin. He was breathing through his mouth.

Forget it, she said, and shook her leg from his grasp, which had suddenly and ickily felt like the hand of a man who worked with toads.

OR SPIRO CHETE AND EATON were in the Jacuzzi hot tub with their heads nestled in the leatherette moulding watching boys flip into the waves off the tire swing.

Why don't we do that any more? Eaton said.

Let's do it, Spiro said.

The truth is, Spiro, Eaton said, I'm afraid of deep water, he said.

They watched a little boy climb on to the wheel, carefully putting his legs through the hole and then lifting off the ramp and swinging back and forth over the clapping waves, the deep bowls between waves, the little arms and legs of children paddling away beneath him.

As the boy released from the swing his leg accidentally hooked in the tire. He dangled there like a pendant over the water. Then he fell too close to the edge head first, a glassy burst of water and then nothing. Eaton looked to the lifeguard, who he saw was fast asleep, head cocked back in his chair and his mouth wide open, whistle draped off his shoulder.

Both Eaton and Spiro stood up and watched the water for signs of the boy.

They raced through the shallow end and Spiro leapt forward and carved into the deeper water where the waves were squashing against the tiled cliffs and pulling back again forcefully. Eaton remained standing in the shallow water up to his thighs. I'm trembling, Eaton said quietly to himself, and turned his hands in front of his face. I feel like I'm going to faint, he said. The water pushed against his legs.

Come on, Spiro screamed from out in the wavy wavy water.

Spiro called to Molly and Petra for help, and they met him in the water and soon they were all searching. All except for Eaton.

There he is! Molly screamed and pointed into the water below her. She began to weep, and she looked to Eaton as if begging him to respond to some question she knew he didn't know the answer to.

Eaton stood there, watched Spiro close in on the point where the little boy fell. He watched Spiro sew into the water, legs kicking up and pushing down into the pool. He waited for Spiro to surface, and when he did, without the boy, now it was Eaton who burst into tears.

What are you doing? Spiro shook his arms in the air at Eaton and then dove again.

Taking a desperate step forward Eaton felt his gut turn over. Help, he cried. Help. Help. Help. Help. Help. Help. Help. Help. Help. Help. Help. Help. Help. Help. Help. The lifeguard shuddered awake, looked around as if he wasn't sure where he was, and then suddenly, clearly in a panic, stood and looked over the pool. Eaton caught his attention and pointed to Spiro dragging the little boy slowly towards the shore. Oh great, the lifeguard said, and he dove into the pool and caught up with Spiro as they reached shallow water. Back off everybody, he said and began to resuscitate the child.

POSSIBLY IT WAS THAT THE LITTLE BOY had hooked his legs into the tire swing, and as he released from the ramp his head jerked back and clipped the end of the ramp and it dazed him momentarily, just long enough for him to lose his balance and fall half-conscious into the pool. And it was Molly and Eaton sitting in the Jacuzzi hot tub together, trying to resuscitate their relationship.

She held his leg. I love you, she said.

He nodded. Me too, he said.

You're impossible, she said and pushed him away. If I bellowed in your ear do you think that rubbery little brain of yours would hear me? I'm talking serious here.

How do I know when you're serious? I am too. I'm sorry. I love you.

Do you?

Yes. I mean, yes.

She sighed. Am I just a set of funny fingers to you or is there something else you find attractive? He laughed and put her fingers in his hands and regarded each digit with care. It was at that point that the little boy began to fall, and upon landing sank and did not surface again. They ran, they ran without even realizing they were running. Molly kept going farther and farther into the rumpling of waves and Eaton found he could go no deeper than up to his thighs before starting to freak out. He stood and fiddled with the seam of his shirt and his drenched jeans burned against his skin.

You've got to help me find him, she screamed to Eaton. I can't find him.

He took another step and trembled and collapsed like a foolish puppet, coughed on chlorinated water. Oh, he moaned. Or it was Molly who moaned. Where was the boy, where was he?

The lifeguard awoke as a bunch of kids rattled his great chair, wailing. S.O.S., the kids wailed, S.O.S. They'd made the little boy's emergency into a kind of game. S.O.S. S.O.S. S.O.S. S.O.S. S.O.S. S.O.S. S.O.S. S.O.S. S.O.S. S.O.S. S.O.S., and when Eaton saw them finally wake the lifeguard up Molly had already pulled the boy to the shallow end. The lifeguard met her there and resuscitated the child.

That's it, Molly said between gasps, her hands on her knees. You're useless. You're the most useless, I can't stand you. That is it.

Eaton followed a few paces behind her as she walked away, and then he stopped, resigned himself to watch her pass beyond the entrance to the women's locker room and leave him. Behind him an enormous crowd had formed around the sputtering little boy, an entire community of poolers, but he didn't hear them. There was nobody around. He was alone. Has she left me, he wondered, or did she just go to change?

PETRA SAVED HIM. Eaton stood and watched, feeling tremendously stupid and incapable. What the heck is my problem? he wondered. She tore out into the water and found him instantly, took him to the shallow end and resuscitated him and turned him on his side and let him barf up warm blue water. Are you okay?

Yes, I'm fine.

Do you have some family, a mom or dad? Petra asked.

I've got one uncle and one aunt. He pointed to a table where his uncle sat reading a snooker magazine, and she told the kid to go rest on one of those vinyl chairs with him.

You people are so useless, Petra said. What the hell were you doing? she said to Eaton.

Eaton started to say something but found there were no words in him. He had met his limitations and they had shaken his hand and laughed in his face. Har-dee-har-har.

And you two. She pointed to Molly and Spiro. Fondling each other like fucking sea monkeys over there in that bubble bath. She put her hands on Spiro's chest and pushed him back into the water.

Now that's jumping to conclusions, Spiro said, climbing to his feet. I would have saved the kid but except for this damn wrist. He waved his pale forearm at her. I can't exactly swim with my tendons like this, he said.

Shut up, Petra said. She took Spiro by the arm and swung him around and kicked him down into the water again.

Thank you, said a woman who introduced herself to Petra as the boy's aunt. That little punk is always getting himself into these jams. But thanks all the same.

No problem.

IN THE JACUZZI HOT TUB Eaton was watching the little boy swing back and forth from one leg and then drop to the water, while

Molly said, All our problems are just a big misunderstanding. It's like a big preconceived event, you know, made to look natural in unnatural surroundings. I love you. I always have.

Hold on, Eaton said, and stood up and examined the water's surface for signs of the little boy. Okay fine, Molly said and stood up, don't listen to me. She looked out to where Eaton was looking. What is it, Eaton? she said. He leapt out of the tub and ran to the wave pool, skipping his feet through the shallow water and forcing his legs into the deeper waves. And suddenly he stopped. He felt a tremble work its way from his scalp down ruggedly through his stomach, his colon, his knees.

He dove into the water. It happened before he could think, before he could lobby against the impulse. He began to do something he hadn't done since he was a boy. He felt ridiculous, but he was doing it: he was dog-paddling—it was the only way he knew how to swim.

He saw a wave bring the boy close to the surface and he stretched an arm out and took the boy by the ear and pulled his head out of the water and lifted him on one shoulder and dog-paddled back to the shoreline. His heart was thudding and his arms were burning and sore and somehow he'd shed his jeans as he'd swum and now his Y-front briefs were all he had on below the waist and he noticed how wonderful and slick the water felt going past his legs. And when he got to the tiled beach and laid the boy down the first thing he did was strip his shirt off, and then he knelt beside the boy and realized he didn't know how to perform CPR.

A woman jumped out of the water and ran towards Molly and Eaton. She was screaming and her bathing suit had crawled off one of her breasts and the bare breast wagged in a funny way as she ran.

Oh my god that's my kid, she cried, her naked breast still naked. That's my little boy, she cried. Is he dead or something? What, is he dead? Oh god. That's my, I'm his legal guardian. I've killed him, the little pecker. I've killed him. She screamed and cried like this and with her one bare breast it looked to Eaton like she was wearing a giant eye patch on her chest.

How do you do this? he said to Molly.

Molly crouched beside him and stared at the boy, who looked dead.

I think it's too late, she said and began to cry. He's dead.

No he isn't, Eaton said. Is he? He isn't dead. He broke open the kid's mouth and hesitated. He looked at the kid's mouth.

Do you have a mirror or something? he said to Molly. We could check to see if it, you know, fogs up.

She checked her bathing suit. No, she said. Sorry.

Oh god, the woman said. I've got a mirror in my bag. Why didn't I bring it with me to the pool it's in my locker, I should go get it. Should I go get it?

Good gravy, Eaton said. He looked as far down the kid's throat as he could, as if trying to find the path to his lungs. Here goes nothing, he said, and put his lips to the kid's lips and closed his eyes and blew a big huff into the boy's mouth.

Nothing. He looked at the boy's face and he thought he could see the skin turning slowly greyer and more slack. He put his mouth down over the boy's mouth again and blew in another time. He watched the boy's chest expand and retract. Again nothing happened. He put his hands on the little boy's chest and pushed, something he also remembered you could do. He felt like a faker, trying to revive a boy like this. He'd had no experience. He was going on a cheap and drugged memory, on diagrams he half remembered and stories he'd overheard. His relationship to emergency aid was spurious at best, and yet he felt he had no choice. It was not about succeeding, it was about saving. And here he was. He gave the little boy's chest another push.

Cough cough cough, the little boy said, and puked up a couple cupfuls of warm blue water. They turned him on his side and patted his back and he gurgled out a bit more water and then wiped his mouth and looked up at Eaton with a confused expression.

Yuck, he said and wiped his mouth. Who are you?

I'm Eaton, he said. This is Molly, he said and pointed to Molly. Hi.

Hi, the little boy said.

Jesus, Benny, the woman said and picked him up by one arm. What kind of trick was that, Benny? What'd you think you were proving pulling a stunt like that?

What happened? Benny said.

What happened? the woman said. She looked down at the kid and held him by the shoulders. She shook her head and then burst out crying. She picked Benny up in her arms and held him there and cried and Benny started to cry too.

I'm sorry, Benny said, I'm sorry.

It's not your fault, she said. Oh, Benny, she said. She held him in her arms and combed his hair with her fingers.

(PERSONAL ACCOUNT) *Yeah, I was at the wave pool, and I almost drowned all right. But nobody came and rescued me. I'm an only* *child and I'm living with my aunt and uncle and my cousins since I was four because my parents went cruising. What happened was that, what happened was that I had these calluses on my feet from my rubber boots? You know what calluses are? Skin that's tough because of rubbing. And in the water they get softer so that's when if you want you can pull them off and chew them. So I was riding the tire swing and I had one in my mouth, right? And I had my arms like this and my legs like this and I was chewing a callus also. But the waves were started and I was nervous about falling and on the tire swing I kind of choked on the callus in my throat. And I also peed too because of being nervous [laughs]. About thinking I was going to drowned, that's why. I fell in the pool and smacked something and I was helding my breath and a wave pushed me all the way to the shallow part and underneath the water I bumped up somebody wearing jean pants. I looked up at them and they were looking nervous also and I choked some more on the skin and then I barfed up the callus and lots and lots of water too. And then the guy with the jeans helped me barf by patting my back. And I'm the only one who saved my life because I can held my breath for a very very very very long time, probably five minutes. Or more even. Want to see? Want to see me hold my breath? I can, watch. Want to see?*

THEY SAT ON THE EDGE of the play pool and watched the infants scream and splash and chew on plastic rings and the nipples of inflatable dinosaurs. Droopy mothers led their babies around by the hand, helping their kids to walk. The babies took unbalanced steps, sometimes only scraping their toes along the surface of the shallow water.

Ga, a baby said. Ga.

Eaton had his head down, was looking between his legs at the water burbling past his feet. She sat beside him and didn't speak. Still he did not know if she was leaving him, if the woman beside him was really there, or whether in a moment he would look and see her gone.

He had swum out with Molly, despite the terrible feeling in his stomach. But they couldn't find him. The water was dark and surging. It caught them in tense pockets and separated them. Eaton was scared. When he kicked his feet he could not feel the bottom and he knew it was somewhere far far beneath him, and his chin kept dipping under the water when a wave rolled past and water would get in his mouth and he was scared he was going to drown.

He's right below you, she told him.

I don't know how.

You've got to, she said and coughed. I took in some water, she coughed again.

He paddled on the surface and looked at the water. She begged him to do it, and he finally did. He went under, and holding his breath very tightly in his chest he pushed into the water, and he saw the boy and he swam towards him. He was just floating there, casually wending in the current. It all seemed pleasant and futuristic. He was still digging through the water when he caught sight of another man—much bigger than him and much faster— coming up beside him, and as Eaton grabbed the elastic on the boy's bathing suit so did this other man. Eaton tried to pull the boy up but the other man tried to pull him the other way. He was confused. They tugged the little boy back and forth under the water. The kid's body shook and his hair undulated like seaweed and his legs flapped. All Eaton could think was that he had to save this kid, and he didn't know what this other man was trying to do. He considered it a possibility that he was hallucinating. The other man bared his teeth, underwater, and gave the little boy a fierce yank, and the bathing suit's elastic unthreaded and broke off and suddenly that was all Eaton had left. Suspended underwater, Eaton held only a white elastic covered in patches of green Hawaiian bathing-suit fabric, and after seeing a field of shadowy legs kicking above his head, he realized he was underwater and about to take in a breath; it dawned on him that he was about to drown. He tried wildly to bring himself to the surface and it seemed to take forever and his whole body was shrieking for a breath. Water bulged and he came up and gasped. A black sparkling void filled his head and he almost fainted straight away. With Molly's help he found his way to the shallow end and went and sat in a corner.

What the fuck did you think you were doing? the lifeguard yelled at Eaton while he pushed the little boy's chest. Who's the lifeguard here, me or you? Me or you, buddy?

You, Eaton said.

The lifeguard kissed the little boy and then turned an ear to his mouth. Fucking amateurs, he said. Or he said, This is my job. That's why I'm here, you doofus.

THEY'D WATCHED THE LIFEGUARD revive the boy, and they had walked over and sat down in the play pool for infants, feeling emotionally drained. They would go home soon, back to their house, and have to start thinking about dinner and things like that. Things like that were creeping back into their minds with a promising resilience. He still had the tatter of the little boy's bathing-suit elastic. He wanted to keep it. Here, she said, placed an arm around him, felt his back shudder. What's wrong? She was holding him close, and the panic of being out looking for the kid still hadn't withdrawn from her either; her fingers trembled like piano strings and the muscles of her heart palpitated.

Are you, are we getting a—? The energy to finish the sentence was not in him.

She rubbed her eyes, No, I mean, I don't think so. We should talk, but no.

He said, I was trying to save him. I didn't know who the heck that guy, who that lifeguard was. He put his head in the crook of her neck and sat there with her. She nodded, Don't worry about it. He held the tattered elastic in his fingers, and she watched him twist it and stretch it, an unfortunate memento of their day, and they wanted to go home and put it at the back of one of the drawers of their dressing cabinet and try to forget about it. They were already forgetting how the day had gone. The waves, their friends, the fear.

MIRAGE/
FATA
MORGANA

MIRAGE

L OOK UP, LOOK AT THE BILLBOARD, slats turning from this to
that, that and that, and back to this, Susan's face comes and
goes. A noontime fog funnels and twists in front of the advertisement and she blurs away behind it, disappearing—then the billboard turns over with a polite mechanical clap and the picture
changes again and pushes the fog away. *Go away, fog,* Susan sings,
as it breaks up into wet silver nothing through raw tree branches
and multicoloured plastic pennants rippling above a car lot. From

the back seat of a car Susan sees herself on the billboard, but she can't see who is driving her because of a blackened pane of glass.

People used to call her the singing retarded girl; who cares? Stick and stones; who cares? She used to sing on the city bus on the way home from school. She used to sing really loud, her songs vanishing in high notes through the slid-open windows, an escaped *"Macarena"* in the air. She also sang "Pretty Woman," Roy Orbison, "Only the Lonely." These were some great songs. She would sing anywhere, anywhere. Sometimes she might catch someone, overhear someone, Hey, there's the singing retarded girl (haw haw), and it would quiet her down as if they had thrown a hook down her throat and reeled out her voice. Until they were gone, then her voice would return. Stand under the gleam of lame white light next to the brick wall of a convenience store and sing. And someone else might say, Nice voice you got there, I definitely think so. Give her a dollar and walk away, and that dollar would go in her pocket and later buy her a slushie.

Sing at home. Her parents were charmed, but it didn't always keep them from fighting. Sing at school assemblies held in the gymnasium with a microphone and music. Up in the foldout bleachers three thousand students (or maybe more!) sat and listened to her, including the Special Ed. kids from her class, who all sat together in the lowest bleachers so the ones in wheelchairs wouldn't have to be alone. Other Special Ed. students were involved in activities like hockey, painting, karate, whatnot. One girl was blind and crippled up and didn't do any activities. Susan had always been a singer—it came more naturally than talking. When she talked it was terrible, all very kind of muddled. Soft and wet, tongue with nothing to grip onto, and no rhythm to follow. She hated talking because it made her feel unnecessarily dumb. She preferred to sing. The lyrics were all her own, and with her music teacher she made up melodies while he played a Casio keyboard. *All the boys are in love with me, I'm in love with all the boys. This is a great day, in each and every way.*

She did this funky swagger when she sang, a bit nasty, a bit lewd, but she didn't go too far because this was her school and she was afraid to get in trouble. Two kids from her class got in trouble for when they were caught screwing in the washer and dryer room. So she couldn't do all her moves here, like the ones she did at home for her parents, because, her mother warned, They might think you're fondling yourself. Her father wasn't as concerned. Ah, he said and ruffled Susan's pale hair, don't worry so much about it, because it's good entertainment. Her mother looked at her father in a careful way, Don't undermine me like that, she said.

On the living-room wall above the television they kept a gilt-framed picture of Susan's twin sister, the healthy daughter who'd inexplicably died at four. Sometimes she talks to me, Susan told her mother while they brushed her teeth for dinner. She talks to me, too, her mother whispered, rubbed the Crest off Susan's face with a damp towel. What does she say? Susan asked. Oh, you know, stuff, like—, her mother said and jerkily bent her head down, as if to shut her mouth. I like to sing for her, Susan said. That's good, her mother said, I think that's very good. I wish she was still alive, Susan said. And then her mother, instead of replying, kind of yawned—an alarming strain in her face—and finally nodded, turned, and walked out of the bathroom. At dinner her father snapped, Why do you insist on filling her with all these

fucked-up ideas? And why, her mother replied in a voice just as
loud, do you insist on filling her with all these four-letter words?
I'm the pirate of love, Susan sang, *coming to steal your heart*.

Before lights out, her father sat beside her with a book in his
lap to read from, help her fall asleep, and said, What did your
mother tell you? Don't listen to her, whatever it was, all right?
Okay, Susan said. Concentrate on your schoolwork, he said,
clasped the book shut. Concentrate on your singing. Okay, she
said. Lights out? she asked. Yes, her father said, and left her alone
to close her eyes in the dark.

SINGING, *CAN YOU GIVE ME AN ANSWER, yes or no, yes-no, that's what
the teacher wants to know*. She waved her hands in the air while
three thousand students clapped. Once the song was over she
bowed and returned to the bleachers beside her classmates. And
later, Listen, a student said, and put headphone buds in her ears,
listen, that's you. Someone had recorded her during the assembly.
She shut her eyes and clenched her teeth and put her hands to her
ears and listened hard to the song, clear and digital. Oh, I have a
beautiful voice, she said, and kept her eyes closed.

Like everything else, soon enough you could download her
songs off the Internet. Anyone in the middle of anywhere could
hear her now. A nebulous kind of popularity surrounded the
tracks that surfaced, and it drove an industry man in a backwards
baseball cap, chinos, and hot Nikes to pay a visit to Susan's high
school, where he sat in the music room with Susan and her
teacher. *Love* your voice, he said, but he was looking at her
teacher the whole time, not her; who cares? He talked. There was
a smile about him that never wavered. He made a web with his

hands and said, Together, and pulled the web towards his stomach and nodded.

Her parents agreed, finally, that it was an opportunity that certainly didn't come around twice, and there seemed to be no reason to hold her back. Without question, she had talent. For days Susan practised her signature so that she could sign the contract that had her best interests in mind.

With her hand tightly squeezing her father's, they took an elevator with a flickering light to a seventh-floor studio where a woman chain-smoked through three rolls of black-and-white film before saying, Shit, this was supposed to be colour, wasn't it? Susan stood in front of a white backdrop facing the electric heat of kliegs, unsure what to make of the click of the camera. My knees hurt, she said. They had her in pink spandex and her face and hair all spackled with glitter. Smile, honey, her father corrected.

Her voice on entertainment television, *I hear the sound of my heart and it sounds like I love you.* Her parents were interviewed, Don't give me that, her mother said, we love our daughter more than life itself. She's a gift, you know, something pretty darn magical, and it's not right how these people treat her, it's not. Her parents were never at ease with interviews. At night they had fights and afterwards apologized to her for them. Questions didn't faze Susan, though; in fact she enjoyed them, nodding amiably, sharing lines of songs made up that day or even on the spot. *Everything is fine, everything is okay, if you are together, you'll float just like a feather.* The whole family became acquainted with tripods and remote microphones and various sizes of steno pad. At night her mother scanned magazines to ensure no one had been misquoted, while her father took long private baths. Susan listened at the door and heard barely a trickle until he lurched up from the water when the tub began to drain.

They bought a new car and it sat in the driveway dazzling and fancy like an ice sculpture, but it was never driven. They didn't call the police when it was stolen, a melted-away image of her success. Now when they drove, it was always chaperoned, usually en route to the airport. *In the sky and on the ground I'll be in your town, I'll be around.* She didn't like flying at all. Landings especially, but also the turbulence. The air, smelling of recycled stale coffee, made her throat hurt. A little boy in a hockey jersey came to her aisle with the airplane safety brochure from the back of the seat in front of him and said, Can I have your autograph? and she looked at this boy and started to cry. The little boy patted her shoulder and said, It's okay, you know, because I brought a pen with me. When she was finished crying she signed the thing and the boy hurried off.

She didn't have to sign her parents' divorce papers, just her father and her mother had to sign. What did that mean, divorce? First she thought it meant one of them was sick. But no, they were just separated, and maybe it was best that they both stay away from Susan for a while, maybe that was for the best, according to a man from the industry. Her teacher can take care of her for the rest of the tour, he said. To Susan it didn't sound like it was for the best, and her parents didn't seem to think so either. In the food court of an airport they looked out a window facing the hangars and watched Boeings arrive and depart, depart and arrive, and they held Susan's hand and finally it was time for her to leave and they parted, her parents going who-knows-where.

She spent her time on stage or alone or with her teacher. A six-piece band of California studio musicians was hired for tours. Theatrical smoke hissed from vents, and from a hole in the stage she would rise up through the white fog that smelled like rotten candy, and sing for an hour and then find herself back in a hotel. You okay? her teacher asked her. *I'm fine I'm fine I'm fine I'm fine.* She didn't eat her room-service dinner. In a corner of the hotel suite there was a stack six feet high of newly pressed postcards with her face on them, awaiting her signature. She never signed her name Susan any more. Her stage name, Mirage, which she'd chosen herself, was written in sparkling toothpaste-thick letters on each postcard. *A song is not glue but Mom and Dad I love you.*

There was someone for everything. *A nice woman does my hair and makeup in the morning, at night she rubs it off, thanks for your help, but the lipstick makes me cough.* And everything was fine. All over windows in downtowns and malls her face appeared, and on T-shirts and on some toys. She did this and that. She slept in different beds most every night, but they smelled alike, and the view beyond all the identical filmy white drapes was never a surprise, and the television always played the same programs. Her mother slept beside her some nights, and then the next she might be gone. Or Susan disappeared, vanished, because no one was around—waking up alone and not knowing where she was. She expected to see her sister, to sit on the edge of a hotel mattress with her and do stuff like fight over the remote control. Because wherever Susan was that night—whatever night—there seemed to be a goodbye at the end of it.

Her teacher had gone back to work at the school, but he made sure to call her every day. I miss you, she said. I miss you too, he said. Susan, I want you to know I didn't want to go away, he said. Where am I? she said, you're not here.

When her songs came on the radio, announced by a panicked voice, she'd sit on the hotel room air conditioner and look out the window at whatever was there, wherever she was, and clench her teeth, and with her head down and her eyes shut so tight she knew she was truly alone. To herself most of all she was invisible. Where was she now? Would she ever know? She could only be seen by others, objectively, remotely, like a distant lamina of heat. Or the sound of her voice coming over the television, somehow more real. The comfort of someone else, of being held close by someone else, had somehow vanished. She told herself, I'm such a beautiful singer.

FATA MORGANA

W HAT DID HE THINK HE WAS LOOKING FOR when he looked out over the flat fields, the minor forest in the near distance, the gophers chirping, all the dry endless summer of his post-marriage? He'd never been so depressed in all his life. How could the woman who gave him a son make his days seem like nightmares? There was no one to turn to, his friends were unhelpful and his parents both remarried like it was a wardrobe change, something new each season. He was alone, the sudden vacuum of it was shock enough, but everyone around made it seem quite trivial, which it wasn't. And all the things she left behind, this and that, that and this, all over the house, stuff she'd forgotten in her panic to escape her life with him. It was painful to find these things. What exactly was it he'd done? he wondered. What could he have improved on, was there even something? As he remembered it everything had been fine between them. They never fought, they talked while making dinner and listened to the radio while doing the dishes, they shared a cigarette on a Saturday evening while watching a new release, they went to dog shows in the spring and they even went to the Baja peninsula one winter for Christmas, they read the same books and disagreed about the television, they liked each other's friends, they laughed at each other's jokes, they had sex once a week, they had a boy, they raised a boy, they had a boy together. But then, no, it hadn't really been fine. They'd been reaching for something, together, that wasn't there, and the closer they'd got the worse it had felt to know how much it would hurt to lose it.

She left a lot of stuff behind even if she didn't forget to take their boy. A sock-puppet monkey she bought at a craft fair, that was something he found beneath the bed one day. He picked it up, its little simian head bobbing, and he put it up to his nose. He detected bath beads, the little melt-away lips that dissolved around her body in a steaming tub and smelled richly of roses, of her. It was hard, the day-to-day of being divorced. He found, for example, a necklace, a birthday gift she'd never worn. He found it under the sink of all places, being used to tie up a bag of toilet pucks. Of course there was a photo album he couldn't seem to put away or even hide from view. It made his few friends wince when they saw it so openly displayed on his coffee table like some kind of prized amputation. The back of every picture was marked, mostly with circas, though, because he'd done the majority of the work after she'd left him and he didn't have a good head for dates.

Glossy and unfaithful to his poky memory, the photo album was just sheaf after sheaf of emotional trompe l'oeils, he'd been fooled by overexposures and shoddy film. Who are these people? he thought. Do they even exist? No matter how much he studied these pictures they never amounted to a woman and a man, together, that he recognized. Only in memory could he love her, the shape of her eyelids.

Man, you need to go out and have a good time, you know? his friend said, pulling off cans of beer for everyone. I'm fine, he said. Yeah, man, said another friend, go out and get laid. I'm fine. Dude, you totally need to go out and get laid. I'm fine. If I was divorced that's the first thing I'd do, is get laid. I'm fine. Friend, I know it's not good to give advice or whatever, but I tell you you have to think outside of your own subjectivity, you know, and get over her. He nodded in pretend agreement. They wanted him to conquer his loneliness through fucking. How the hell was he supposed to do that? Or how could he *not?* And how would it help, either one?

It was a relief when the friends stopped coming around and he could spend his hours just looking out the bay window he'd installed himself (with help from a television program) and watch the dust race across the field and sticks bouncing along behind trying to catch up. He loved windstorms, and also those intense heat waves after rain when the acreage would turn to liquid, all hot and wavering. To see limpid azure ponds where he knew there were no ponds, beautiful or otherwise. And his ex-wife calling, How *are* you? and what was the correct way to answer that? What was the answer she would *least* like to hear? Or the answer he most wanted to give? The truth? he asked her. Well, of course the truth, she said in the voice she saved for insects and chores. He said, I don't know where I am. There's no one around. How's my little boy?

On television one afternoon he watched a talk show and the host had a retarded girl on for an interview. The girl was a singer it turned out, and pretty popular by the sounds of it. The woman leaned in close to the retarded girl and pressed her hand against the girl's hand. Mirage, the woman said, you are an inspiration. Okay, said Mirage. The woman turned to her audience, the camera, and said, Mirage has been on tour now for over a year, her album is selling worldwide, and she has never looked back. She turned to face Mirage again, What gives you the courage to keep singing, to keep up this busy schedule, and most of all, what gives you the power to love so much? He watched the retarded girl named Mirage on his television. Soft around the eyes like sometimes retarded people are. She made him think about his own little guy, and even though they rarely saw each other since the divorce that didn't mean he didn't love his son and miss him. He turned the volume up. Mirage said, I really love to sing, and nothing I can do is like singing so it's what I love. The woman asked, Who do you sing for? Who do I sing for? Yes, the woman said. Well, Mirage said, I sing for everybody in the world. I sing for my teacher. I sing for my mom and dad. I'll sing a song for you. The woman leaned back, Would you? Okay. Mirage made up a song, a short one. She sang a song, her voice sort of gentle and rich and lonesome, a little song that rhymed. The audience clapped, some stood up from their chairs and clapped above their heads. That was wonderful, beautiful, wasn't it? She looked at her audience as if stunned, and everyone clapped. Thank you, said

Mirage. Your songs are all about happiness, aren't they? the woman nodded. I think so, said Mirage. Mirage, the woman said, and put out a commiserating hand, your parents are recently divorced, how does that feel? This question made the girl cry, and the woman wrapped Mirage in her arms and they wept together. No one made a sound. And in his quiet home, he took a deep breath, but suddenly on the exhale he was crying too. How absurd, how fucking awful. He was really bawling. He called out his ex-wife's name and felt sick doing it. He slid from his chair and on the floor he kind of rested while the show continued, pressed on while he tried to restore himself. Every day is a new beginning, the woman looked out at him, at his small den, at his small life. Things will get better, the woman said. Could she see how he lived? Could she somehow see his life in the dark pupil of that camera's polite mechanical eye? Was he in there like a hint or a kind of apparition, visible in there, somewhere, somehow? Was he known to her, somehow? It's the very hardest thing, Mirage finally managed to say. I miss my mom and dad and I don't know where I am. The woman nodded, You're doing fine. You're right here. We'll be right back.

SPINES A LENGTH
OF VELCRO

TWO SUMO WRESTLERS ARE IN A RING staring each other down,
their spines a length of Velcro. The sun is out and the sky is
huge and it seems that everyone else is drunk. But the sumos must
stay totally focused. It is the sumo way, probably. Their legs step
apart. They hunch over. They put their hands on their knees. The
bulges of fat along their beltlines look like half-melted nougat.
Over their bowl-cuts each of them wears a black helmet that looks
like hair tied into a bun—helmets that keep slipping over their
eyes. I can't see! yelps one sumo. Neither can I! pipes the other. A
teenage girl who's refereeing tightens their chinstraps another

notch and says, God, you've got small little heads. When her hands come up to their chins they can feel her fingernails scratch their necks and there is, for a wiggly instant, a new thrill that runs straight down into their legs. Your heads are too small, she says. They say nothing. For one thing she's wearing a sports bra they can both see through her top, and for another they're about to kick each other's ass so they need to concentrate.

Around the ring adults are gathered clutching Mason jars of keg beer, cheap party beer and lots of it, slapping their knees at the sight of their kids inside those rented getups, a father saying, Kick his ass, as he sweeps away a glob of beer foam from his moustache. I've got twenty bucks on you, don't embarrass your dad now. He shows his kid the bill in his hand and laughs. A nice crisp bank-machine twenty riding on him. Show your dad what kind of mettle you're made of, he says, and shakes his sumo by the arms. Let's hear your war cry.

Arr, says the boy.

Don't be a wussy, his father says. Again, he says.

Arr, says the boy. He's squinting. He had to take his glasses off and have his little sister protect them while he wrestled or he might've broken them otherwise. He hopes it looks intimidating. He hopes he looks vicious with his face all scrunched up like this, instead of just looking like a blind kid trying to keep his balance in a fat suit.

There in front of him he sees the indistinct fuzz of his father in a white Fruit of the Loom muscle-shirt doing a little shadow-box. Twenty bucks, right? Don't forget that.

The mother of his sumo opponent, a woman with a curly runnel of hair down her shoulders and slick fingernails with a tendency to scratch the air as they approach a man, comes up beside his father and says, That little son of yours couldn't wrestle his way out of a T-shirt.

Unlike you, I suppose, his father says.

Oh, nasty, she says, lip curled.

Everyone is looking forward to some meat. The scent of BBQ'd hot dogs and hamburgers passes over them in streamlets. A cardboard box full of white buns from Costco sits beside a row of three blazing propane grills. There are circular buns with sesame seeds bagged by the dozen so that you have to separate them from each other, and long tube-shaped buns with creases along their tops. A jar of relish fell to the ground earlier and has become a sort of illicit rendezvous for bees.

Here is a short-sighted little boy about to wrestle the kid on his block he never even talks to, even though their parents are friends. A little boy who excels at book reports and math quizzes and province-naming. He learned to run fast thanks to certain larger boys. Now he's number one in track and field in gym class. He is weightless, zoom, the speed of light. And yet he is still tormented by the same night terror he's had since as long as he can remember. He awakes from a gasping dream with his heart door-knocking at his ribs. In the dream he's being smothered by something large and unutterable, choking, almost killing him, almost. Little boy who is just establishing his first real crushes on girls, which, if he imagines these girls at night as he drifts off, brings the suffocating dream back almost the second he falls asleep. And suddenly he's got a crush on this referee.

She stands in the middle of the ring with her legs apart, the referee, her Adidas tearaway pants tight against her thighs. She says, Bow.

The sumo wrestlers bow and fall over.

Afternoon's sharp light catches on the folds and puffs of their costumes and exposes the hundreds of fabric dimples on their skin like yawning pores. Their legs are disproportionately short but they sure are fleshy. A cuff of tarp-skin at the bottom of each shin reveals sport socks underneath. Their dumpy inflated bodies are a bit elephantine, sacks of skin exploding with more skin. Strange suburban baby-monsters. And they've got those heavy diapers on, the kind that real sumo wrestlers wear.

She hoists them back up again. Careful, she says, this sweet teenage girl, the oldest kid on the block, the daughter of an enter- tainment lawyer currently sitting on an extendable Kmart lawn chair made of white and green vinyl weaving and an aluminum frame, with his legs crossed, with his hair creamed back, wagging an Italian leather espadrille at the end of one toe, talking steadily on his cellphone and jabbing his index finger like a rapier.

Aren't you gonna watch, Dad? she screams over the crowd that has formed.

He puts a hand over the phone, In a minute in a minute.

Mawashi. Sumo diapers are called *mawashis.* Also *shimekomis,* after the way they're wrapped.

Well, she says to the two kids, then are we ready or whatever?

I'm ready, the boy without his glasses says.

I'm totally ready, the other boy says, the little punk with the mole on his chin who lives next door in the house with the biggest yard. There's always a few hundred toys of different shapes and sizes on the lawn and myriad action figures meticulously burned and maimed left on the roof of the one-storey house. I am so *fucking* totally ready, he says.

Don't cuss, his mother says, and smiles at the other boy's father. It's not appropriate.

He's sweating, this short-sighted mini-sumo. He's getting seriously hot inside the suit. There's sweat *purling* down his temples. Even his *ankles* are sweating. Body inside a body. The sun has blanched the sky, the tops of cars burn white-hot, the siding on houses is soft to the touch, the grass on lawns is a dry sienna from its tungsten glare. Sprinklers make supplicating arcs. The heat does not yield. How long, he wonders, can he take the heat like this? Wrapped up in so much flesh like this?

Orbiting the sumo ring the fathers are getting quite inebriated, laughing and waving and yelling at them to, Go at it, go at it! They siphon out beers and debate the merits of their children and families. What did you call my wife? I didn't say nothing. I think you did. Well, I think you think wrong, buddy.

The block party will conclude with American fireworks, but for now this will do to entertain. The neighbourhood's own pint-sized Takanahana, its own little Akebono.

Dust piles up along the edges of houses from the wind. The half-blind sumo's sister performs an imitation of a car alarm being activated. She's got it down to the pitch and volume and everything and she's only seven.

Why did he agree to this? he wonders. The little boy didn't look too pleased when he saw the suits. To get inside his sumo outfit he had to lie on his back in front of the costume and slide feet first into the meat of the sumo, inching his legs through the dermis to the ankle like a ghost creepingly taking possession of a body. Oddly the inner padding of the sumo suit was sleeping-bag plaid. His arms had to squeeze through the plaid blubber until his hands passed through elasticized wristbands and then were immediately slipped into mittens. Mitts, not gloves—these sumos have only one huge plump finger on each hand and the requisite opposable thumbs. The referee sealed him in from the spine—by way of Velcro—and then folded over a flap to conceal the seam (for verisimilitude). Then she hoisted him up to his feet and said, Looking good, sweetie. His legs buckled. He wasn't sure if it was the weight of the suit or some kind of erotic feebleness. He waddled over to his place at one side of the ring, facing the other boy. Now he is ready to wrestle.

You kids look pretty adorable, the referee says.

Ha! his sister squeaks. She wants to be their girlfriend!

Haw haw, says everybody. The fathers, the mothers, their grade-school friends, even the teenage referee laughs, the whole block party laughs. Their girlfriend. Not only funny because she's a teenager and they're just boys, but because of what they're wearing. All that mallowy flesh and those cute-as-hell kid cheeks squooched out from their chinstraps.

He looks at the punk kid standing across from him. Two idiotic cartoon fat men being laughed at by a whole cul-de-sac. Something in the angry humiliated stare of that kid tells him he's in trouble.

My kid's gonna whup yours's ass, his father says.

Care to put some money where your mouth is? the other kid's mother answers.

I'll put something where my mouth is.

Oh, nasty.

More keg beer is siphoned improperly into jars, big head for a little blonde. And everyone drinks too fast, not thinking about tomorrow's hangover.

The girl has a palm up at each of them, holding them back. The short-sighted boy sees a scoop of cleavage as she leans down to straighten his helmet again. The punk kid can see into the sleeve of her shirt all the way to her smooth armpit. Are you ready now? she asks.

I *said* I was ready, the punk kid says.

Are you okay without your glasses? she asks the little boy. He can smell berries when she's this close to him. He's so red in the face it's a wonder he hasn't melted, and he can only answer her with a timid nod.

They're ready! she says.

The neighbourhood cheers. A makeshift bookie works the numbers; tens and twenties pile up in a sweat-ringed ballcap. A Dalmatian barks. A balloon is let go from the fist of a small child. The sun winks away with the passing of a scant cloud. The contours of shadows change ever so slightly and only for a moment. The wind calms down. More bets are made.

Don't mess this up, his father calls out, and then he stumbles over to his kid's side, puts an arm around his upholstered son, leans down to whisper, And I mean do *not* mess up.

The boy just tries to stay upright—it's all he can do.

Beyond the ring and the parents, past the tables and condiments, beer kegs, and bowls of mashed potatoes, the lawyer, the referee's father, is still on the phone, and his gestures have gotten worse: simple but intense karate, on the verge of full-fledged kicking.

No, he says. No, is what I said. No. Did I not say no?

The referee counts to three, slicing an arm down at the ring with each number. ONE, she yells. TWO, she yells. And then, after a coy pause in which she looks to each boy and gives them both a little wink, THREE!

The sumos lunge at each other—stumbling tripping practically falling, and still they feel nothing when their chests collide with an airy *plap*. It's like two pillows battling for a place on the bed. Soft combat. They raise their arms, as if that'll help. The blind kid gets a mitt in the face, and when he bites the hand it tastes like the underside of a wig.

The block party goes wild, amused as hell by the two kids as they paw and slap at each other. Like a Walt Disney cockfight right here in the road in front of all their houses, during the first heat wave of the summer on a torpid long weekend meant to celebrate this country's birthday or something.

Use his weight against him, someone suggests.

Pull him out of the ring, a father yaps, spills beer all down the front of his shirt.

Kill him! someone screams.

The referee dances around them looking pretty and it's the worst thing ever for this half-blind kid, who wishes he could make this whole scene suddenly stop. Everything posed in a stillness he's produced with his own superheroic mind. The first thing he'd do would be to go over and stand on his toes and kiss that girl right on the lips. He could do that and no one would ever find out. Then the next thing he'd do would be to beat the crap out of this stupid kid in front of him, because he can't seem to get this punk's little mitts out of his face. Every time he pushes him away the kid comes back even harder with the mitts up. And the world hasn't come to a standstill at all, no, everything is moving faster and faster, with his father wagging two twenties *and* a ten in his face, and in fact at any moment he's sure he's going to lose his balance.

The other kid, the punk with the mole on his chin, it's obvious from the way he scrabbles and claws with all the childhood mania he can muster that he just wants to get this over with. He wants to whup this shrimp and get out of this costume and end the humiliation. His mother is more impressed with the kid's father's muscles than with how quickly he's going to slam this four-eyes to the mat, and a teenage girl (human kinetics, she once told him, that means I'll get to work with bodies) skipping around and reminding him not to bite, or head-butt. It's awful. He feels sick and stupid.

So he whups the kid, the blind kid. Takes him by the arm and heaves, sends them both caroming towards the edge of the ring. They fall on each other like lovers, the blind kid on his back with the boundary of the ring beneath him.

I win, he tells the blind kid as they lie there waiting to be picked up.

Big whoop, says the boy.

Loving it, the audience is loving it. Half of them whine and put their hands over their eyes and the other half howl and make *cha-ching* noises, their fists pumping the arms of invisible slot machines. Money is doled into people's palms all crumpled and hot. They stand the sumos back up again. Suddenly the fathers are acting like trainers, trying to fill their sons with renewed confidence, rubbing their bellies and patting them on the cheeks.

All right, his father says. Next time go for the legs. You can see the legs, right? Without the glasses? That's the key next round. Legs.

Next round?

His father gives him a sip of beer from the jar. Cheer up, he says, this is great.

He wonders if he might faint. Monsoon-like waves of nausea pass through him, and he needs to be held up by his father to keep from collapsing. His sumo helmet has been dislodged and is pinching one ear and chafing the skin around his jaw.

Please, Dad, the boy says. I feel sick to my stomach.

Not now, okay. At least win one round.

Please, Dad.

But his father has already sunk back into the sudsy crowd of parents surrounding the ring, boozy and demanding and weird, and he's left alone again to fight his way free. Everything is blurry, a big nebulous haze of embarrassment. He watches all the parents, all these adults with full-time jobs and bills that come in the mail in brown envelopes with plastic windows, all of these people here in front of him, jumping up and down, poking each other in the ribs, barking and spitting, laughing over losses and wins, pinching each other in places they shouldn't, and talking in flirty artificial voices (that's not the way his father talks to *his* mother)—and he realizes that even once he's left the ring it's not going to be any different.

And the teenage girl is doing somersaults around her dad, and he covers his cellphone again and says, That's great hon', I'm on the phone.

Everyone has their wallets pried open to dig for bills. They smooth out wrinkles in old fives, sift through change for loonies and toonies. Their palms are moist. They cry out bets to the bookie and stuff their money into the ballcap. Everyone is watching the boys and no one is watching the parents.

His sister makes the sound of a car alarm going off.

The sun is very hot.

They wrestle again. And again.

SHAVED
TEMPLE

Do you want me to? Sure, I mean, only if you want to, I don't want to force you or— No, I mean, no. Okay, then, okay. Okay, then I'll do it. Am I forcing you here, to do this, I mean? No, no, not at all, I don't care if we do it, it might be fun. What do you mean, do you mean it'll be fun to do or that I'll look funny? No, I didn't mean it that way, no. Do you think I'll—do you think I'll look handsome? Oh god, let's just get it over with. Well no, forget it, because it's not important, it's not that important that I do this, or that you do this—it's not integral to, whatever, or, you know. Oh, I know. Because, hey, let's

just forget about it, we can forget about it, how about we just
forget about it? Okay, we'll forget about it, but are you sure,
because— See, you're wavering, you don't really want to. Oh, you
prick, I can't believe you. What, come back here, what did I say?
You were testing me—look, I couldn't care less, we can do it, we
can not do it, I mean, all I have to do is plug the razor in, it's—
But see, you don't want to do it—why are you smiling? I'm not
smiling, it's, I think I think it's more of a grimace. A grimace?
Yes, it was a grimace, like, why am I being treated this way?
Treated like how, what way? Like a tool for this, for you and
your psychological mind games and whatever, and your ideas. I
don't like the track you're on, it's dark, a dark track, and I didn't
mean to take you to a dark place like this. Forget it, just let's do
it and get it over with. Are you sure? Oh, I don't care, I really
don't, shave no shave I don't care. Why are you sitting down? I'm
going to try and calm myself. What? I'm going to close my eyes
and, you know, I'm going to meditate. Right now, but my hair,
my shave— Right now, I'm feeling tense. Did I make you tense?
Tense-ness is in the air, that's all, it wasn't you specifically. I'm
sorry. Don't apologize for who you are. I'm not, no, this isn't
who I am, entirely, it's not the entirety of who I am. I know. This
is a single molecule, like a moment, of who I am. I didn't mean
to imply— No, no, neither did I— That this was the entirety of
you and your— Look, I want to, I really do, I think it's going to
be so cool, so if you want to, maybe you could stand up again?
Make up your mind. I have— I want it, and if you want it, then
that's cool. Cool, yeah, very cool. What *does* that mean? What
does what mean? Your tone. My tone, my tone means nothing,
it means I'm inwardly rolling my eyes as in, like, this is just

about enough. Okay, okay, so I'll zipper shut, and you do it—but careful because— I'll be careful. I don't want to get hurt. I said I'll be careful.

HIS NECK BENT DOWN, his chin pressed to his chest, his eyes firmly closed. His hair hanging. His neck bent down, in his ear there is a tingle, a buzz, a hum. Does she love him? Does she love him or what? What will happen? She brings the razor over, throwing the black cord over his head, his neck bent down, chin pressed, eyes closed. Hum, the razor hums. She folds over his hair, away from the ear, the razor in her hand, steady now. His scalp is grey. As she drives the razor across his temple. Hair begins to fall. Clips of it drift to his shoulder, to the floor. His neck, his chin, his eyes. Does she? Maybe she doesn't. Yes, it's possible that she doesn't. His pale scalp, with the back of her hand she knocks away stuck hairs. Begin to wonder. She sweeps against his ear, along the back of it, cleaning, sweeping, knocking. Neck, chin, eyes. A bare strip of skin above his ear where now a coarse grid of stubble shines. His hands clasped palm to palm in his lap, maybe or should he pray? With his eyes closed, of course, his neck bent down, and his chin to his chest, so yes, maybe he could at least try. In a chair, while she steps over him, leg over his lap, another leg over his lap, something like that or what. Does she? Her legs over his lap, not to stop, no, not to stay and no, not to play a minute. Fool around. Does she? A leg and then the other leg, to pass over him to the other temple. Not so good, not really so good, is he? After all. Ah, she sighs. With his eyes closed, chin to his chest, neck bent down. She folds over his long hair to shave the temple and says, Ah. What does Ah mean? he wonders, as she folds the hair up away from his temple. Brings the razor down beside his ear and drives it across his scalp. Hum. Hair falls in clips. What now? What now?

SHEEP DUB

WHOSE BABY HANDS WERE SOFT and instinctive, clenching indiscriminately around fingers laid in her palm, whose legs shot into the air like sensitive feelers, probing and tasting the air of her crib; whose stomach was as soft as kneaded dough and bare for a mouth to press against and make loud raspberries; whose baby cry she never lost even when she was six, crying when I forced her out of my room and pinched her toe when slamming the door, crying when I told her she was stupid, crying when I strangled her, and crying when I told her I didn't like her; whose memory was idiot savant–ish, or photographic at least, remembering things from when she was less than a year old: the colour of the shirt I wore the first time she had a fever and was taken to the doctor, the name of the dead barber that used to cut my hair before he died—whom she'd met once when she was two; whose hair, as a baby, began to grow in leafy tufts from behind her ears and turned long and flowing and the colour of bittersweet chocolate; whose name for fear was *the Sheep*; whose nightmares accosted us both because she insisted on sleeping in my bedroom; whose first word at five months(!) was *Ben*, my own name; whose favourite food was bananas; whose smell was always slightly of bananas; whose constant reminder was that I didn't like her, that I was as close to hating her as a brother could be, that she was not wanted around me; whose own name was Christine, is now long dead.

I WASN'T FAR ENOUGH AWAY from the maternity ward, not far enough away that I didn't have to hear my mother's shrieks, the high, anxious noises like the kind she made when she'd almost cried enough and was about to fall back asleep. I was in the hall, on a folding chair a nurse had opened for me, so that I could see into the room where my mother was birthing my sister. Inside, my father wasn't making any sound, and I didn't know what his role was in the delivery—if he was necessary the way he was for the conception. Now and then a nurse jogged by me; one slipped on a streak of coffee I had seen a man loose from the geriatric ward spill earlier. The old man had passed me, shaking, and as I'd watched him and heard at the same time my mother's screams it had seemed as if it was all coming from him. He was screaming, he was shaking; he spilled some coffee, kept walking. I was supposed to be reading an *X-Men* comic. A family of mutants. The blue beast.

Next day I came back with my father to visit for the second time.

You'd like to see her, my mother said.

Made my way across the room towards her bed and saw at once that my mother had huddled against her the baby, swathed in hospital towels. I hooked my hands around the cold railing above the mattress and stood on my toes to see my new sister's face.

Meet your brother, Christine, she said, tilted the baby towards me. She had eyes that were puffed and shut, and twists of blue and red veins like hair all over her skull. Her mouth was tiny and caked with stuff, as was her nose.

I saw her yesterday, I said.

Did you? I can't remember.

My father folded onto his knees and petted his new daughter's face, casually wiping some of the stuff from her nostrils and lip corners.

The most beautiful baby, he said carelessly.

Blocking my own view of her, I saw for the first time the bare patch of skin on my father's scalp and the thinning striations of hair surrounding. He was ambling towards baby himself, the way Christine was bursting away from it.

My mother said to him, Hope your hands are clean.

WHOSE MEMORY WAS IDIOT SAVANT–ISH, or photographic at least; whose favourite flavour of ice cream was banana-mint; whose designated bowl for eating banana-mint ice cream was an old ceramic onion-soup bowl with a chipped handle. At three years old, her nose met the edge of the kitchen table so that it looked as though she were peeking up over the top to pilfer the food before her. She swung a spoon up and dipped it into the bowl and brought a dollop of the dessert down to where her mouth was, out of view.

She said, This is our medicine. She picked out a nugget of mint and held it. Then with two fingers she placed it at the back of her throat the way she'd seen it done. The way she'd seen it done with medicine.

The wicker garbage basket in the bathroom was always filled with empty amber bottles, all labelled in dot matrix print with my mother's name, the doctor's name, the name of what the bottle used to contain.

IT WAS A GAME SHE PLAYED. Standing at the window in the living room while I puzzled over math problems or the loops and hairpin turns of p's and z's, she would press her finger against the glass and point to something outside.

What's behind that house? she would ask.

Shut up, I said. I'm working, I said.

What's behind it? Nothing?

Shut up.

If there was two of me, I could find out with no one knowing.

She turned to the window again and looked out past the glass.

What's over there, behind that?

I stood up from my math book and kicked it aside, went to her, took her arms in my hands and shook her. She saw me coming and flinched, wound her shoulders up to her ears and opened her mouth to cry; I shook her, saw her eyes stutter and toggle. I could feel that she was small; her bones clacked together like the joints of a marionette. I shook her like that, there.

Told her, Shut up.

Letting her go she throbbed, dizzy on her feet. Christine welled up in the eyes with tears, and before I could make it back to my homework, she had me at the waist. Wrapped around me and crying, or about to cry, her open mouth allowing drool to dampen my shirt, she stopped me from moving.

Please, Ben. She hugged me tightly.

I gave her a knock on the head with the heel of my hand. Let go.

Her crying worsened and she said again, What's behind that?

I said I didn't know, I didn't know what was behind the hedgerow that she pointed to because I'd never been allowed across the street.

I could see the coin-sized grease marks her fingers had left on the window.

The glass and wood that separated us from outside was thin and delicate.

Never, my mother said, ever—cross the street. All right? Follow the sidewalk.

In bed—when all light aside from what my nightlight cast had been carved away and we could see one another only by the rare shapes relieved of shadow—she would attempt to mimic the inflections of our mother's voice.

Never ever, Christine would say, pausing to sigh, letting her eyes shut and open like someone veering too close to sleep, cross the street. All right? Follow—the sidewalk.

She also said, What's that? whenever there was a noise. And I could hear her frantically twisting in her sleeping bag, unleashing her arms and sitting up.

What was that, Ben?

WHOSE NAME FOR FEAR WAS *THE SHEEP*; whose nightmares accosted us both because she insisted on sleeping in my bedroom; whose first word at five months(!) was *Ben*, my own name; whose sleeping bag was kept unrolled below my bed, with a pillow and a plush E.T. doll.

What was that, Ben?

The doorbolt sliding back, a knife lifted from a kitchen drawer, the creak of a knee joint. The Sheep: she could hear it raise a heavy front leg and drop a hoof to the carpet, and then another leg, and another, another. Each hoofstep a muffled thud coming closer, up the stairs two at a time, the hard blow of nostrils becoming audible as it made its way to the door of my bedroom.

Can I sleep with you? she'd whisper. Ben?

Stay in your sleeping bag, I said, on the floor.

But now even I could hear the Sheep's nose sniffing at the door, smelling us through the cracks; it sucked the doorknob between its big lips and spun its tongue along the brass to taste where the palms of our hands had lain; it bit down and tried to wind the handle open.

She was in my bed, beside me under the covers, without my noticing how she'd got there, and I could feel her shaking, could feel her fingers clench and tug at my pyjamas.

Oh my, she said, like our mother said it. Oh my, and then my sister started to cry. Her crying was severe; I'd wipe away the hairs that webbed her eyes, which remained wide open, dilated, black and raw.

SHE ONCE DESCRIBED EVERY PATTERN on every one of our father's ties. She drew them with Crayolas on loose-leaf and we hung them on the fridge with real estate magnets.

WHOSE HAIR BEGAN TO GROW from behind her ears in leafy tufts and turned long and flowing and the colour of bittersweet chocolate; whose job it was—in return for candy—to regularly inspect the wicker garbage basket in the bathroom for our mother's empty bottles. She fished them out from the pool of Kleenex, mint dental floss—and I kept them in an old sewing box under my bed. At five I learned to crack their childproof caps.

I kept mostly candy inside our mother's discarded vials. Like a pharmacist, I used a letter-opener to divide a selection of the candy between us and we surreptitiously ate as we sat and watched the television.

Jelly beans, Mike & Ikes, Nerds, Tart 'N' Tinys, Sweet Hearts, Runts, Pez, licorice Goodies, Rain-Blo.

Let your mother sleep, Christine would say, and she'd lie back on the carpet, fold her hands behind her head—slaked, coloured sugar powder crusting at the sides of her mouth.

At six I was allowed to visit the confectionery at the foot of our block without being accompanied by my mother. Christine was also invited, so long as we held hands through the entire trip.

We followed the neat lawns and fork-tined fences to the confectionery, dust bowls raising themselves in cones off at the horizon where houses were yet to be built, where the construction workers left their trucks when they came in to pave the new roads or wire new lampposts. I choked up Christine's hand inside my own as punishment for walking too slowly. I made my grip so tight her fingertips flushed purple, squirmed.

She didn't complain.

Hurry up, I said and yanked her forward.

At the store, the boy behind the counter—whose thin moustache disappeared completely at the centre, and whose breath smelled of digestive biscuits—tipped towards us, smiled, and said, Looking for the rush? and we nodded shyly, made for home with our candy, where I would fill the amber bottles with the confections and catalogue them accordingly. Certs, Tic Tacs, and other mints were separated, as well as the more serious collection of sneaked Tylenols, Anacins, and Rolaids—which our father left around in half-eaten rolls.

There was also, in an amber bottle all on its own, pressed against the bottom by six lumps of cotton, a single white pill that I had found below the sink. This was one of our mom's *real* pills. Christine and I often thought of that pill, and we regarded it as a treasure, studying it every day to ensure that it hadn't been pilfered. It was very small.

I HAD A FRIEND OVER FROM SCHOOL, a boy named Andy. And we sat in my room and I doled out my drugs to him and he pretended to be affected by their properties. I carved out three Sweet Hearts, four Certs, and a Rain-Blo and told him to take them all immediately or he would die. He did so, and then, with a burp, went into a clonic fit, a brief and comedic seizure that portrayed the drugs' side effects.

Thanks, Doc, he told me and shook my hand.

I served myself a prescription of Runts, swallowed them fast.

The more prescriptions I filled for myself and Andy, the wilder the side effects got, until Andy was flailing about, slamming against the walls, and pulling his cheeks out as far as they would stretch, as I butted my face against the mattress of my bed.

What are you doing? Christine came in without knocking.

Help, I screamed to Andy, I'm having a streak of violence. Get me some drugs before I kill her. I leapt from the bed and came at my sister with both arms raised, hands splayed and ready to strangle.

Help, I cried. Andy worked fast at designing a prescription for me, not fast enough. I had her against the wall, my fingers locked into a tight cage around her neck. Her face puffed and the capillaries in her cheeks came to the skin; her eyes watered and became ringed with blood. She made little gasps and her teeth drew shut. She kicked weakly at my shins; her fingers hooked to my shirt. I could feel I was holding her from falling, that her body was giving way.

I swallowed what Andy put to my lips and, once sated, released her.

She found her breath again while holding me, still, holding me. Her head against my chest. Not making a sound aside from the air climbing in and out of her lungs.

Leave, I told her. I have a friend over, I said.

WHOSE FIRST WORD WAS *BEN*, my own name; and then more words: *banana* (a command), *David* (our father's name), *six* (the news at six), until she began to repeat the monologues on afternoon soap operas, the lyrics to songs on the radio, or the number of times the phone had rung in the last three days. By the time she was five she would give me a synopsis at the end of the week of all that had happened in the last seven days. Her degree of accuracy astounding, she seemed to clone our lives, doubling every event. She would perform, verbatim, dialogues between our father and mother, fights and capitulations; she would describe scenes in microscopic detail; she would, in effect, dictate her diary to me.

CHRISTINE CAME TO ME, knelt down to where I was working and said, I feel bad-weathery. It was something our mother said if we asked her why she had just swallowed some medicine. Watching her raise the heel of her hand to her mouth and swallow with her head cocked upwards, then massaging her throat with her knuckles. A glass of water afterwards.

I invited Christine to my room, showed her a bottle with dot-matrix type on it reading: Take two daily. AM then PM.

Take two of these every day. Uncapped the bottle, handed it to her. One in the morning. One before bed.

She nodded. It's nothing serious. She twisted the bottle in her hands and considered the contents.

Thanks, Ben, she said.

I waved her out of the room.

She was to take Junior Mints for the next month or so, and I made sure that she did not take more than she was allowed. I counted them.

Watched her drop them in her mouth as our mother did, with the heel of her hand. A glass of water afterwards. Twice a day as prescribed.

THE SHEEP MADE THE WIND HOWL, made the tree outside my window scrape its stiff elbowed branches against the pane of my window, made the high heels click on the sidewalk; the Sheep made these sounds.

Two minutes later, two minutes past any sound—a cough cloaked by doors and walls, a car passing with a swim of light across our ceilings—any sound, and two minutes later, the time it would take her to gather the courage to get out of bed and go to the hallway, she would knock on my door. A series of tiny, one-knuckle taps like code. Tap tap tap. Tap tap.

I said nothing, did not reply to the knocks, knowing it was her. I imagined her head screwing around in the darkness of the hallway, alert to the Sheep, waiting for a serrated tooth to carve into her back.

She knocked again.

Ben?

The door opened, hissed as it brushed against the carpet of my room.

Ben. The Sheep. I heard it.

But she imagined something more feral. A sheep with dense, oily wool, stained with ash and mud, smelling of the bitter held-in upchuck of nausea, with jagged coiled horns like nautilus shells and joints as stiff and rotten as old wood. It would trample her, kick its front legs into the air and hammer them on her neck and ribs, snapping her, then bite at the split skin to tear chunks off to eat. Its breath was cold, loud, its eyes like black beans.

Ben?

Shut up, I said, did not move.

Can I sleep with you?

No.

She took the sleeping bag and pillow from beneath my bed, slid into it on the floor. I heard her fishing for her doll and then putting it beside her head as she always did.

Stay there, I said. I don't want you near me.

Found her the next morning up against my back, making noises in her sleep.

SHE SAID THAT OUR MOTHER'S HAIR was *auburn* and then asked me what the word auburn meant.

I REMEMBER AT NIGHT, when our father came home, he was in clothes I never recognized, their pleats, their tailored seams. They were as unfamiliar as he was. The front door would open and at first I wouldn't recognize him. He would go to our mother on the sofa to kiss her and wake her, and then, soon after, to the shower.

Don't kiss my lips, she said, and rubbed her mouth with the back of her hand, you've been out all day.

He put his hand on her forehead; she pushed it away.

I feel bad-weathery.

I'll have a shower, he said, and left to start one running.

Beside the toilet there was a rack of race-car magazines, some with women dressed in bathing suits on the covers, some without.

COME TO ME, SHE SAID, and barely moved her hand. Her palm cupped, scooping. I came towards my mother, stood beside the couch where she lay.

Be good to your sister, she said.

I am, I said. I'm good, I said.

A hug. She raised her arms for me to climb between them, hold her.

No, I said.

Leave then. She let her arms fall, elbow then wrist. Her chest rose, her mouth opened as if to release a sigh, but no sound came. I felt I had hurt her feelings.

Stayed beside her a moment more and considered giving her the hug she had asked for, thought about it, walked away. Went to my room and shut the door, attempted to think about nothing.

FOR HALLOWE'EN CHRISTINE wanted us both to go as Ghostbusters, and my mother offered to make us the costumes. She built us special backpacks made of cardboard and Tupperware, all painted black, with vacuum cleaner hoses fastened to them that fit into a loop on our belts at the other end. We had matching grey outfits and rubber boots. Christine had never walked our neighbourhood, aside from the route back and forth to the confectionery, and she sat beside the window in the living room on the day of Hallowe'en and followed the sidewalks with her finger against the glass, planning the areas she would cover.

What's behind that house? she asked me. Can we go there?

I don't know, I said. The television was on.

Are there houses behind?

Don't know.

Mom coming, or just Dad?

Dad.

When the sun fell and the street became dark it was harder for her to see across the road to where she imagined we would start

our route—the place she'd first put her finger. Squinting, she saw
the lamps outside flicker and glow, spreading cones of orange
light down on the sidewalks.

A child came to our door and rang the bell.

You're a ghost, my mother said.

Tick or teat, the ghost said, one eyehole around her nose.

Christine stared at the child, watched the girl follow the candy
bar our mother gave her down into her pillowcase. Watched her
run back down our driveway.

She didn't eat dinner; wasn't hungry.

Mother put us in our costumes, attached the hoses to their
proper places, and fussed with the collars of our suits.

Take a picture, she said.

No film, our father answered.

Great. She stood up and went to the kitchen, filled the dishwasher.

Let's go, Father said, and went to the door and put on his
shoes. He looked at his watch. Let's go, he said once more.

Christine pulled me down to whisper something in my ear.

I CAME HOME AN HOUR LATER and showed her all I had gotten.
She looked back at the window.

All this came from our block? she asked.

Didn't even finish the block, I said, started sorting the candy.

Going to bed now, our mother said once she'd seen my loot.
Heard the door to her bedroom shut.

Thirty-two kids came, Christine told me. Want to know what
they were? She was still dressed in her costume, though she had
not left the house.

No. I put my candy into the medicine bottles.

Can I have one?

No.

Before going to bed I studied the single white pill that was our mother's. Its edges were soft; it could easily dissolve.

THAT NIGHT THERE WAS NO MOON. It was cold. I had blankets up to my chin, and I rubbed my feet together to keep them warm. There was no sound.

I looked to where my closet was, expected to see nothing. My closet where I kept my clothes and a basket of old toys. Light came from within the closet, breaking through the slats of the door. The light was whitish-blue and dim. When I attempted to look away I found that I was not able to move, paralyzed. Something was inside my closet.

From outside my room a sound came, and I forgot about the light as quickly as it dimmed. There was no light.

I heard the noise again, and then, soon after, Christine tapped on my door, opened it, hissing as it brushed against the carpet of my room.

Ben?

I felt like crying for some reason, but didn't let on.

Go away, I whispered.

No, Ben. I hear the Sheep.

Don't worry about it. Go back.

She came inside and shut herself in the sleeping bag. We listened to the noise again.

What is it? she asked. It was coming from our parents' bedroom.

Shh. I looked to the closet again but it was normal.

Ben? I could hear her sniffing back tears. Can I tell you what came to our door tonight?

I don't care, I said, having difficulties breathing.

The sound came louder now.

Christine whispered, A cat. Three pirates. A television set . . .

Oh, the sound said; the silence afterwards ate everything.

I'm scared, Ben, Christine said. Can I—?

I was scared too. I hadn't moved and I was frightened to try. She opened the blankets and fell in beside me, breathing hard through her mouth. She took my hand. I could see the Sheep.

Christine, I said, it's in Mom and Dad's room.

It is?

It's killing them.

Oh, the sound said.

Christine squeezed my hand. We continued to listen.

We have to save them, I said.

I'm too scared.

Come after us next.

Oh, the sound said.

We opened the door, peered into the corridor. I put my hand out, watched it be swallowed into the black. The hall stank of soap and something foul. The Sheep. Christine clamped my hand as we stepped out of my room. The whitish-blue light now came from the slit between the door and carpet of our parents' room. The tufted hair of the carpet was flickering in light from the source.

Oh, the sound said.

Christine pulled me down to whisper something in my ear.

She said she couldn't remember anything any more, felt guilty, was frightened. I put my finger to my lips to tell her to be quiet. I saw that tears were streaming down her face.

Our feet made no sound as we made it from my bedroom to our parents'. The doorknob, cold and brass, made no sound as I wound it open.

Oh.

Neither of us was breathing. I opened the door.

OH. The sound was louder now. We saw that our parents' television set was on, with the sound turned down to nothing. On the screen a woman's face was burrowed in the belly of a man.

I could feel Christine's knees knock against me as they shuddered.

Oh, our mother said, sitting on top of our father.

SHE WOULD TELL ME ALL that had happened in the last seven days, the Hallowe'en. She would describe everything that she could remember, every microscopic detail, every word. But she wouldn't remember much other than a cat, three pirates, a television set.

WHILE OUR MOTHER WAS IN THE HOSPITAL, near Christmas, I found Christine on the floor of my room, lying flat with a hammer beside her. She had broken open every bottle, had eaten all the candy. A dusty purple film coated her lips. She looked sick.

Those were mine, I said. Saw wrappers from the candy I had received at Hallowe'en, saw the remnants of what I had bought from the confectionery, and all else gone as well. She had eaten everything, not a thing left.

I'm overdosing, she said.

Get up. I yanked her arm and lifted her to her feet. She repressed a belch and ran to the bathroom. I shut the bathroom door, and then my own door so I wouldn't have to listen.

Christine had been given a few tranquilizers, was asleep in her room.

We all need some rest, my father said and squeezed his temples. Go to bed. He smiled a small smile and folded down to his knees to look me in the eyes. Put his hands on my shoulders, opened his mouth to speak, didn't. Casually, he wiped my face, though I don't know why. He stared at the floor, and when I looked down, too, I saw that there was nothing of consequence there. He took his eyes from the carpet and looked at all that was in the hallway besides me—didn't look at me. Finally he laughed. He made a single, numb laugh come out.

Ha. Stood up again and shut the door to his bedroom behind him.

I lay in my own bed, the covers up against my chin. I wasn't asleep.

Soon I heard the door to my bedroom slide open, saw my sister, her head drooped.

She said, Can I sleep with you? Her voice was slurred and slow. She said, Don't feel so good.

Yes, I said.

She stumbled over, almost tripping once, and fell down beside me, and as I covered her over with the blankets, having to move her arms and legs into more suitable positions, I saw that she was already fast asleep. The medicine my father had given her to relax her, combined with my entire stock of pills, had made her drowsy.

She had barely made it to my room. I knew that she had also eaten that single white pill of our mother's, because it too was gone.

I tried to sleep, but couldn't.

I lay in my own bed, the covers up against my chin. I wasn't asleep.

When I opened my eyes it was as dark as when they were closed. The air was crisp. I looked to where my closet was, and since it was dark, expected to see nothing. My closet where I kept my clothes and a basket of my old toys. There was light coming from within the closet, breaking through the cracks in the door. The light was whitish-blue and dim. It did not frighten me. When I attempted to move towards it I found I could not, paralyzed. Saw from between the slats of the closet door a slight movement, like an animal shifting its weight from one heel to the other. I could see the Sheep in the whitish-blue light.

She had eaten everything, not a thing left.

I discovered I was sitting upright in bed. I remember wondering if I should go to my closet to open the door and let it out, but no sooner had I thought that than the closet door creaked open. Like the bellows of an accordion, it opened and folded against the wall. The light was still there, and in the light was Ben.

This is what I remember—without Christine's help I remember this. I remember standing, facing Ben in my closet, each of us regarding the other. I didn't look so young. My hair wasn't as messy. When I blinked, Ben blinked too. But it was not my reflection—the Ben in my closet walked towards me now, and sat down beside me on the bed, our knees touching. We wore the same pyjamas. We both turned and looked at the closet. The whitish-blue light still shone, and I could see the tenebrous lengths of my clothes behind.

Ben's voice was not like my own, deeper, slower. He said, I feel so bad about it.

We looked to one another and then I decided to get up and walk to the closet. Ben stayed sitting on the bed as I made my way to the closet. I nodded, not sure why.

I stepped into the closet and turned around to look at Ben on my bed. I saw that Ben was in the closet so I slid back into bed.

The closet door shut. There was light coming from within the closet. The light was whitish-blue and dim. It did not frighten me. When I attempted to move I found that I could not, paralyzed. I saw from between the slats of the closet door a slight movement, like an animal shifting its weight from one heel to the other. There was a noise outside my room, and as quickly as I thought to look at where the sound was coming from the light dimmed and disappeared. There was no light.

I rolled Christine against my back, her head towed along behind, draped her arm over me, tested the skin at her wrists, the thin tendon cords there, and the pulse of blood. I held her hands inside mine the way I did when we went to the confectionery, I held her that tightly, and I felt the slow, shallow exhalation from her mouth against my neck. Each breath coming later than the one before.

ANY NUMBER of REASONS TO ACT AS ONE DOES, UNDER THE CIRCUMSTANCES'

1

I T MAY BE TEN, OR MAYBE JUST PAST. There's ice in the corners
of the outer window panes, dense geometries of frost that street
lights glitter through. And when they turn and peer out these
windows to see beyond, Eli and Serita, making caves with their
hands against the tempered glass and dipping their eyes in, they
see the black coming off the sky. Not even stars in that sky.
Possibly there is a moon somewhere but it is either concealed or
someplace else. They can hear the neighbour's dog barking like a

maniac next door even though they've got the volume on the TV
up pretty high.

Eli's slim hand explores the back of her skull, mitted by her
stiff black hair. How long has it been since the last time he was
this close to her, close enough to catch the orange-rind smell of
her lipstick, how long—it's the closest he's been to her since the
school dance in the fall, while they waited at the wire fence in the
student parking lot for Serita's father to chaperone them home.
He turned and kissed her chin—missing her lips entirely, so
nervous. One more year and Eli will have his driver's licence and
he'll be able to take her home, instead of seeing her father's or his
father's eyes flicking back and forth from the road to the rear-
view mirror, watching for surreptitious hand-touchings and other
sexual indictments.

The television is playing the movie they have rented, *Twister*.

He trolls his fingers through her hair, finds the maze of her ear
and pinches the lobe. Stop it, she giggles, and strokes his hand
away with her shoulder. With index and thumb he comes at her
and tweaks her ear again, smiling. She swats him away. Ouch, she
says. One more time he gets a good hold of that soft pendant of
flesh and yanks it some, making her wince.

I'm sorry. He lets her go free.

You, she says, and jabs him under the ribs.

Ostensibly, Serita has come over to help him babysit his little
sister, to help him with Angie, ensure she brushes her teeth,
maybe even flosses. (She enjoys watching him tuck Angie into
bed, the way he gets down on both knees to turn her nightlight
on and checks to see that the row of stuffed Disneys along her
window ledge all have their heads facing the right direction. It

impresses Serita, the care he gives his little sister. Not quite the way her older brother treats her, but whatever.) When in fact she has come over—and it's clear to everyone—she's come over to be with Eli once Angie's been put to bed, to watch a movie and be next to him on the couch. She's come over to make out. She liked his style back in the school parking lot. He didn't want to plug up her throat with his tongue, or suffocate her with exhales matching her inhales, he just wanted to plant a light one on her and reel away. He's the first boy she's been allowed to date since her family moved here a year or so ago.

I'm not worried about that little sprite, her father had said at dinner one evening, scooping some khulla keema from his plate with a chappatis from the Safeway.

It's true, she thinks, he does look like an elf or something.

A tornado picks up a whole farm, crushes it, sends it vomiting from great windy vortices across the yellow valley. Can you imagine? she says, bends her neck back. His hand goes moving up again to grabble along the margin of her ear. Watch it, she says, her shoulder flinching. He glances quickly at the smooth arc of her eyelids and down the scoop of her neck. For grade ten, he thinks, she's seriously good-looking. In the hallways of school he's seen her walk with enormous volleyball steps. It's like she's always ready to plunge forward and greet something mid-air.

A tractor rises from the ground; a barn collapses upwards.

I saw a train wreck one time, but nothing like this, she tells him, and he's wondering if he should try to kiss her again.

He brings his free hand up to her knee and past—towards the remote on the coffee table. I think it's a bit loud. As he leans forward he keeps his hand awkwardly clinging to its place in her hair; she has to twist a bit to let him do it. He turns the volume down. His sister sleeping upstairs and all. Noticing a Victoria's Secret catalogue half concealed under the *TV Guide*, she wonders if upstairs in his parents' bedroom there are silky things.

She wants to kiss him, but he seems absorbed in the movie. She can smell baby powder on him, on his face maybe. Does a three-year-old still need baby powder? she wonders.

Bill Paxton's character is secretly wishing he were back together with his ex-wife. Played by Helen Hunt. Under a bridge, they have a moment of peace as the eye of the storm looks them over with its narrow retina, but soon the wind growls and they're holding on for their lives again.

Seeing this in the theatre would be hell, she says, even though she saw it on the opening weekend. She doesn't want to hurt his feelings by telling him she's already seen it.

Too much, he says. But he doesn't mention that he did see it in the theatre, a couple of times actually.

The neighbour's dog barks again and again and again and it causes Eli to make a fist.

When we were kids we were mean to that little dog, he tells her.

Really?

We used to chuck rocks at it. He hears himself say it and hears how unfavourable it sounds. He takes hold of that earlobe again and pinches it like bubble wrap.

You jerk, she laughs.

But she's attracted to hearing about what he was like as a kid, especially the little cruelties. Looking to the floor she sees a set of Fisher-Price toys. Legless Fisher-Price farmers are lying face down. The plastic fence around the sheep and horses, and dinosaur, has splayed apart, and the red plastic doors of the barn are wide open, revealing a roost full of hens. She recalls from her own childhood that when you open or shut the red barn door a cow moos. When she lived in Manchester; she remembers this toy from that long ago. It's as though a tornado has roiled through this farm, too. His sister's toy farm on the floor of the den.

It's soothing and also rousing to have him combing through her hair, to feel the sharp edges of his fingernails and the warm heel of his hand against her skull, neck, and ears. She imagines they are trapped somewhere, together, because of a horrendous work of nature. Her own Bill Paxton, her own twister. Waiting for him to pinch her again, waiting for that to come and startle her so that she can attack him back, both hands locked at his waist.

Do you want something to drink? he asks.

No, she says, maybe later, then takes her chance and plunges lips first towards his face.

2

A BEAGLE. A DOG NEXT DOOR. A brown and black and white dog, about twenty-five pounds, the kind of dog with black lips and tight jowls, this dog being a beagle, this beagle being about ten years old now, owned by a neighbour, a stubby man who's always waving goodbye to his house as he drives away in the mornings, always waving hello as he pulls up in the evenings; this beagle who spends and has spent most afternoons alone in the backyard, this beagle whose bark is more like a body-piercing than a dog sound, who has irritated everyone on the block since he first came to the neighbour's house, this barking beagle thus driven to insanity by children coming home from elementary school, who, without regard for his mental well-being, insisted on hucking gravel from the alley at this beagle, and laughing with merriment as he barked and barked and barked and growled and finally began to attempt literally to eat his way through this neighbour's fence, this beagle named Shoopy—according to the brass coin hanging from his collar—this beagle began to attempt to chew his way through the fence in order to get at these kids and bite them, chew through his owner's fence in order to continue chewing through these elementary-school kids' legs, this beagle, who every day at about a quarter to four got pelted cruelly with various-sized pebbles found in the alley, getting stones in the eye, at the hip, knocking at his feet, and saw no choice but to try and defend himself, to try and bite and chew through the yellow-painted slats of wood that contained this beagle from the kids beyond, who took every opportunity to taunt and injure this beagle. This dog. His dog mind reduced to chew, not chew; a bizarre canine binary. Who even now whenever someone passes in the alley—though it has been years since the last time anyone threw a stone—is impenetrably conditioned to bark and bark and bark and growl with the feral zeal of a far more fierce and starving animal (say a cougar, or a gorilla, or even a *rabid* dog), and then proceed to dig his canine canines into the fibre of this beagle's owner's fence and attempt to gnaw his way past to whomever is walking innocently through the alley, because this beagle has the memory so brutally etched in his brain of being pelted with stones from the alley just a few two-by-fours from his muzzle. A very sad thing this beagle. People are frightened to death of Shoopy when they walk by, because he is so truly mad that you can actually watch as splinters are crushed between his teeth and swallowed. A terrible kind of Pavlovian nightmare, really, for Shoopy, in which abuse has been the substitution for treats. The neighbour has tried to train this beagle out of his destructive anger, by hitting Shoopy with a rolled-up copy of a Victoria's Secret catalogue whenever he catches him with teeth against the fence boards (this didn't work at all); or with better results by trying to hold the dog in his arms like a child after a night-terror, trying to ease away this beagle's conniptive shivers with love and attention, saying, Shush, shush, there, there, and watching his pet, his beagle, slowly calm in his arms, the warm tender flesh of his arms, because, of course, this beagle has had problems with bowel movements and ailments of the digestive tract, having gone to the vet a number of times for the same problem, which is, of course, the removal of wood particles from his innards. Oftentimes difficulties are with shards of two-by-four stabbing into the skin of his stomach, or a fibrous mush clogging his intestines. This beagle comes in from a horrible day of rage and can't sleep for stomach pain, can be heard crying by the neighbour and his wife, whinging in his basket in the echoey kitchen. This beagle, who recovers from the hospital and is right back out there, eating the fence and barking, though it's been, how long, maybe three or four years since anyone has directed a single pebble at poor Shoopy. Because that's all this beagle knows to do now: chew; it's sad.

3

WHEN HAD BAKED SALMON TASTED SO GOOD, when had a chocolate torte been so indulgent, when had they been out together, alone, without the kids, on a weekend—had it been more than a month, more than two, how long?

They're at Milestones, Grace and Marty, and having a great time. They'd stay forever if they could. With a table near the window, as Marty had requested, they sit and pick at the last of their desserts. And whenever a pause comes to them, they turn and look out over the street that brought them here and watch as cars hum by. He takes her hand very gently and squeezes. The smile is real and satisfied, the whole evening somehow approved by just her smile. And now, with the meal done and their plates swept away, they each unpeel their striped mints and split the bill right down the middle.

Just like when we were in university, Marty says with a grin. Grace nods and takes a final look at the restaurant. A younger couple, undoubtedly prettier than themselves, is being seated and given menus.

Am I still attractive? she asks. Oh, you know what I mean. Never mind.

Marty takes her hand, God, of course. Of course.

Should we drive around a bit or see how the kids are, she wonders, half to herself, a thought more than a question. What with that volleyball girl over.

He knows not to answer right away, stares through the hoop of one of her pink Bakelite earrings, and waits.

I'll bet they're fine, she says, and brushes smooth her skirt. But I'm pooped.

They go home.

Snow attempts to fall again, as it has been doing all day. Single flakes toss through the air and fall in crystalline algorithms onto the frozen grass. The bitter math of winter. They drive past their son Eli's high school on the way home and Marty pictures his son somewhere in there, even though the place is dark and it's Saturday. Marty's been out of school for so many years the long corridors and lifestyle seem an enigma to him. There is no way he's going to remember how he felt about life then, so long ago.

All around them cars spin out of control on black ice. She drives the minivan home and parks it in the garage. They lock the doors and she hits the alarm. A bird sound chirps. They come out of the garage to go in through the front door.

The neighbour's dog growls at them and gnaws at the fence.

Shaddap, Marty says to this beagle, and swings his hand as though hucking a rock.

They get inside and find their son on the leather couch in the den with his girlfriend Serita. Both have that wide-eyed look, even though they're unmistakably separated by a whole couch cushion. The space between them is conspicuous. They've been necking.

What are you two doing tonight? Grace asks. She knows it's an awful thing to ask.

Her son looks at her. Nothing much, he says, we rented *Twister*.

Serita tries ineffectively to look small and gawky, bending a wrist over and biting at her knuckles. Grace sees two empty glasses stained with Coca-Cola and a two-litre container of it beside them on the table.

How's Angie, asleep?

She's asleep.

Do you need a ride home tonight, Serita?

No. I'm gonna call my dad.

Tell him the roads are a disaster.

Okay.

Smiling to each other, Grace and Marty travel upstairs, delighted at the recognition of their son's delicate entrance into sexuality. Marty pats his wife on the bum.

They check on Angela. She's sleeping face down so they turn her head to one side. Their little baby. She smacks her lips and waves her arms in the air without waking. Her little feet are covered by her sleeper. In the dark, the bluebirds-and-robins wallpaper seems less pleasant, Marty notices, and suddenly he feels morbidity step through him and out towards the moon, wherever the moon is. He shakes off the feeling, knowing that far too often lately he's been ruminating on his age.

Let's go to bed, hey, he says to Grace, puts his hands on her arms.

This night's over too soon, she tells him, and he agrees.

Shivering from the winter draft, he creeps naked under the blankets. He can just make out her body in the safety of the unlit room; her legs spread casually, about six inches.

How long has it been, she thinks—not knowing that he's thinking the same—how long has it been, two months? She contemplates an image in her mind of orgasm, that abstract sensation with all its spices and perfumes. As he makes motions of surrounding her, she conjures a phantom sense of what she may achieve tonight, as though above the bed she sees a mirror image of herself shuddering in some sort of ecstasy, her legs wrapped around a pipe of sex. Anything void of associations; she wants that blind desparate walk into passion to come back again, like the kind when she was younger, and less tired.

He asks her if what he's doing feels good and she answers that yes, it does. I want you to feel good, he tells her, so just say the word if it doesn't.

She says nothing.

Okay? he asks.

Yes, sure, she answers, then shuts her eyes.

He kisses her on the stomach, around the navel, down to the first coils of pubic hair and then back up, kissing up past her breasts to her clavicle. Finally kissing her lips. She barely moves.

She doesn't want this evening to end. She wants it to remain frozen, here, with him, all alone.

He's not yet aroused, though he desperately wants to be, wants to show his wife of nineteen-and-a-half years that there is passion, still, after all these millions of nights together. And kids. Guiltily, and with little premeditation, he allows a race of women to hurdle through his mind. Cashiers at the IGA, his old high school history teacher, a whole list of models from catalogues his wife sometimes gets in the mail, Xena the Warrior Princess. He kisses Xena's stomach.

I want you, he says with sincerity, and then to himself, I want you, Xena.

He laughs.

What? she says, wondering if her thighs are making him laugh.

Nothing—just a funny thought went through my mind.

There's a scream downstairs and the low rumble of emergency, the clicks from timber being snapped from a house's foundation and one by one firing their nails like sperm.

Casually, he lets his hand run along her. She bends her arms up and spreads her fingers against the wall. She pushes herself down.

Could you do that for a while? she asks him.

Sure. Gives her a wet kiss on the chin.

Shortly, it seems to him that he's been doing that for some time, so he implies he wants to enter her. She guides him as he lies down above her, and soon he is inside.

No so fast, she says.

He goes in slowly.

Would you scratch my back? he asks sheepishly. She graphs a number of red lines into his back and chest with her fingernails. He tells her that feels wonderful. She wants him to caress the pits of her knees and he does so. She is pleased. Most of all she loves the way he smells, so—woodsy.

You do this to me and I'll do that to you, she says, and growls in a funny way.

They lie like that together, briefly commenting on their circumstances, labelling each new event, exploring each other's sensitivities, and picking at the detritus of their fantasies, until their night together is over.

They sleep while dogs bark and weather moves.

THE RUNNER
after John Cheever

GENE'S MARATHON BEGAN. His run, a run, *the* run. His legs—
the real one and the prosthesis—seemed to float over the
road as it hummed effortlessly below his feet. He followed the
broken divider line stretched out down the middle of the
highway. In the dying fields to his left and right he heard the electrical song of crickets. A veil of clouds was draped over the
horizon. The sun above. The moistened sweatband across his
forehead. He ran past dilapidated gas stations and the long blades
of grass around the guardrail of a bridge. His sore muscles. The
lifeless wind. He ran over the bridge while water below wheeled

and drove against the tired yellow bank. His amazing leg, his
gorgeous bright red lungs.

When he opened his eyes to find he was in a Fitness Club and
not the ginseng fields of B.C., Jean inevitably returned to his
thoughts. The smell of sweat hung in the air like funeral flowers,
productively mournful. His marathon was dedicated to Jean.

He ran in place, his footsteps landing in place. He fought
against the backwards drag and did not make any progress, aside
from when he changed treadmills. His legs seemed to float over
the rubber tread as it hummed effortlessly below his feet. He set
the treadmills for interval training, to mimic a highway, to
imagine a run up and down hills.

He applied lip balm.

OVERHEAD, THE WHITE-SWEPT VANCOUVER SKY was clean and
cold and halfway numb. It was the sort of afternoon when everyone worked out indoors. And everywhere Gene looked, men and
women were pumping madly to the point of explosion, a muscled
pandemonium. With a sort of desperate nostalgia, he watched the
flexion of many different groins. These days, everything
reminded him of Jean.

No, he wasn't even going to think about Jean, he felt great and
it was going well so far. Here he was back at the original Salko's
Fitness Club. He was living in the moment, no matter how familiar the place was, no denying *that*. This Fitness Club was basically
identical to the one he'd left behind back east in Toronto, his and
Jean's bankrupt franchise. It was true that all across the country
patrons came in regiments cast from the same mould.

Clones, Gene thought, I'm one of many clones.

He looked. What he saw was nothing new. People bench-pressing two hundred, two-fifty, three hundred pounds, arms snapping back like bird wings, smelling of overworked glands. Deeply masculine grunts ricocheting off tilted windows. The flick of eyes from side to side, mirror to mirror. The surgical squeak of sculpted flesh. It was all here, it was all for him.

CAN I GET YOU SOMETHING? asked a woman, small and pretty like a birthday candle. Her head bobbed back and forth and she wore a sleeveless undershirt that read, I Am Salko Approved. You need something, anything, a drink?

I could have one of those green algae drinks, Gene said.

One spirulina coming up. I'm Lucinda, by the way, she said, waggling her hand at him as if he was shaking it. Then, inexplicably still facing him, she jogged away.

While running, he thought about small and pretty things. An insect bundled in the core of a tulip rubbing against pollen. A flat stone patting off water. A woman's baby-blue-painted toes twiddling in sunlight. He numbered these thoughts one, two, and three. The challenge was to feel nothing, to be an emotional vacancy, his skull an empty room.

He'd decided, while driving west across the country in an off-white rental car, to start again from scratch. If such a thing was possible. It was a long drive, he had time to mull. Highway One is the longest highway in the world; a man had tried to run from one end of it to the other—a mythic road in a way, however ambient. Gene tapped his prosthetic foot down as he accelerated up a switchback. A little desperate cloud held to a place in the sky above the road. When it rained in the Rocky Mountains, Gene stretched his seat belt up and wiped his eyes on it. The rain reminded him of Jean. His Jean.

Salko was walking towards him.

Originally, before moving to Toronto, Gene had owned a Salko's Fitness Club in east Vancouver, and it'd been a successful venture. He was savvy; he understood that a fitness club was made of one part high-quality equipment and two parts good parking. It was where he'd first met Jean.

Salko walked steadily, but casually, towards Gene. Nothing stopped him, but he seemed to gain no distance.

There were seven treadmills in this Salko's, and Gene had run on five of them already. Two more to go and he could move on, that was his plan.

Salko was right beside him. His bantam T-shirt was stretched fiercely against his chest, and below he wore what looked like your basic pair of boxer briefs.

Shake my hand, Salko said.

They shook hands.

Great to see you, first of all. And secondly, do you like this, Gene? This is new and improved. What you're looking at is surface, Gene. Same basic ceiling. Same colour scheme. Gene, I hadn't told you before for reasons this and that, too complicated to get into right now obviously, but we've updated here on the coast. I should have told you but I didn't, so there you go. Salko Fitness has been revised. They don't call it renovation any more, they call it revised. I like that. They term it like that because of new technology, which is what we've done here. Excuse me.

Salko produced a small white herringbone comb from a pocket somewhere behind him and ran it twice over his scalp. He put the

comb away, passed his thumb and index finger across the bridge
of his nose and sniffed violently before continuing.

Behind the surface we're connected, Gene. There's all around
us the yang of technology. And what with five Fitness Clubs in
the city, at ten grand per, that's simple math.

He pinched his nose and made another caustic sniff.

When you're done, Salko said, what's say you come to my
office?

Sure.

Salko snapped his fingers and speed-walked off, waving hellos
to customers and touching women on the hips.

Here's that spirulina you wanted, Lucinda said.

Hey, thanks. He took it, peeled off the ribbon around the cap
and drank back the green slough. He wiped his mouth. The girl
was still standing beside him, fixated it seemed, so he handed back
the empty container and she squinted at him in a way that
somehow made her whole body quiver.

Okay then, she said and jogged away, backwards, melting from
small to smaller.

He returned to his run, a repetition of the run he'd done
minutes before on the treadmill to the right. As he mapped out
the city in his mind, it occurred to him that he could run a dogleg
route of treadmills that would end at his old Fitness Club on the
east side. His marathon could take him all the way back.

THERE WAS A REST STOP BY A LAKE where the grass was long
enough to brush his knees, and he stepped off the highway and
leaned against a tree, cracked his neck in both directions. He
examined his prosthesis; it was holding up well. With a white

towel he pampered himself and then went and knocked on the door to Salko's office.

Let me show you something, Salko said and pulled him in. He directed Gene to a window. They were looking at a woman using free weights.

This is a two-way mirror, Gene, I just had it built up. Right in front of Gene's face a woman was pumping weights, her face splashed with red, the muscles around her armpits taut and frightening. Her eyes were on the mirror, and he was behind it, watching her thrust.

Don't stand too close, Gene, is what they tell me.

I can see why you like this.

Gene, it's good to see you.

Seems like only yesterday, Salko.

Not really.

No, I guess you're right.

Fuck it, is what I say.

Bygones be bygones, how about?

Water off a duck's back if you want, Gene.

Thank you.

The woman was pure brawn. He watched her pump. Sweat dangled and fell from her jaw and travelled in a sinewy line between her breasts. She was incredibly boring, almost like a marionette with limited mobility, or a dreary video loop, pump pump pump pump pump pump pump. Gene could barely register she was there at all. She was looking at him, but she was looking at herself. Pumping her feminine musculature. The pumping like a word stuttered until it emptied of sense.

Salko said, I saw a good porno last night called *Let's Fucking Showtime*. I wept it was so good.

Do you have a PowerBar or something like that I could eat?

Do I? Who do you think I am? He laughed once, Ha, and went to his desk, where he removed an ivory casket from a drawer and laid it on his crystal coffee table. He unhinged the lid and there inside was a batch of PowerBars in glistening packages. Salko tore open two of them and gave one to Gene.

These are seratonin boosters. It's like they carbonate your brain.

Sounds perfect.

Here's to sugar on your strawberries, Gene.

Likewise.

They chewed.

Ah, that's better, said Gene.

Delicious.

They sat together on Salko's eggshell-white leather couch and chewed.

It's time to breathe, Salko said. I was forgetting to breathe there for a moment.

I plan to run all the treadmills, Salko.

Look, I realize I was acting calloused. I was sorry to hear about Jean. There, I said it. Damn, why is it always so hard?

No, Gene said. That's not what I mean. He squished his finger into the yellow wax of his balm and applied it to his lips. Never mind about that, he said, puckering, and turned to look out Salko's window, past the necklace of treadmills to the Burrard Street bridge and the brewery. He watched traffic pass endlessly over the bridge towards downtown, beat after beat against the valve of a stoplight. He saw the sky as blue as a vein.

He said, What I mean is I'm going to run on all the treadmills in all the Salko's in Vancouver.

Okay. I like that. I don't get it, but it sounds like a challenge.

I'm going to get going.

Let me introduce your marathon to my staff, Salko said. Have you seen my fucking cellphone anywhere?

I'm standing up.

Godspeed.

HE CROSSED THE BRIDGE. Above him a cloud like a pale muscle flexed atop a mountain. The wind arced over the windshield of his convertible, bracing and mechanical, frigidly northern. Gene's fingers were cold, the knuckle joints were locking, clawing. He couldn't flatten out his hands against the steering wheel. Shivering, locking, bracing, and mechanical.

At the front desk a woman greeted him by name, aimed a banana at him, which he took, which he pulled the skin from and ate, thinking nothing, absolutely nothing, as he made his way to the treadmills.

His marathon began again. His run, a run, the run. He ran. He ran in place, his footsteps landing in place. A small town appeared on the horizon, the flat lights of a family restaurant and stop signs and small children with coats on, waving to him as he ran by, some kids carrying streamers, their parents nodding in approval—never having seen a man do something so bold.

By all appearances the Fitness Club was the same one as before. The seven treadmills all faced the window, the walls joined at familiar corners, doors led to similar rooms, even stains had formed in faintly recognizable shapes on the pilled grey-blue carpet. The lack of difference was only intensified by the minor inconsistencies in repetition: one less stall in the men's washroom, a slightly wider foyer, two vending machines instead of three. Like a twin trying desperately to individuate against genetic law. Not that it mattered, for he was already in a Saskatchewan of heaving wheat fields fanned by a gritty wind, a blistered tarmac on eroded highways. Golden death on all sides, below the maw of a parched sky, the dry killing breath of god; goodbye. His every muscle clench was a gesture of heroic antagonism towards the heat of a prairie hell. The road ran nervously straight to the horizon and trembled there against the blue. Yet each step brought him no closer to his destination.

HE TOOK A BREAK. Something about the way his lungs burned suggested now was a good time for a rest. On a bench he sat and unfastened his leg and laid it down beside him, grabbed a white towel from a shelf and wiped his nub and then the rim of the prosthesis. A man known as Baby sat next to Gene's leg.

Hey, Baby, it's good to see you, you look great and all that.

Well, sure. And how about yourself? I haven't seen you in, what?

Yeah, what?

Eight or nine?

That long?

I suppose not that long.

Five or six.

I guess not even that long.

It's fantastic to see you either way.

Baby nodded and began to massage his own arm, fingers into the muscle. Then he massaged the other arm, and then his chest. There was the occasional sound if Baby cupped his palm on soft

skin and pressed down quickly and air burped through his fingers.
The massage was involved but not intrusive. Gene didn't find it
unusual, he'd seen Jean do that kind of thing, and he'd probably
done it himself sometimes without even thinking about it. The
body required maintenance and attention, and there was also just
the sheer self-indulgent pleasure of exploring the fine product of
all that hard work.

You look great, Baby.

You look great too, Gene.

Don't lie, it doesn't suit your complexion.

Where's Jean?

What's your real name, Baby?

My real name? He looked at Gene incredulously. You're
asking me this now? Where's Jean? We used to have so much fun
together, us three.

Come on, Baby, Gene sighed, that's a real thing to say.

What? What's a thing to say? How should I know what's a
thing to say? No one talks to me these days.

Jean died months ago. Last winter.

Baby said nothing. He put his hands to his face and took a long
breath. Then he bent down and unzipped a bag he had at his feet
and dug through sweat socks and extra shoes, deeper, until he
found something he liked. He put what he'd found at the top of
the bag so that Gene could see it, and then he zipped the bag shut
again. It was only noon but Gene didn't mind the idea of what he
saw there. He had a vision of a highway made of treadmills and
wanted to plant his feet on that rubber map.

Where'd you get all those multivitamins, Baby?

What is this, *Law & Order?*

I could use something to re-oxygenate.

You're covered.

Let's take a drive, Baby, I have a car.

I have a mix tape.

I'm hitching on the leg, I'm standing up.

I'm already standing.

AT THE NEXT SALKO's—the third of six—Baby hung around quietly as Gene performed his marathon. To be honest, Gene was beginning to feel a bit tired. A stinging sensation around his eyes made him want to sleep. Nevertheless, he forged ahead. He focused on his legs. There was a kind of music to his jog, the rhythmic chug of his feet and the hum of the treadmill. He ran and ran and ran and ran and ran and ran and after a while the running made no sense and he became concerned he might stumble and fall in a pile of useless limbs. But the legs kept going.

HE RAN PAST A STABLE and an acreage where brown and black horses slowly ate feed, and there was a sunset like a shrinking pool of orange juice, and a fine rain, more like a mist, wet him down, and then ultimately it was dark. Half an hour later, after treadmill after treadmill, they were back to sitting together, Baby and Gene, but now Gene was woozy, laminated in sweat, as he swerved through a bout of nausea. Maybe this marathon was too much for him. He waited for saliva to relubricate his mouth.

You know that girl Lucinda? Baby asked, pointing her out in the corner of the Fitness Club.

I just met her today. What's she doing here?

My impression is that she likes you.

Gene said, Think she'd like to see the nub?

They shared a laugh.

In the distance Lucinda crept behind a blue recycling box.

Baby said, Can I ask what exactly it is you're doing here?

That might be the cutest thing I've ever heard you say, Baby. Who taught you to talk like that?

Gene strapped on the leg and went back to the treadmills. He said, You see how I have two more treadmills to run here?

I guess so.

It's a marathon, Baby. He smiled and started to run.

Baby looked concerned, with his legs crossed.

When Gene's first Fitness Club opened it was voted the number-one place in the city to meet sexy singles. Membership doubled. He met Jean on a Friday evening.

He kept running despite all these distracting thoughts, these horrible little tidbits of his past that came back uninvited. His skin leg was sore but he kept running. His stomach had cramped, his soft useless belly, but he kept running. Sweat fell in his eyes and his ears hurt and his lungs shrieked in pain. He was dehydrated to the point that his lips had gone all dry.

Remembered how Jean's lips were like bath beads. He remembered how even in the mahogany casket with all that heavenly silk, with those lips sewn shut, they were still as smooth. Unpleasantly, he remembered kissing Jean's lips as though performing some lurid funeral rite. It was the only delicacy he'd allowed himself. All he could think of at the time was how he would've pawned Jean's teeth and toes, if need be, to pay off the fucking debt to the Fitness Club.

That's a lot of running you're doing, Gene, said Baby.

It's for a worthy cause, Gene replied.

What?

My health and well-being.

It might only take a colour that flits by to make him think of Jean. The ripe shine of an apple. The smile of a spandex thong.

On the last treadmill his skin leg suffered a series of sudden and painful spasms that developed into an odd double limp. But he kept on because of basic guilt. The more he'd loved Jean, the more he'd failed to notice himself, and his body had begun to slacken and deflate. He'd outlived Jean despite being out of shape because of, what? The corrupt whimsy of cancer?

I don't want to think about this, he'd said to Jean on the phone that night.

Fine then, Jean pouted, you always make me feel like shit.

Come home. You've been at work all day. Don't be like this.

Don't be like what? You think I can't work because of it, but I'm not as weak as you assume I am. I'm not tired.

Suit yourself.

But Jean failed to come home that night, so Gene went in to work the next morning, looking. It was the first time he'd been there in months, it was the first time he'd really been out of the *house* in months. He'd been doing the accounting from home and never had to go anywhere. He'd let Jean, terminally ill and stubborn as hell, do everything. It hadn't occurred to Gene until he had to shatter the frost from the car door that it was even winter. There was snow everywhere and icicles on the sides of houses, which broke off occasionally and disappeared into piles of white.

He sat and warmed the car. He drove cautiously. When he unlocked the Fitness Club and searched the office and found nothing, he discovered he was prepared for what would come next—something crucial in his heart went inert. He knew Jean was in there, he could feel it, and in the washroom, stuck between the sink pipes and the toilet, he saw Jean lying dead.

When he dialed for an ambulance he knew it was a doomed gesture, that when he gave the address of the Fitness Club it was a kind of eulogy.

THE MARATHON HAD BEGUN to take on the flavour of something romantic. The loose hurt of muscle exhaustion went straight from his toes up the back of his neck. There was no denying he was on to something here.

The automatic glass doors shifted away from Gene and Baby as they entered the next Salko's.

He ran. The first six treadmills were hell. He swooned and almost collapsed reaching for the handlebars of the seventh, overheated, rushing with multivitamins, sticky with sweat, out of his mind.

He took a pause, went to the men's room and wet his face in a sink, started to cough. The pallor of his face was of no distinct surprise, but the thick yarn of blood that spun out from his mouth and the red stream from his nose were a concern. He tilted his head back and swallowed, very slowly. He lowered his head, and it felt heavy enough to tear right off his neck. His eyes shut and opened, and shut. In the sink, bloody water, he had a pool once, a big pool with water as blue as ice, and they kept it clean with salt, and Jean would swim every morning, at least thirty laps, so beautiful, nobody in the world—, arms milling through the water, taut shoulders, rippled lower back, ripple, the bloody water goes

down the drain. Was it blood? He couldn't remember what he'd
eaten earlier. It might not have been blood, this stuff from his
mouth. The stuff out his nose was definitely blood, but the
thicker stuff he wasn't so sure.

Anyway, it was mid-afternoon, and regardless, he'd have to
pick up the pace if he expected to make it to the last Salko's, the
one he used to own, before it closed.

He ran in place, his footsteps in place. His breathing was
erratic, highly unconventional, full of worry. Rare lines of cedars
on either side of the road looked like the eyelashes of shut lids. A
car passed and he watched it zoom by and saw a cat sitting on the
sill of the back window. He collapsed face first on the floor after
he'd completed the last treadmill. Something in his mouth tasted
like cork.

Baby threw a cupful of water on him and it exploded on his
chest and it was incredibly refreshing.

I'll call an ambulance, a woman in a slick unitard said, a dainty
nervous hand up to her mouth.

Not necessary.

No?

No. Forget the ambulance. Gene got up unsteadily. I just need
a moment with my trainer, Baby.

Trainer? Baby said.

Gene's stomach was a raw fist, and his skin leg was burning
sore.

No ambulance?

A moment with my trainer and everything will be back on
track, Gene said.

They went to the parking lot and fell into Gene's car and

relaxed on the leather interior. Baby looped a belt around Gene's left arm and raised a syringe in the air. This is adrenalin, Gene, it'll make you feel alive.

Hit me, Baby, one more time.

And then, for a long winning moment, everything was made of stars. His pupils dilated like twin moons as he convulsed on the back seat. He floated. He sank. Orbits became windstreams, windstreams turned into ruler edges, ruler edges into elegant micromatter. Micromatter into pure noise. His ears heard everything. Sounds that Baby would never hear. The click of feet, step after step, beat after beat, like the good valves of the heart. The ingenious structure of the leg. In the absence of flesh, the ability to reproduce that structure in steel and Kevlar. To actually hear cells dying. Desiccated skin into particulate dust. The curl wither crisp of cellular death.

He'd scraped the calf of his prosthesis and now steel pipes were exposed like bloodless bone. His hair was stuck to his ice-white forehead. His tongue, fat and purple in his mouth, choked him. His heartbeat was shovel after shovel of graveyard dirt.

I have to go now, said Baby. Is that okay with you? Will you be okay?

You have to go now?

It was very great to see you, Baby said, and pulled out an interesting smile.

Gene panted. He said, That's not what I meant. Another memory had vaulted back to him. Jean at the dining-room table drawing big dicks on their napkins with a ballpoint pen. When he saw what Jean had done, he took one of the napkins and ran it under cold water. He said, You've just ruined good damask.

I thought it was funny.

Well, I don't find you funny.

I'm sorry. I thought you liked my cute pranks.

Slowly, over months of washing, the men began to fade.

HE ARRIVED AT THE FIFTH SALKO'S FITNESS CLUB—the last one before his own. The light through the windows was turning a shade of dark, and as he ran he saw the blip of street lamps appearing throughout neighbourhoods.

Behind him an aerobics class was doing floor work. A miniature woman led a group through a series of leg exercises, scissoring and spread-eagling to the tom-tom thump of some dance music. Twenty women of different ages, body types, colours, and intelligence, all toe-slicing the air in tandem. Their lives distilled down to a half-hour regimen. An aerobic reduction of need: And just three more, two more, and one; just two more, two, and one; just one more, and one. And one.

WHERE WAS HE NOW? Nearly to Lake Superior maybe. Somewhere in Ontario maybe, but there were few images to accompany him, only an empty pocket where he used to see the world.

I'm right here, she said.

He turned and there she was, Lucinda, all five feet of her, hair tied in white trimming, pretty as a gift.

What are you doing?

I don't know.

He pointed to his prosthesis and said, It needs grease or the pistons will wear out.

She made a coy gesture and didn't answer.

His run, a run, the run.

His run through Ontario had gone as well as it could have, under the circumstances, and Quebec he remembered by the snow all soft and cold on his cheeks as it melted to water and dripped from his chin. With each treadmill he was that much closer to success. His exhaustion felt fatal, though, and however he moved there was pain to follow.

IN THE CAR WITH HIM WAS LUCINDA. They drove along the artery from Terminal to Commercial towards Gene's old Fitness Club, along the dim trail of business, night having accrued.

I'm so ready now, Gene said. He loosened his shirt at the neck. I mean, I'm really ready to give it all I've got. I'm so pumped.

I shouldn't have come along, Lucinda said, holding the dashboard in her fingers.

Close your window, I'm freezing.

The top is down.

You're a gem, Lucinda.

I'm worried about you, Gene.

It's good for you to worry. You're my trainer.

I'm not your trainer. Don't touch me so soon like that.

Am I touching you?

Yes, you were.

I'm pure impulse now. I'm verb only. I'm all alone. I'm nothing.

I said don't touch me.

Am I touching you?

Yes. You are.

The verb to touch.

ALL THE STARS CAME OUT IN THE SKY like bits of crushed glass. A blunted wind closed in. He parked the car in an alley surrounded by slick blackberry bushes whose thistles needled out with blood-red tips. The gravel lot was illuminated by a triple billboard.

Oh, Lucinda, Gene whimpered, what am I going to do?

She said something.

What did you say? I didn't catch that. Was it important, what was it?

She said something.

Oh, Jean, I don't understand what's happening to me.

She said something.

Gene started to cry. I'm horrible, I'm so horrible.

Finally they stumbled from the car, Gene and Lucinda, and came around the front of the Fitness Club to find that it was locked.

Through the windows he saw that everything was not the same. The lights weren't on. The darkened machines loomed like massive skeletons, jutted ribcages and spines. They lay in shambles, disassembled and useless. Steel wires dangled from the gutted ceiling and the walls were stripped, the floor bare.

What's going on here?

Oh, man, Lucinda said.

Gene went to the door, his hands clenched and weak and bent from exertion, he pounded on the door, but it didn't open. Now, for what, for whom? Why did he do all this? For nothing?

Give me something to throw at this place.

That wouldn't be so cool, Lucinda said.

He peered in the window, saw all the treadmills exactly where he'd left them, along the back. He saw the unlit purple neon swirl above the front desk that read Salko's. He felt the anxiety of these inanimate objects lying waste, with their pulleys, gears, winches, wires, and keys, imploring activity and yet always to remain lifeless and solid. Their rate of decomposition was so inconsequential compared to our own dash towards oblivion; that's why we trust them, Gene supposed.

He unbuckled his leg from his hip and held it in his hand while hopping on his skin leg.

He felt weak from all the running. His muscles each had their own fits. His skin felt cold enough to slush right off the bone.

We have to break in, he said and grabbed Lucinda by the arm.

Let go of me, she said, pulled herself away.

Gene tried to slap some sense into her but missed.

Damn it, Jean, he whined as he tossed his leg at the glass. A small spidery crack formed in the window, and his thigh split as it fell to the sidewalk. He looked at the prosthesis on the concrete and then up at the window and saw that neither was damaged nearly enough, so he threw the leg again. This time as the glass trembled the ankle burst, firing the foot into shadow while the calf and thigh broke up and spat out wire and springs.

Stop, Lucinda cried. Gene.

What?

Can't you hear the alarm inside? We have to go. He watched as she ran off towards the car, waving for him to follow.

This is not good, he said and threw a piece of leg at the Fitness Club, which did nothing except loosen more bolts.

Now a moment of weightlessness.

During a marathon there's a point when you seem to lift off from your legs, as if the agony of their work is somehow split from the rest of you, and you simply glide gyroscopically atop these independently pumping limbs. The pain doesn't so much go away but loses its attachment to you. And then suddenly you're sort of flying. The opposite can occur as well, the moment Gene fell back on the sidewalk, disabled by pain and weight, legless and sucked to the ground. Bruising his hip or maybe breaking it.

The marathon goes on. He crawled towards the Fitness Club window with thigh parts in hand and hammered them against the glass until another crack formed. Pretty soon, he thought, I'll be inside and I can finish the last lap of my run.

He said, Let me in, please.

To run through Canadian forests, deciduous, turning red in a collapsing sun. Fields in ochre, curl wither crisp of goodbye leaves. To run through an explosion of dandelion seeds, the white hair spinning through hot wind—, a jetty of logs threading out along a lake where muskrats clean their morning fish, so close to the finish line, so close. His heart punching at his ribs. His last muscle to retire.

His arms went numb and his leg slipped from his fingers. And sirens in the distance, underneath the ringing in his head or the Fitness Club. His broken white highway line was locked from him, the improper finish to his marathon. His leg in pieces as if frost had shattered it from his hip.

THE UNFORTUNATE

NOT A MONSTER, BUT NOT SIMPLY DISFIGURED, the boy was born during a cold snap. His mother was in labour for three hours before she relented to the forty-five-minute drive to the city hospital. I don't want those doctors looking at me with those, with those instruments, she said. They lived on an acreage with pigs, goats, a few dogs. It wasn't a farm and his father wasn't a farmer, but he sold hot-water heating to farmers, and that was close enough. They lived in the country, and on a winter day such as this a woman might prefer to try to give birth in her living room on the wall-to-wall rather than brave the freeze.

Sixty kilometres of white ice between here and some idiot doctor. Her husband smoked and sat in his easy chair and watched CNN while she sweated and grimaced. Are you ready to go now? he asked her.

No, she said. Damnit.

The unborn boy's older brother was in another room looking at catalogues that had come in the mail, women's apparel.

Ah, shit. She stood up with her big belly. Go get the Pathfinder warmed up.

Now for the second time her husband became a father. The child came out head first as usual, with an unusual head. A nurse backed away. The doctor squinted at what he saw. He delivered the baby from her and lifted it into the light, cleared the newborn's mouth with a deft turn of the finger, told her she'd just had a, Well, let's see, okay, it's a boy.

Another one? she gasped.

Her husband lovingly untangled a splatter of hair that stuck to her white forehead. A boy, he said, that's just great.

The doctor slung the baby in her arms and she saw him for the first time, his little body, fresh skin, head shaped like a football, and she said, Damnit, what is this?

After keeping the boy under observation for the next few days the doctor sat the parents down and told them he had suspicions.

What suspicions? the mother said.

Well, the doctor put his hands in his lap and looked at them, it's too early to speculate.

Her husband reared up from his seat, Too early to, you mean you don't want to tell us because you, what suspicions, answer the question my wife asked.

Please, the doctor said, please. The husband flattened his shirt and sat back down.

AT FIRST HE HAD DIFFICULTY LEARNING TO WALK. His head was way too heavy. They would find him ambling sideways, dragging his head along the carpet; he'd be sitting up and suddenly his head would tip backwards and he'd start crabbing forwards; lying flat on the floor he'd run in circles; when he stood up his head would still be on the carpet. This kind of thing. His older brother watched him roll around, Goddamn dud brother. You're the kind of creature that gets killed in other cultures.

That's not nice, his mother said. Take that back. She returned to her knitting, a game show on the TV for background. The Panasonic there in the corner was next to the gas fireplace they had rigged up to a clap mechanism. Clap and the fire ignited. Clap again and it vanished. On the TV someone spun a big wheel and clapped and the fireplace stuttered explosively. His mother looked at her knitting, then the TV, then her youngest son, as if they were connected somehow, in a way that didn't seem to please her.

His features, his pencil-dot eyes, for example, were pinched together as if all tacked to his nose; the back of his head formed an equidistant cone to the cone of his forehead; and sad blond whiffs of hair came out of nowhere on the pink baldness of his scalp. It was common for the child to get headaches, and later, as he matured, these headaches turned into migraines and nose-bleeds, earaches too. If he got a cold or the flu he might go blind for hours at a time. He begged for the phone to stop ringing when it wasn't ringing.

HIS FATHER BOUGHT A HORSE. One morning he took his baby boy out to the fence, holding him on his shoulder. The wind was nimble and snow travelled through it in dancing flecks. The sun was white. The horse came to the fence and snurfled. Look at that brown horse, he said to his son, that's your horse, I bought it for you, happy birthday. He had just turned four. What a beautiful animal, hey kid, what a beautiful animal a horsie is. The boy leaned an arm forward to touch the horse with a finger but his head was too heavy and he slipped off his father's shoulder and fell in the snow. He cried. The snow was cold. His father brought him back inside huddled in his trembling arms, I'm sorry, I'm so sorry, goddamnit.

They had beef stew for dinner.

Why'd you buy him that horse when he can't even ride a horse? He's only four.

I've boughten you lots of things. I can go and buy your brother something too.

But he can't ride a horse.

Just eat your dinner.

Afterwards they had vanilla cake and sang Happy Birthday. The boy squealed and then started to cry. His brother gave him something stick-shaped wrapped in a newspaper and a wrinkly bit of ribbon and he tore it open and there was a Mars bar inside.

Don't eat that all at once, his mother said. You'll get cavities.

Once they'd eaten and had put the boy to bed, while sorting the dishes into the dishwasher, she said to her husband, We can't afford a horse.

Now you too? Can't I enjoy this?

I'm the one sorting through the bills.

It's too late now.

Later that evening his father went back out and rode the horse at a gallop and lost track of time and he rode and he rode and when he got home one of his ears had been frostbitten and finally a week later a small chink of dry red ear fell off. He put the piece of ear in a Sucrets tin and put the tin at the back of a drawer in his office desk.

THE COMPANY HE SOLD HOT-WATER HEATING FOR didn't cover the cost of his gas when he had to drive halfway across the damn province in his Pathfinder to try and convince some hick couple with three TVs and three VCRs and a giant cardboard plate with six remote controls glued to it to get hot-water heating instead of the oil heating they were used to. The man of the house never even looking him in the eyes, just going from remote to remote, flicking and switching and suddenly recording. The prairie wind outside was full of icy razors. Arriving home late that night with nothing to show for the time, goddamnit, he stood and watched the horse graze through chunks of hard snow. The horse pushed around in the snow and found yellow grass to eat. His father never rode the horse again and eventually the horse became unhealthy. They fed the horse and cared for it in all other ways, but it was never ridden. The horse became skittish and would run in tight circles and rear up; or for many days the horse would stand at one corner of the fence and look at the ground, and at night it would fold up at the knees and sleep, and again, like the day before, the horse would stand and stare at the ground it had just slept on. And the horse did this for what seemed like months.

THE BOY TURNED FIVE and they brought him in at the doctor's request for more X-rays, covered him in a heavy black blanket, It's okay, honeycakes, it's okay, I'll be right on the other side of the door. She backed away from him and the door shut and the boy was alone, Mama, the boy said and wept.

Flicking on a switch, snapping the X-ray against the lit glass, the doctor detached a pen from his shirt and traced the icy glow of the boy's skull. He looked to the parents and took a deep breath and nodded. Is that, well, that looks like an awful lot of bone there, the father said.

The doctor nodded, At least three inches at the back, here, well, four, and again, here, at the forehead.

The mother chewed her lip, held her husband's hand firmly in her own, Is that a good thing, no, no it's a bad thing, right?

No, yes, it's not a good thing, the doctor admitted.

Damnit, the mother said and stood up, I hate all you doctors, you know I fucking hate you, you're telling me he's stupid.

No, no, that's—

Helping put on her son's mitts, toque, then wiping her eyes, out the door, and back into the SUV. The long rutted road below the Pathfinder, out past the last restaurant in the nearest town, the curling rink, and then nothing but dead wheat and white loaves of snow.

FOR DINNER SCALLOPED POTATOES, ham shank heated and with gravy, fruit salad with whipped cream, string beans, Can I show you my marks? his brother said and ran and retrieved some tests from his grade three class.

Oh, you're so smart I can't believe it, you're the one, I tell you, in this family, going all the way to university, isn't that right? she said, turning to her husband.

That's right, he said.

He's a genius, isn't he? his mother said.

You can bet on it, his father said.

Pretty soon you'll be teaching me things, she said.

Can I have a girlfriend? his brother asked.

His mother frowned. Concentrate on your grades and girls will be begging for you, and stop thinking about girls, don't think about girls.

Mama, the boy said.

Hey, it's suppertime here, his mother said, pipe down.

Mama.

What did I just say?

His brother said, Shut up, you dud.

Don't call your brother a dud, how many times?

The boy turned and stuck his tongue out at his older brother and then got his head pushed against his supper plate, food up his nose. The family laughed, his father crying, tears, dabbing a napkin against his eyes, Oh I'm sorry but that's, I'm sorry, that was like a clown running face first into a pie instead of the, you know, the opposite. His father had to sit back from his meal and just breathe for a moment. Meanwhile the boy could feel another headache coming on, rippling outward from behind his eyes, across his skull, screaming behind his ears, down his neck.

He was blinded. The headache got him. His mother guided him to bed, They're just teasing you okay, okay? The boy nodded. You got to understand your brother, he's a very smart boy, and it's not, you can't blame him really, he's very smart like your father says.

THINGS WERE BAD AND THEN HE WAS A TEENAGER and things got worse. In high school his desk directly faced the desk of his teacher. She had an electric pencil sharpener she used on her chalk, and it made a tortured noise as it ground down to a point in that little battery-powered box. The entire class sat behind him and he could hear the soft murmur of their rude voices, the seedy stamping and stretching of legs and arms. He could hear it but see none of it. If the teacher sat at her desk—which she always did—it was inevitable that the class had to look over his deformed head to see her, and he knew this, but there wasn't anything he could do about it.

Sitting in the desk behind his was this girl with curly hair. A note was passed forward while the teacher read passages from a book of Canadian stories. The note came over his shoulder pinched between the fingernails of the girl with curly hair, Somebody passed this to me, it's for you. A folded note on loose-leaf, he opened it and saw a drawing of a thick square-shaped boy with meaty fingers and monster arms, goofball short legs (like his own) in ill-fitting pants, and a football complete with stitching replaced the head of the boy. This was a caricature of him, he knew that, he wasn't so stupid.

He turned and looked at the girl and she was blushing. He stood and faced the class and spoke in a steady voice over his teacher's lecture, said, Fuck you, you fucking fucks.

And was sent promptly to the principal's office where they seated him with a line of delinquents to await guidance coun-selling. He fell into the same slouch as the other boys, the preg-nant girl. The handicapped kid. He sat there, the dud, and tried to will his head to shrink. But no, it wouldn't.

Sit down, the counsellor said, right there, and pointed to the only chair in the room other than the one behind his desk. How are you? he said.

What d'you mean? the boy said.

Hm, he wrote something on a legal pad. I was looking through your, through the list of your classes, the counsellor said. History, do you like that?

The boy looked past the counsellor to a map of the world taped to the wall behind him, I like it okay.

The counsellor nodded and smiled and nodded, What do you plan on doing this summer?

I don't know, I thought I'd get a job.

That's good that's good, so I wanted to ask you before we really get started, before I get into—, you know my son is in your history class, and also your algebra class I see, do you know him, did you know my son went to this school?

Yes.

Oh good because, before we start, I thought maybe you might know how he's doing. Yes, ha ha, sometimes a father doesn't know everything, even if he's a guidance counsellor, ha ha, things a boy keeps even from his dad, I'm sure you know how that is, well.

What do you want to know?

Have a pear, the counsellor said. He gave the boy a pear. Try it, go on, give it a big bite.

The fruit was rock hard. He put his teeth against it and dug them as far as they would go into the meat.

That's good pear isn't it, it's delicious, personally I love pears.

The boy nodded and broke the piece down into smaller pieces with his back teeth until he could finally swallow it. The counsellor dropped back into his chair. That's good, so, I guess I want to know, and don't misunderstand me, but, I worry of course, a father, well, ha ha, is he on drugs?

Oh, the boy said and put the pear back on the counsellor's desk, it's not ripe.

I'm sorry I thought it was, I'm sorry, is there anything else—?

No, thanks. No, he's not on drugs as far as I know.

The counsellor rubbed his hands together, Good, that's nice of you to be honest with me, thank you, now. Tell me, tell me about what happened today in class.

There was a knock on the door and a secretary's head appeared and rolled her eyes at the counsellor and he was up out of his chair and told the boy he'd be a moment, and the door shut and he sat in the leatherette chair and waited, let his head rest against his shoulder.

IN THE HALLWAY DURING A BREAK he stood in front of a change machine flattening a five-dollar bill. He took the bill and pressed it against his chest and studied the diagram on the machine and then followed the directions and put the bill to the machine's lips. The bill came spitting out. Having some trouble? she said, the girl, suddenly she was right there beside him.

Oh, he said, well I—

It won't take wrinkled bills, here. She opened a little bag slung over her shoulder and gave him a perfectly flat five-dollar bill. Try that, go ahead. See, she said, voila, change. It came jangling down and he collected it. What was that note about that made you freak, she said, you know, in class today?

A sproing of hair fell across her eye and she tugged it beneath a clip, Someone drew a picture of me with a football for a head, he said, and she looked at him very seriously in the eyes.

That's sick, it's really, doesn't that hurt your feelings, because if it was me I'd be bawling, I used to, this is so embarrassing but, I had a limp? My hips were at an angle, I wore these special leather pants all the time? Oh my god, you can't tell anyone this. You won't tell anyone, will you? She put a hand on his arm.

I won't say anything.

Okay, she smiled. I trust you. These leather pants were so painful. They were cut so I had to walk against the natural angle of my hips and—

Who drew it? he asked her.

Who drew what, I don't know, how do you, why would I know?

It made me mad, he told her, how am I supposed to change the way I look?

Sure, you can't, it's not your fault.

I wish I looked normal too, like I could get special leather pants for my head, people think I'm stupid because, and I'm not stupid, why'd you give that to me?

No, I don't think you're stupid, I always thought—, no, okay, you know two desks behind me and on the left?

On the left, he shut his eyes and lifted his left arm, Yeah okay I know that guy.

Well that's who drew it.

He made up a plan in his head. Beat that kid up.

WHEN THE SNOW STOPPED COMING DOWN and the clouds broke away and the days got colder and the evenings even colder than that, their old horse started to look weaker. His knees nearly giving out, either that or they'd lock and the old horse would stand in one spot for hours, afraid of falling over. Even with the TV on they could hear him braying, Maybe it's time we put the guy out of his misery, his father said.

He took his son outside behind the old grey barn and showed him how to use a shotgun, firing old books off a chopping block, not so much for the aim—he'd have his son stand right over the book—but simply to get used to the recoil and the noise. The horse tramped about, the smell of cordite and the terrible crack of the gun puzzling him.

Ah, maybe we shouldn't do this, his father said.

Okay, he said.

Don't chicken out like that. This is an important lesson. You know everything dies?

Yeah.

Well then. Okay, his father said, I can't watch this, I'm too old myself. Good luck, and he went inside.

The boy stood there with the gun against his arm. The air was cold and the barrel of the gun was cooling fast. He loaded another two shells, walked over the creaking snow towards the stable and the horse. Climbed over the fence, the horse taking a couple steps away and then no more, tossing his head and then staring at the boy, two quiet eyes looking, watching.

He aimed the barrel, closed his eyes, and did it. The horse froze, then buckled, slumped to the ground.

The screen door clanged shut and his father came out. He

walked towards the fence and almost stumbled. He said, Oh.

On flattened snow his old horse lay, head turned back, blood coursing out hot and steaming. The boy looked down at the miserable horse and said, I feel like I'm going to be sick.

His father fell on his knees, You stupid stupid boy, you think I was serious, my god this was my horse, I can't believe I let you—, why didn't you, you fool, you're so goddamn stupid.

The boy replied, You told me—

Why didn't you ask me, you could have asked me why, haven't you got a mind of your own, to do something like this, stupid and senseless? Falling back into the snow beside the dead animal his father gasped for air and pawed at the gore and liquid of the old horse's life. This would be what the boy remembered of the day his father lost it.

He returned his father's gun to its rack in the shed and walked over to the stable and looked at all the hay, the hay the horse slept in.

He picked up a shovel and wandered out the back door and walked some distance into their acreage, stabbed the blade at the frozen ground. It took him nine hours to dig a hole six feet deep, and the next day, when he got home from school, another three and a half to get it deep enough to fit the horse in. He brought a skid over and found he could get the horse on it by using its stiffened legs for leverage, tied some rope to the skid, and dragged the horse across the snow to the hole he'd dug. He shovelled the dirt back over the horse and packed it down and within three days the snow had it covered so thoroughly it was impossible to remark on which plot was the horse's and which was just plain dirt.

THAT NIGHT HE WENT TO BED EARLY. He lay in bed and looked at the walls in the dark. He thought about things. That old horse trembling and collapsing. He heard the TV coming from the basement all grunts and moans, then heard his brother coming up the creaking stairs, shifting foot to foot, and the bathroom door shutting. His brother, now a high school senior, still without a girlfriend. The bathroom door opening, his brother come knocking on his door. What is it, what d'you want?

Do you have any soap?

Soap? No, I'm sleeping, what d'you need soap for?

There's none left.

What d'you need it for?

Having a Jacuzzi.

It's midnight, and you've had, you've already had two today.

I know, *dud*, I know that.

Well what d'you need another for then, and don't call me a dud.

There was a pause before his brother said, It's none of your business what, where, and why, goddamnit, and then he heard his brother walk away.

His father came and knocked on his door and he thought it was his brother, Go away. The door opened with a splice of light and he saw his father standing in his housecoat, I'm sorry, Dad, I, I thought you were—

His father raised a hand and made a fist and punched the air, Ah-hoo, his father barked, this is the new, you see, this is the new time for you and me, the new whatsit, the new epoch, get a job, you hear me?

Yes.

Good, get a job.

All right.

All right good, get a job or, or you know. His father tightened the belt on his housecoat, turned and walked away leaving the door open. The boy heard his mother quietly say, Don't give him a hard time, he's simple, right, don't be so rough.

The hot-water heating kicked in and he could feel his lips begin to dry out before he fell asleep.

THERE WERE VERY FEW PLACES in the school to hide during lunch. He had to spy out empty classrooms and eat in the back row. High schools were not developed with the solitary in mind, and so when a group of boys appeared at the door to look at him he wasn't surprised, What're you doing in here? the kid said, stepping through the doorway. The kid had an awful grin and a stale giggle. He was the one who'd drawn the caricature.

I'm eating my lunch, what does, what d'you think I'm doing? he said, and put a final bite of bologna and macaroni sandwich in his mouth and crushed up the plastic wrap and shoved it into the paper bag.

The kid smiled, I came to say, you know, that I'm sorry about, you know.

About what? the boy said, a headache so close behind his eyes he could feel the hard melody of it. Now was when he should start beating this kid up, but he was too afraid.

To say I'm sorry about that drawing, he came closer, that was, you know, pretty mean of me. The boy leaned against the desk behind him. I mean, that wasn't very nice of me, the kid said, smiling. I feel kind of bad about it, the kid said, here let me apologize. A fist came up and connected at the boy's jaw and he was turning out of his desk, the remains of his lunch going down with him, and another fist.

When it stopped there were more boys around, smiling but silent, and the kid who drew the picture was flushed and tired. You like that? the kid huffed.

The boy climbed up from the floor and sat back down in the desk, his head lolling from a headache—now he was stinging blind, What d'you think? he said.

What did you say? the kid said.

You asked me if I liked that and I said, what do you think?

The kid looked to his friends, You just can't get enough, can you? What, freaks can't get enough, is that it, is that it? A sloppy tired punch just above the ear, Is that it?

After they left he stumbled out of the classroom with a bloody nose and out the front door of the school, paid the fare to ride the bus to the nearest town and sat in a Chinese Canadian restaurant watching the owner feed a stray dog overcooked rice and bits of grey hamburger, You what? his mother said when he got home, you can't do that, what're you, stupid?

No, Ma, but look at me.

His father folded down the day's newspaper and slid each section back into order and then looked up at the boy and said, You can't just, see, you'll have to get a job or, I'm sorry, that's right. He was still in his housecoat.

His brother was watching TV in the den and eating mini-pizza-bagels. He stood up and went to the bathroom and came out again in five minutes without flushing the toilet or running any water, Well there's no way, his mother said, if you ever thought you were going to be like your brother and get to go to university, count that out, not even high school, I don't know what can you do without high school, what job can he get?

His father leaned back calmly, Oh there's, I mean there's a type of job that, manual work, I think that should be your goal. And then he fell off his chair. More than once at each meal his father would lose his balance and fall off his chair and his mother would have to go and pick him up off the floor and prop him up in the chair again saying, Bend your knees damnit, bend them.

THE NEXT MORNING HE RODE HIS BROTHER'S BIKE to town and stopped in at the family restaurant where the curling teams met after games and he had an interview as a dishwasher. No, the manager said, and he walked out the glass door while an electronic alert bell went off. He got back on the bike and tried the gas station, the hotel, the store, the wallpaper warehouse. It seemed that no one had any work for him. When he got home he parked the bike in the shed and walked back to the stable and picked up the shovel and went out and started to dig a hole. When the hole was deep enough he filled it in again. He came in the back door and took off his boots and jacket and didn't answer his mother's questions, What the hell're you doing out there, is that, is your dad paying you, no, what? He had a shower instead. And then he sat and ate dinner. Thank you for dinner, he said and went to his room.

At 6 a.m. he pulled himself out of bed and dressed and went out and started to dig another hole. At nine he came in for some raisin toast and cinnamon butter. By five in the evening the sun had already guttered and the wind had picked up and he'd finished filling the hole in.

At the same time the next day he was out again, no snow coming down, the sky a veiny blue and a gelid white sun burning off the ice and his work was a bit easier. And by the time summer rolled along he'd dug a hole every day for the past five months—that was one hundred and fifty holes—and he'd filled in just as many.

I'm watching you out there, his father said.

It's good work, he answered.

When I was your age I worked for money. I got paid. What you're doing, I don't know. His father rubbed his nose furiously.

Well. I work and don't get paid. You get paid and don't work.

HE STARTED TO GO OUT in just an old pair of shorts, no shoes even. The dry ground was warm and soft, and then cooler and wetter as he dug deeper. The smell was rich and mellow. He began to notice the crease of the hole's chilled shadow as it drew up his body and he was comfortable with a hole's size when he could stand completely in its shadow. That was when he'd begin filling it in. There were worms now that it was summer, and dead mice, and long milky insects like he'd never seen before. He dug a hole and sealed it up. His fingernails were black, there was no use trying to clean them. He'd forgotten about his old high school, as far as he was concerned they were all dead and buried.

What are you doing out there, hey, yeah, hi, what is that, a hole you're digging?

He leaned against his shovel and ran his hand across his forehead and cleared away the sweat, It's a hole.

He walked towards the car stopped on the rural road beside the split-log fence and saw his guidance counsellor behind the wheel of a Toyota, Why're you digging a hole, is that something, may I ask why?

The boy walked towards the car and stopped at the fence and looked at his guidance counsellor, then looked at his own dirty feet. I've been digging them all year.

What, since you, since you left school?

That's right, I guess that's when I started.

His guidance counsellor turned off the engine to his car and leaned farther out the window and looked at the upturned land behind the boy, the random wildflowers dribbling red here and there, the long ambient stretches of umber weed, the wavering heat exhaling and warping the low sky. Looks like you have, well, is this a job, I mean, for pay?

No, the boy answered.

It isn't, well, I guess you're just passing the time then.

I guess so.

His guidance counsellor nodded.

What're you doing out here? the boy asked him.

Oh, ha ha, I came to see how you were doing, I came to see, but it doesn't look like you're interested in school any more.

No, the boy shook his head and kicked a clump of dirt from his shovel, no way.

Hm, well, can you take a break? I thought, it's pretty hot out, I'll buy you a beer.

He squinted his eyes at the counsellor, I'm not old enough.

That's all right, I know a place.

ON THE STAGE A LONELY COWBOY RUBBED THE STRINGS of his guitar and his bony partner played a Casio keyboard with programmable drum sounds, bass sounds, and a little sick trickle of piano. There was an exit sign above a door near the men's washroom that read IT. The whole place smelled of stain and salted nuts. The boy wondered if that was the scent of puke or just old beer. He saw a farmer sitting on a stool at the bar repeating numbers off a ledger into a cellular phone. The boy's head felt kind of loose and soft and he rested both hands on the red shag-covered table between him and his old guidance counsellor. A delirious man approached them and showed them the contents of a greasy paper bag, Fish, the man said.

There was a freshwater salmon in the bag, No thanks, his guidance counsellor said, and the man continued on to the next table, saying, Fish.

The boy watched the foam deplete in his mug of beer. I phoned your parents when I saw you weren't at school, his counsellor said.

The boy looked up, Why'd you do that?

I was, it's my job, that's what they pay me for, I was concerned, I mean, also, it wasn't just my job, I was concerned.

What'd they tell you?

The guidance counsellor turned the handle of his pint towards him, raised it and drank, put the mug down, They said you found school too hard, that you didn't do well on tests.

That's true, the boy said, I didn't.

Well okay, but, hey, I'm asking you, hear it from you.

Fish.

No, no you already asked us . . . hey?

What? the boy said.

The guidance counsellor leaned forward, Why'd you leave school?

He raised his head and pointed his eyes to the ceiling and then rolled them down again and he was hoping the whole world would be different, but it wasn't. He said, You think I'm going to tell you that I couldn't handle school because I have a head shaped like a football, well, that's what I'm telling you.

From the stage the cowboy singer said into a microphone, This one goes out to all the women, how many of you are women?

The guidance counsellor turned his head to the band and then looked back at the boy, And you think I'm going to tell you that I think that wasn't a good reason.

HE CAME IN ONE NIGHT COVERED WITH DIRT and showered as usual and came out to watch TV for a change and there was no one in the house, he was alone. He went to his brother's room and opened the door and looked around. In his parents' room he found a photo album with pictures of him and he suddenly real-ized how ugly he was. He went back to his brother's room think-ing about pictures and found a bunch of curled-up photos of naked women stuffed into film canisters—and an unopened box of ribbed condoms. Your father had an accident, he's in the, they've got him in the hospital, he fell trying to sit down to dinner again, his mother was wailing as she fell in the front door.

Should I go see him? he asked while trying to help her off the carpet.

No, god, no just stay here.

Well, what's wrong?

Goddamnit, I'm no doctor, honey, I'm not a doctor, I don't know. I need to be alone right now, okay, honeycakes? She pulled at her hair. Give me a hug, she said.

He gave her a hug. Now go away, she said.

He started up the stairs towards his bedroom.

I love you? she called after him, almost as a question.

I love you too, Ma.

Later his father came home and laughed and laughed, Ha ha ha, for what seemed like too long and then fell asleep.

HE DUG ANOTHER HOLE AND FILLED IT IN. The next day the same. There were lumps like blackheads everywhere, fresh earth shovelled and packed down again. The oldest winter holes had sprouted odd little green tendrils here and there.

Hi.

The boy walked towards the car, What time is it?

His guidance counsellor looked at his watch, Five-thirty.

He threw the shovel against the side of the fence, I said, didn't I say six?

Yeah you, six, yeah, I'm early, should I leave and come back?

No, come on. They walked into the house and he introduced his guidance counsellor to his family, shaking his father's shaking hand, How do you do, I'm fine, his mother said, Well I've heard your voice so many, sheesh it's nice to finally meet the man, his brother said, Yeah hi.

You needn't introduce me to your brother, the guidance counsellor said, winked, and followed the family into the living room where his mother had set out a bouquet of flowers she'd bought a couple years back, made of polyester.

I'm going to have a shower, the boy said.

There's no hot water, his older brother said. It ran out halfway through my Jacuzzi.

I'll have a cold shower, and he left them alone.

Dinner was spareribs, steamed carrots, corn on the cob, boiled potatoes, lime aspic. They drank iced tea. Outside a cherry sky turned purple then black and dancing clouds of mosquitoes followed the smell of cooked meat to the screened windows and waited there. Well this is the best meal, I mean, these are the ribs to end all ribs.

His mother blushed, Normally the man of the house would make, but today, she looked to her husband whose drooping head almost touched the table, but today I was the meat chef, ha ha.

It's just delicious.

His mother said, Leave room for the dessert I cooked, well hold on. She brought a pecan pie from the oven and they sat and ate it à la mode, and then his brother disappeared, then his father, so it was just him, his mother, and his guidance counsellor.

Let's move into the rumpus room, his mother said and clapped the fireplace on. Bring your drinks.

I'm going to bed, the boy said.

He shook the guidance counsellor's hand, I'll talk to you soon, the counsellor said.

His mother smiled like a precious schoolgirl.

BEFORE THE SUN CAME UP he started another hole. He noticed construction right on the horizon, way off there in the distance.

They were putting up a Petro-Canada gas station, he could see the sign.

At dinner that day his father said, I think, what we think is that you should be starting to look for a place of your own.

His father was old now, prematurely grey in the hair and in the eyes, limbs thin and stiff.

The boy finished chewing and shut his eyelids for a moment, You want me to move out?

His brother put down his fork, See you can't justify it, you can't just live here not educating yourself or bringing in any money either, just, you've got to—

His mother interrupted him, Honeycakes, each person's got to learn his own way how to live and—

You all talked about this?

His mother started to cry.

His father said, Oh we talked about it all right.

The boy walked into the living room and pulled out the old Nintendo and untangled the entrails of black cord and hooked the thing up to the TV and sat playing Super Mario Brothers 2, thinking about what he should do next. The music was plinky and stupid and he felt nostalgic. His reflexes were a bit off, but he was surprised to know that he could still remember where all the secret bricks were, the extra lives and gold coin hideaways. He bounced on the hardback shells of big turtles. He made his own way.

HELLO, SHE SAID. HI, HE SAID, sorry, maybe you don't remember me, I was in your history class, I sat in front of you? Oh, she said, and then, will you shut up I'm on the phone—just a second okay?

Okay. I'm on the phone, shut the, shut the door, okay, yeah, I remember you, how are you? I'm fine, how are you? Good. He sat back on his bed and realized he didn't know what to say, she sounded vital and alive: he said nothing. Did you drop out or something? she said. I guess so. Wow, what's that, I mean, do you miss school? No, he said, I've been busy. What? Working, I've been working on the acreage. That's cool, that's good to keep busy. There was a pause. Look I'm sorry to call but, it's that I need a place to live and I don't know anybody, and I had your number. Another pause, he wound his finger in the coil of the phone cord. You need a place to live, you're getting your own place? I guess so. That's cool, she said, man, that's, I mean, that's *really* cool. Do you know anybody who needs a roommate or something? No, I mean, no. Okay, sorry to bother you. No, don't worry about it, shut up, sorry, my little sister, I better go, my parents.

After hanging up he thought about her hair, the way it dangled in front of her eyes in perfect coils. He needed to use the bathroom but his brother was having a Jacuzzi so he sat and held it and thought about her and then let her disappear again the way he'd been able to let her and everyone else from school disappear, and he fell asleep, his head to one side, large, heavy, and thick with bone.

THE NEXT MORNING HE MET HER at a steakhouse where she worked as a busser. On her break they ate steaks with steamed broccoli and french fries and she looked older and he loved her for a moment. Have you been to that, to the mall in the city?

No, he said.

You've never been to the mall?

I've been to some strip malls.

Oh, it's, you'd like the real mall. They have a store that's just hats.

Maybe I should go there.

But yeah, no big deal, she said. It's pretty boring at the mall. Just like everywhere, I guess.

Is this a good place to work? he asked.

No, the manager's a prick.

I'm looking for a job, he said.

Well my dad got me this job, maybe, do you, well.

He put his arm against the frame of the window and looked out at the gas station and the field behind it, My dad doesn't know of any jobs for me.

He picked at the last sinew of his steak, he watched a car pull into the gas station, it was the guidance counsellor's car. His counsellor got out and filled the tank, leaned down and someone stepped out, it was his mother, she went inside and paid. They drove across the street and parked in the parking lot of the steak-house. Hey that's the guidance counsellor, she said, holy look at that, that's not his wife 'cause she's, you know, she divorced his ass, do you see that?

Yeah, the boy watched them cross in front of the window of their booth arm in arm and go towards the door.

Maybe it's sweet to see him like that with another woman. Think she sucks his tooter? I wonder if she does?

That's actually my mother.

The steakhouse door opened and the boy kept looking out the window. They were checking for a table, he could see them out of the corner of his eye and saw them jolt at the sight of him, he kept looking out the window, the door opened, they went around behind the steakhouse and came up quickly to the guidance counsellor's car and drove away.

Oh my god I'm so embarrassed. That was your mother? Well, but, did you know that? Your mother and him? I feel like such a loser.

No, he said. I better go, he said.

She took her napkin off her lap. Really, okay well, thanks for lunch, I, well, I'm glad you called, I mean, feel free to call anytime, I'm so *bored* this summer I can hardly—

Sure, he said, I will. But he never did.

HAVE TO SAY I'M GLAD YOU CALLED, thought maybe I wouldn't hear from you again, ha ha. I think you're going to like this guy. He's got a good sense of humour. They drove down a highway and he watched it become autumn and wondered why things went so fast even when it seemed like he was doing nothing. He sat where his mother had sat as a passenger how many times? his arm out the window.

Been busy? his guidance counsellor asked.

I worked for three days washing cars but they fired me.

Why'd they fire you?

Because of my head, the mechanics didn't like looking at me.

That's ah—, he said.

The money was pretty good.

They drove a little while longer. I think you'll like this guy, he's a bit of an oddball but you know, heart of gold, listen, about—

But they didn't talk about it, the conversation quieted, they went over a hill.

A blackened rusted barbed-wire fence followed the road until they came up to a steel gate and the guidance counsellor stepped out of the car and opened the gate, returned to the car and drove along two bald streaks in heavy grass. Dragonflies followed the car, How are you?

Good, how're you?

I'm fine, good to see you.

Good to see you. The man leaned down in his lawn chair and picked up a bag of tobacco and began rolling a cigarette in the lap of his sweatpants, It's sure fucking hot today, I'd say it's the fuckenest hottest day we've had this summer.

The guidance counsellor looked up at the screaming sun and then back down. Under the shade of a plastic awning rigged to the front of a little house no bigger than a fist sat the man, It sure, it's hot I'd say. The boy watched the man twist the paper up, lick it, light it, and smoke it.

Fucking addiction I tell you I tell you, he spat at his feet. What's wrong with your head there? the man said.

The boy stopped. The guidance counsellor smiled or squinted. I've got a malformed skull, I've, well, there's too much bone.

The man waved a hand in the air, Yeah yeah I can see that, but why's it red and flaky like that?

The boy put a hand to his scalp, Oh, oh, that's a sunburn, I, well, I don't grow much hair so—

Fuck, the man said and pushed some smoke from his mouth. Well that's the crapper, and no hats I bet.

No, the boy said, no hats.

Beside the house was a chicken coop bigger than the boy had ever seen, above which a white haze hovered. The floor of the chicken coop was flush with movement, white puffs skittering and circling, feathers floating up and scooping down through the air. There was a chicken-wire door to the coop and a flatbed truck parked near the door with big tractor tires covered in the splatter of offal. The guidance counsellor waved a hand at the man, This is my brother by the way, I'd like you to meet my brother.

He stuck out his hand and the man put his cigarette in his mouth and passed his hand to the boy and the boy shook it.

It was a few degrees cooler in the shade. That's a lot of chickens you got there, the boy nodded his head in the direction of the coop.

Is that the fault of your school, bro'? Don't you teach kids grammar? The man rubbed his armpit.

I'm a dropout, the boy said, and the three of them had a real laugh.

The guidance counsellor sat down on the slat-wood deck next to his brother's chair and smiled at him, What, what, why're you looking at me that way, what?

Nothing, just, no, nothing, the counsellor said.

Well fuck, see, this is why, are you trying to figure out what's going on inside this slushpile up here? He poked his head with his finger. Because there is no way to parse this gooey mess of a brain.

The guidance counsellor laughed and wiped some ash from his pants, No, no, and I don't want to know.

D'you see they're building a Petro-Can up there? the man said.

It's going to have a restaurant attached to it, I saw.

I heard it was an Internet café, the man said with a laugh. I'm just kidding, but wouldn't that be fucking funny?

WHAT YOU'D BE DOING IS THIS, the man said as he unlocked the door to the chicken coop and walked in. Chickens instantly surrounded him, pecking and clucking. He picked one of the chickens up casually by the neck and gripped it by the head and with a deft turn of the wrist broke the chicken's neck. The chicken's head fell to its breast and dangled there loosely while it went into spasms. He dropped it to the ground. The chicken ran butting into other chickens, doing hectic backflips before finally falling over dead. He picked the chicken up and threw it into the back of the truck. How does that look for you? the man asked.

The boy nodded, I can do that.

All you have to do is break their necks, I'll hack their heads off.

Okay.

He walked through the door and was attacked immediately by chickens. Little pecking beaks. The noise was infuriating. Don't think about it, just grab the fucker, go on, the man said and gestured. The chickens gobbled and jabbed one another with their dirty orange faces. He reached down and found one kicking between his fingers. He brought the chicken up off the ground, not so much heavy but unwieldy, and grabbed its head and cranked it around.

No, no don't let it go it's not dead yet, it's not dead, give it another twist.

He heard a crack, or felt it in his hand, and let the thing down, watched it freak a bit and then die.

They broke open a few beers and sat under the awning, Can you work every day? The boy said that he could. I'll pay you a nickel for every chicken you kill.

He looked to the guidance counsellor, That's good pay, don't worry.

A nickel doesn't sound like much, but think, it doesn't take long to kill one chicken.

I need a place to live, do you—, the boy said, have you heard of any?

The man put down his beer and began to roll another cigarette, Well fuck, I've got, up in the barn, I renovated the attic, it has a bed and whatever, there's a toilet and a sink—I was thinking about it as a guest room but.

I'll take it, the boy said.

Ha ha, the man said, all right.

His guidance counsellor smiled, See, now, see this is good; more beer in the fridge? He stood up and opened the screen door and went inside.

The man sat forward in his lawn chair and picked tobacco off the floor of his porch. Fucking heat it's the fucking crapper, I hate it.

HE TOLD HIS MOTHER HE'D FOUND A JOB and a place to live. She said, Oh that's just, goddamnit, look at your father. His father was in the living room wearing a housecoat and his head was folded over the edge of the easy chair with the TV blinking and dimming in the background as if maybe a tube had broken inside it, but no, it was just a rock video on the religious channel.

And you're going to just get up and go, what about me? said his mother.

He wondered if his father was asleep, and then said to his mother, I thought you wanted me to find a place, get a job, for my own good.

Haven't you been listening? Your father, he's sick. The doctors say.

Now he noticed that his mother was very agitated, her eyes were silky with water and her clothes were on all backwards, she whispered to him, You can't leave us like this.

But you said.

I need your help, honeycakes, please. I'm not a doctor.

I should get away for a while, he said.

You, I don't, I don't, hold on, she picked up the ringing telephone, hello? yes, here it's for you.

For me?

Of course for you, here, she handed him the phone, his brother in the living room took notice, breaking his concentration on his textbooks.

Get back to studying, his mother snapped, don't pay attention, I don't want you learning anything stupid from your brother.

Hello? he said into the phone. They talked, he told her to come over later if that's what she wanted, she did, she wanted to come over, Okay then, come over later. There was a beep but she ignored it. His heart tripped when she said it. There's a beep but I'm going to ignore it. Come over later, he said again. When later, When it's dark, All right when it's dark.

HERE ON THE PRAIRIE THERE WERE MORE than just stars, there were layers of stars that threaded together into gauzy strips, diaphanous against the empty black face of the universe. The fabric static of the universe, he said in a way a man might say something like that to a woman. Under a wool blanket they huddled in the chill of the summer night on the back steps of his family's house. She was warm and smelled of an expensive soap, a soap she must have bought at the mall in the city; he couldn't help but imagine her life. She said, Can I come and hang out in your new place? He said, Sure. They watched the family goat off in the distance mount a shallow body of rocks, stand erect and watch the tidepools of stars motionless but alive in the sky. What d'you think is *up* there? she put her head on his shoulder and shivered dramatically. I don't know, I see stars and planets but of course they say there could be more. I saw this show, it was about space, she said, her eyelashes brushing against his neck, and they, well, how did it go, I can't remember, but it's like the universe is still getting bigger. I'll bet it is, he said. She leaned away from him and he looked at her. Can I touch your head? she asked. Okay, he said. He wanted to close his eyes but he wanted to watch her. She lifted her hands out of the blanket and put her fingers on his temples. She smoothed the random tufts of soft hair and brushed the dry skin away, she followed the dips in the skull and the nearpoint at the back. Down the nape to his shoulders and then up behind his ears. She kissed him, I'm only seventeen, she said.

Well, he said, I think— In his brother's room he remembered seeing that box of condoms. They were ribbed. But he couldn't very well go in there now at two in the morning and ask to have a couple. He said, I don't, no, but if you think, I mean.

She kissed him again, on the peak of his forehead this time, My uncle runs the confectionery, she kissed him on the lips.

Sure, he said, I know the one, come on, he pulled her out of the blanket and looked down her body.

She followed him to the house, I can't come, right, he's my uncle, he'll—

He sat her down on the couch in the living room, Sure okay, sure, just wait here, is that okay? Okay, don't make any noise or you know—

She ran her finger over her lips and whispered, Zippered shut.

He drove without the headlamps on, his heart rattling. He parked and ran in the confectionery doors, Hi there, her uncle said. Hi, he shuffled up and down the aisles picking out candy bars, a jar of pickles a box of condoms, a newspaper, Okay that comes to ten eighty, the uncle looked at the boy casually, dropping the condoms into a plastic bag with the other items. Thank you, he said and ran back to the van huffing and scared out of his wits.

He drove down the cobbled road towards the house and at the main gate he pulled over and decided to walk the rest of the distance so as not to wake up any of his family. He spilled the contents of the bag onto the seat of the van and put only the condoms in his jacket pocket. The air was cold and the night was dark by the half moon. The wind seemed to sing a high note, giving him the first edge of an earache. Now and again he stumbled over the freshly turned earth of some hole he'd recently made. Nervously he broke open the box and separated a link of condoms and transferred them to a pants pocket, put the rest back in the box. He crept up the stairs to the house and tenderly put the key to the lock and screwed it around and clicked open the door. Removed the key and careful not to let it touch the other keys on the chain hung them on a peg. The hall was dark and he walked through it towards the living room.

She was on the couch, below his brother, her body moving as he'd hoped it would move against his own. They had not heard him. He'd been very quiet coming in, he was sure of that now.

YOU CAN'T LEAVE, NO, YOU CAN'T, NO, you'll leave your father like this, she cried, tearing the clothes he'd packed out of his Samsonite. He put them back in his suitcase only to have her throw them out again.

We bought you these goddamn clothes, these are ours, we goddamn paid for them, dig holes all year, these, none of this is yours. She turned the suitcase over and dumped his belongings on the floor of his room.

His brother came and stood in the doorway with his hands solemnly in his pockets.

Get the fuck away from me, the boy said.

I don't know what happened, his brother said. What can I say?

Get away from your brother. She pushed him out of the room and shut the door. She started working at the Scotch tape, putting his old rock posters up.

In his parents' bedroom his dad was sitting bolt upright on the Sealy with an *Us* magazine in his lap open to a picture of a robot. He waved a hand to the boy and smiled, Okay well, it's been great, I mean, you'll come for dinners sometimes, right?

He said, I think I might but it's hard to say.

His father nodded, Great, and coughed. I remember when you were born, he said, and everyone thought you were going to die, with that big huge head, but I thought no way, not this kid, he's tough, and hey, look at you now, what do you weigh, how much?

About two-twenty.

All muscle too I can bet by the look of you.

I guess so.

I'm proud, really, no, I think it's just great.

Okay, he said. Dad? he said.

What? his father said.

I'm sorry I shot that horse, I shouldn't have shot the horse.

His father said nothing. His father made no noise. He looked at his father, saw his eyes shut as though maybe a strong thought had passed by, but he still didn't say a word.

His mother screamed from another room, See? He's all deliri-ous, he's sick, I can't help him I'm not a goddamn doctor, I'm not and he doesn't know that.

His father laughed through a grim rasp, She's hysterical but it'll pass. Don't worry about me, the stinky stretch is over for this one, he pointed to himself. No way, he said.

AT DAWN HE WOKE NATURALLY and he was in a new bed, much lower to the ground, a softer, less resilient bed. The attic walls were stapled with old newspapers, the plumbing pipes protruded like knuckles from the dry skin of the walls. He washed his face in the sink and opened his little beer fridge and made himself a bowl of cereal, and someone said, Can I come in? and a pair of

hands hoisted themselves up the ladder and his guidance counsellor followed behind them.

Hungry? I can make cereal for you.

Love some.

They sat and ate. It's warm up here.

It's a bit too warm, the boy said.

I think he'd let you make a few more windows, if that's, you
could if you wanted.

It's a good idea. He poured them each another bowl.

I stopped, maybe you already knew this but, I stopped seeing
your mother.

The boy put his spoon in the leftover milk. I didn't know that,
no.

Yeah, I did.

Why?

Why? Oh I don't know, your mother, she's an interesting
woman. But she wasn't with me because— I know she was
wanting some guidance that's all.

Some guidance.

She was, that's right, but I couldn't give it to her, she thought
I could, but ha ha, I'm not very good at my job, I guess. She's
having troubles dealing with your dad.

I'll say.

Look, the counsellor said, my son, he's not ready for this kind
of thing. He doesn't know about any of this.

I don't think I do either, the boy said.

The counsellor nodded, like a child being reprimanded for a
small misdeed.

How are you? the counsellor asked. How are you doing?

He thought about this as he stood up and gathered his clothes and began dressing, Don't worry about me. He shrugged. I think I should start work now.

The guidance counsellor wished him luck and they stepped down the ladder and into the barn and the guidance counsellor said goodbye and went to his car and the boy went to the coop.

He gathered up the first chicken by its pimpled, bony legs and swung it up and clenched its neck, broke it quickly, threw it into the truck. The other chickens pecked at seeds. He raised another off the ground and killed it just as fast, That's good work, the man said, leaning against the coop. I eat lunch at noon, come on over to the house. The boy said he would and got back to work. He snorted feathers from his nose and blinked them out of his eyes. The coop was hot and there was little shade.

By his twentieth chicken he was lathered in sweat. He went up to his attic and ran a towel under tap water and wound it around his big head then went back to the coop and began killing chickens again, one by one, throwing them into the truck. At any time two or three of the chickens in the truck would still be kicking and flapping and stirring around in there atop the growing mound of dead ones. White feathers floated everywhere, the more he killed, the more this seemed to raise the feathers off the ground. When he broke their necks he noticed this sometimes caused a spasm that released a puff of feathers all at once. They were sticking to his body, he was dappled with white.

By noon he'd killed two hundred, You'll have to work faster than that to make any money, the man noted. They ate tuna sandwiches and drank beer, it was good to be in from the heat because he was exhausted and dizzy. Either that or I'll have to raise it to ten cents a chicken, he laughed. He rolled the boy a cigarette after lunch and they sat on the porch and smoked and watched a dust storm in a neighbouring acreage peel away a layer of dry weed.

You see they put the lights up in that Petro-Canada sign?

No, I didn't see that, the boy said.

I guess we'll have to go to that restaurant sometime soon and check out the waitresses.

Sure.

You smell like dead chickens, the man said.

I've been killing them, the boy said.

That's too fucking funny, you've been killing them, well no shit.

The boy laughed, And I'm going to go back there and kill some more.

Go to it, the man said, and the boy walked back to the coop, picked up the first chicken that came near him and broke its neck. He threw the bird into the back of the truck.

Later that afternoon they drove to the city, to the mall in fact, to sell a dozen birds to a butcher. He asked the man if they could stop a moment to take a look at the mall since he'd never been.

I'll wait in the truck.

He stepped out and walked in the front doors. The air was cold and the floors were smooth and the light was odd. He looked at a rack of baby clothes and watched a man do karate chops and then a row of children try and imitate the chop. He listened to music come from the ceiling and he thought to himself, So this is a mall, and then he felt naive. Someone bumped into him and screamed when they saw who they'd bumped into, and then burst out crying and apologized for the whole thing. A group of teenage girls huddled closer and closer together as they passed him and he decided that he didn't like malls all that much. He smelled the food court and then saw the corona of food outlets around the tables. Old men sat with their coffees, men that reminded him of his dad but were in fact much older, and he wondered when he'd next see his family, and the thought made him sad, because he really didn't ever want to see them again. And he asked someone in a pet store, Where's the store that only sells hats? Hats? the clerk said, a store that only sells hats? The clerk looked at the boy's head. There's no store that only sells hats. The boy nodded, I thought there was, I'd heard that there was a store here that only sold hats. No, there's no store like that. Is there another mall? the boy asked the clerk. No, this is the mall and there's no store that's just hats, there's a store that only sells nylons, women's stockings, but no, not hats. Okay, the boy said, thanks for your help, but the clerk had already walked away.

HIGHLIGHTS
FROM THE YOUNG BOY
VS. THE RAM

DARK PERINEUM, SLENDER CHAINLINK, hot stuff. This one's for the title, people, it's down to the wire here now, and heart valves are working overtime let me say. There's adrenalin tonight, in the veins, in the air. Under the canopy there's standing room only, it's badly ventilated, fogged-over eyewear everywhere. Oh, that didn't look good, hold on, testicles adangle, like the kind of sort of ripple of a purple night's sky. Young boy, all light drained across his high-kicking thighs—raindrop jewels of sweat plucked from the shoots of his pubis. Lathered, a glinting and musky patina over his pale skin. The milt-fruits of Bacchus and so on.

He has come here to win, for sure no question. *Sexualis adoles-centi*, watch him bust a nut on the mic—stay tuned. Sneeze, pardon me. And might someone die tonight? Keep that in mind. Thoughts of mortality, like it or not, go whizzing through the mind. We're talking here about death. To fear it is to be miser-able, to avoid it is to be pathetic, to deny it is impossible, who said that? So crawl into battle then, like for example into bed, or you know what I mean. Like to wake up late last night with your name in my head, and all the pillows laid out at the wall you used to sleep against, and then a breakfast for two ninety-nine, a pair of sausages, two pancakes, and already I'm so tired but I can't no I mustn't go back to your sheets and blankets, no. That kind of thing. But just let's keep in mind that here, in the ring, great slinking death is always the third party in an unknowing, unde-sirable threesome. The seductive fascia between two intimates is the Saran of death's cling, and so forth. A young boy, a ram, etc. . . . best not to ruminate. But here we are, in the womb of the world, the great umbilical woods of our past lives, or whatever—best not to ruminate. Young boy with two eyes like confident slaps of buttery paint. And the ram: all dander-headed and termi-nally ill—his only hope is to pull a full-on Saturn-style move and swallow young boy whole, so speculate the experts. Like in myth, you know—you know about myth. Words from the wise, sure. From up here the view is good despite the pangs of loneliness. What do you call it when you're afraid to be alone but also afraid to be with someone? I keep my mouth one splayed hand's length from the microphone as I was taught in school. So I don't pop my p's and whatnot. I watch the levels; I'm careful; I do what I'm supposed to do. Maybe I should mention our sponsor

_____. So now listen then, hear him breathe. Intermittent huffs like a slow fuck. Maturation of a gut, the first soot-whisper of a moustache, young boy—still, he has a lot of good years ahead of him. Whole lot of mounting and visible pubescent anxieties let me say, what with that like clipped little mouth, whirly coif, no pockmarks yet, not much going on up there. Truant and finally expelled, story goes. Attention deficit maybe, or plain old simple, maybe, or the victim of a fetal thud—hard to say, but yes. His grades are well known publicly, no reason to dwell. Always has been more of a player on the social circuit when you get right down to it. Linked, tabloid-wise at least, to the movie-of-the-week twins; not confirmed, no. The ones with their own dolls— darling cuties in these days in court suing their parents. And his face everywhere you go, dazzling, trance-inducing, whoop there it is; his body like a toy to play with, to adore; he looks good in a white leather cowboy jacket; his own line of boxer briefs. Ah yes. We watched him grow up. And anyway, look at him now, just fantastic. A real handsome young boy, not yet old enough to drink or vote or drive a car. Finds the muzzle and plugs the nostrils—way hard—a good grip on the scruff. See the heaving tire around the billy's ribcage. Long matted hair, vague expression, nearly deaf, priapic reek, and practically rotten, old ram. A fighter in his day, sure. Household name, sure, but that was long ago. Can't ignore the flab now though, no. Smelling of the bitter held-in upchuck of nausea; a dry halitosis of antique acids, impossible to ignore, even from way up here with nobody else around. Almost a viable weapon, that mouth-wise funk. Meanwhile. Gets in close, works the body, uses the hooves rope-a-dope style against the bushes, nice. And oh, ram's horns dig deep, nice. Oh, but young boy tweedles it and comes around for a big dee-dum, very nice. Tapioca-coloured, perfumed by ambrosia—girls going mad-like, pinched thighs and fainting spells and hot earlobes and practically honey-soaked bumblebees helixing around him tugging little parchment flags to herald his arrival, here there now, and he pretty much has this one tonight. Stay tuned—

—And we're back—under the moist canopy, what with the new moss carpet and everything. All such pubic names: the twisted ulota moss, the bottle, the curly thatch, dusky fork—I could go on—the common beard, lanky pipecleaner, goose-necked, electrified cat's tail, and ah yes, the goblin's gold. The hairy screw moss. Ah yes. It might be summer but still it's so damp. What with the dew-dropped cow-wheat, fine muslin-cloaks of mist, a puff of air against the bangs, what have you. The fine peel of hot arbutus skin all shattered piles among the liver-worts. Ah yes. Hugely white silk straps of sunlight looped between the blades of giant ferns and black cottonwood trees. All locally farmed, I might add. The baritone smell of ancient wood. Sneeze, pardon me—allergies. Emissions of dream-dark sap trill down the maples, the cypresses, quite a place. And let me say, up here where I am, all alone, let me add, it's a splendid view. Way up here, in a space close to nothingness, for sure, a kind of sort of preternatural void. Bodiless voice from where, when you think about it, where? There are moments of tenderness between a ram and a young boy that I cannot, no, can never be privy to. Brief, yes, but more than I can ever really ever hope to have. Like the faint beat of two thrashing hearts touching or close to touching. Like how soft is the skin at the very tip, really, is it so soft as to not even feel authentic, possibly? We want it more and more, yes, and a little faster every time. Let's talk about something ancient but taboo. Fear of sin, of age, of death etc. . . . Something which includes too much stubble. Something approximating carnal, or at least onanistic. A ram and a young boy. Reach in, ram, and scoop out his die-cast plastic heart and replenish, or whatever. Let's talk about something else. Arms like hoary brackets. Nails unfiled and scrappy drag across the pilose nethers, a soft hesitant penumbra there and the joint of the wrist and the bend of the groin. A delicate procedure which causes pink lips to brush up against black ones—a spittle bridge, kind of disgusting. Opponents back away and lunge again, a scumbled blur of limbs spletting together. Sneeze. Oh, I don't feel well all of a sudden. Please, let's just be quiet for a moment and close our eyes and beg a bit, just a bit, that this silence, stillness, emptiness, what have you, will never end. Cannot end. The lung of the wind is tired now, has been blowing for so long. Below me on soft earth, soft like what, like rich ground coffee ready to percolate and awaken, the mystery of a shadowplay, the sorrow of a battle, a kind of sort of tryst. Wake up to a pair of eyes you don't recognize. Who are you, where did you come from, don't leave too soon, but don't stay for too long. Cough cough, excuse me. Ah never mind, it's not important.

Before the show, YOUNG BOY: I just plan on, you know, I'll go out there and work it the way I was taught to work it, and with the, yeah, all the fans behind me one hundred and ten percent-like, and I figure, as much work as I've done—training, whatnot—I think my concentration is the key—I've got an excellent chance. And my singing career to think about. I've seen the ram, yeah, I like what I've seen, a lot of respect for—, and you

know, longevity and all that. But it's most importantly about
focus, which I have. And not thinking about the singing career
and the upcoming tour. I've got my trainer. It's a matter of
reflex—hoo ha—and tactics—hiy—and skill—huh—and concentration on the moment and what's at hand, most importantly.

Just one more question, Are you at all afraid that you might
die?

YOUNG BOY: Die? No, what, I mean, well, hold on, what?
What do you mean die?

—Alas, talk, behind-the-scenes discussions and such of
unhealed injuries, still. Burns to the *circumvallatae papillae*, scars
running backward, inward, along the dorsum of his tongue, hard
to say how that will— Oh, here we go: Spent-knot, finger-slip,
wedgie. That was quite a move. Did I say alas? Lonesome
circumflex gets the hoof, stretched from the shoulder—is that the
famous painter loam-side? Turn the smoked kliegs on him and
see if we can't get a smile. His whipping signature curlicued over
above-mantel canvases globally, top ten for sure. Oh, it's just a
look-alike, a poncey Caravaggio wannabe, or whatever what have
you. I said alas, I'm sorry. Anyway, meanwhile. Red slut-streaks
run parallel in sets of five down each side of his back, young boy,
up to you know what, last night maybe even. Got to wonder: did
she suck him, his powdered nozzle, still brassy and boyish, and
such a gentle spray? It's on everyone's lips, the question, smoothly
cut and formed. Did she, who she may be is your guess as good
as mine, but did she suck him? Performance, out here tonight,
by the looks, yes. And deep I might add, and pumping, I might
add, and with jewels of slobber among rivulets, I might add. By
the looks. We watch him because he fulfills us, did I already say

that, but the fulfillment leaves us barren. I mentioned that
already, didn't I? But can you remember the last time someone,
anyone, someone you barely know, flattered you, made you feel a
shudder, a body tang, a certain sense of appetite for whatever, for
you know what? Young boy, we flatter you because we want to be
you. Cough. Just for a moment to have the gumption to only for
a moment say something meaningful and honest and scary. To
say, I'd like to kiss you right now, or even just, I think I'm doing
okay, I don't need another drink, but thanks for the offer. And to
wake up, share the crusts with you, a dot of cold jam on top, and
still the fuzzy feeling of a sleepy half-nervous brain to keep us
quiet. —Holy crow, admire the jaw-action on that ram, speaking
of jaw-action. And big-mother digastric muscles here there now.
Yellow-rimmed eyes Milky Way black—no telling what he might
do, grizzled old bastard. Big grass-stained teeth like that there.
Ropy angora-type hair like that there. Ankles white bone like that
there, chunk of fungus caught in the frog of his hoof—ouch,
smack-dab on the young boy's sternum.

Earlier in the week, YOUNG BOY'S MOTHER: I asked him
to quit it with the wrestling but no, does he listen, no, does he pay
attention to his other obligations, no, does he know his father's
not well, no sir, no he doesn't, too busy, hm.

—Call out a name, fans, the name of the one you love. Say,
When I see you it's suddenly night, and all the stars come out. Or
say, You appear before me as if a flock of red birds has suddenly
fluttered from a pine tree. Say, I love you, I really think I might.
Say, You prolong me. Those here to see the ram are tufted like
giants, tit-hair white and mellow. Pink skin like the pink skin of
shaved farm animals. Foam nautilus coils above the ears—a set

of horns for nine ninety-nine. Cloven at the heel. Wheeze, cough, excuse me. A hiss of cheers, the wave. Crimped seaweed streamers and the like. Along the sidelines paper cups with logos on them, little corrugated jackets slipped over their midriffs. Plastic lids punched. Litter tossed in passionate exclamation from the crowd. Love, unlike heat, does not rise, and I am so cold. I might add. A soft pass—ignored—underbelly dimples flash like drops of juice—ram's on his back now and it doesn't look good. Listen, hear the ram: sort of hacking sound. Sponge-web membrane of the old goat's lungs click together, bogs of phlegm giggle in there, not too pretty, burble up and gather on the lip-edges like a nicotine belch. Immodest whisper of long transparent eyelashes butterfly against young boy's chest as the ram butts up. Young boy's nipples like the single buds from a salmonberry. The rough coral twine of the ram's horn dipped in the pollen of meadow death-camas lilies—up past the precious areolas up—chin-smack—maybe I spoke too soon. He deflects, chuckles it, and what have we here? Estimates, wagers, anyone? The ram's making a nice comeback. Seen him like this before with the kids, very smooth operator—here we go, and that's an elbow to the kidney, nice. Gasp, gasp, excuse me, something in my throat. Toe cuticles as black as hash oil. The fatted cleft at the bottom of young boy's spine now stained by dirt and mulch. Crushes a whole shelf of mushrooms across his ass. Orange mock oysters and jelly creps and ruddy panusses. We're talking big panusses here now. See him shake that thing, let's have some of it over here. Acrid burps of spore-smoke as his ilium wedges down on a bed of spiny puffballs. Signature sweet-knot move from the ram here there now, got to admire such a sort of kind of curmudgeon.

Nose hairs older than this boy, truth be told, oh—knuckle sandwich. Hold on, teeth pop and spindle off their dangly nerves. Spoke too soon, regarding the ram. Note the blood. That's dark blood, rich blood, important blood. Limp-headed ram, looks not so good all of a sudden, how shall I say? Googled eyes, a bit slack and wobbly and shaky at the hind legs, how shall I say. Let's see that again, here we go, see: From off the thud young boy uses momentum to soleus compression to ligament wind to bicep pump to tendon stretch to elbow grease to tricep twing to carpal articulations to palmar ligament clench to fist to punch, to punch, to punch, very good very good very good. Can't say for you all but I like a good old knuckle sandwich, have to admit. A clock-cleaner, a windmill, a pounding, a sock, an upper-cut, a coldcock, I'm going overboard, aren't I? Tonight's Slow Motion Instant Replay brought to you by_____. Gag, excuse me, gag gag, pardon me. I need a glass of water, sorry. Sorry. So sorry. I am so sorry. Let me say, no moment now free from anxiety, no rest stop for that, no last call; one last caress, no. To hide under the duvet and just cuddle and coo, no. Nights spent wondering what that tenderness is to the left of the navel. Days spent tired and restless and ultimately frightened and weak. Let's talk about buying chocolate milk in a gas station, becoming enthralled by the lights, the overhead fluorescent beams along the island, the stir of an engine, the final mouthy gasp of exhaust floating up into the midnight of it all. Let's talk about a gas station some more, do I pay at the pump or do I go in and say hello, buy a shiny magazine and look at the pictures of people I'll never meet or know in any way; let's talk about bowel movements, no, on second thought. Work alone and sleep alone and forever afraid. Got to wonder, is this what I was meant to do? Am I scared because I, somewhere, who knows where, I made an untraceable error I will never ultimately be able to fix? Is guilt the ink-shadow of desire? Is it better to regret something you have done than to regret something you haven't done? Got to warn you, I might throw up, there's big waves of nausea now, I admit. While down below me: Barometric pressure causes young boy's cremaster winch to wind—up scrote-sac up—the dapper hat of his penis given a certain frost as well. Jherri-Curl twirl into a fadeaway flipper and aye, the ram's going to feel that one in the morning. In the morning, alone and hungry. In the morning, with befuddled memories. In the morning, lamb, desperate, tired. In the morning, to try and rise and make something of the day, break-fast a glass of water. Cough cough. In the morning newspaper his face will appear in front of him like a cracked mirror. In the morning he will fall back into bed, heavy with remorse, old, a doleful punch-drunk knell between his ears. In the morning, nothing. In the morning. Nothing. Ah, it's so true that we are all alone in the failures of one step at one faltering step at a time. It's all over before you have a chance to clap off the light. Young boy all arch and all triumphant, yes, for sure, for now, for here. Those ones dressed as satyrs in the bleachers not too happy by the looks. Tear off the face putty, expressions of sorrow underneath the makeup. Gag. I feel sick. Genuinely overcome by illness. Joy, cough cough, for some though, cough, excuse me. Barf. Excuse me. Barf. A glorious effluvium of semen-white imported tropical birds blurts skywards, disappears into the sun's hot egg. Now from tree and hollow and, sneeze, everywhere, hundreds of chorus girls appear and erupt, cough, in song, skirts flitting up their thighs like so many venetian blinds. Retch, oh, now I feel horrible. What I'd do for a drink. Something luke. Something with the bubbles removed. It's over before you know it. Young boy has won, I repeat, the young boy has won. Retch. Risen off the earth, young boy, cradled in a sproingy bed of jubilant arms, gasp, retch, cough, sneeze. I can't breathe, someone quick. Numbness in the extremities. There's something large and obstructive and possibly yes the possibility is there that it is psychosomatic in my throat, please. Oh. Why thank you. Drink, drink. Thank you. I think I've seen you around, what's your name? With the match now over, choke, keep in mind that the two part ways. Leave not together but, cough, alone. Separate. Young boy, ablush and fondled, frothy crowd, all but yanking his limbs from their sockets. The symptoms are starting to fade, thank you. They love him; he's allowed to disremember. Ignored, the ram, still face down in the dirt and schist. A sad sack of mutton, a terrible ending for a champ. Sneeze. I like the way you've done your hair. Gasp.

W

A CHILD IN THE DARK, GRIPPED WITH FEAR, comforts himself by singing under his breath. He walks and halts to his song. Lost, he takes shelter, or orients himself with his little song as best he can. The song is like a rough sketch of a calming and stabilizing, calm and stable, center in the heart of chaos."
—Gilles Deleuze and Félix Guattari, *A Thousand Plateaus*

1

DESCRIBE THE BOY IN DETAILS that will bring him back. Blond hair in a hassled bowl-cut overdue for a trip to the barber's. About four feet eight inches tall. Weighs maybe seventy pounds. Arms long and thief-quick for cookies, Twix candy bars, loose change. They ask him to describe his boy, his son, and he has no alternative but to piece him together from memory. Knows a few songs by heart. Likes to watch cop shows because of the mad gunplay and interrogation scenes. The brick walls with the two-way mirror. *I didn't do it, I didn't take the boy.* The cops and their guns, the criminals and their guns. Under the arm, the leather holster clasped like a harelip around the silver tooth of a regulation firearm. Eleven years old, the boy is. His birthday is November 11, 1991. His name is Eliot. Blue, well, more accurately, cobalt eyes. Wears a pair of thin brown glasses with inevitably greasy lenses because he neglects to wash them except if nagged. Dimples. A mole behind his left, no, his right ear. No, his left ear. He has a mole behind one of his ears. A white scar above where his appendix used to rest. A smile that could kill you. *Hope that smile kills you dead.* A little boy of no more than eleven years old. Last seen wearing an X-Men T-shirt with three-quarter-length white sleeves; a pair of grape-juice-stained Gap pyjama bottoms; rainbow Adidas socks. Last seen as he was being tucked into bed, under the flattened meringue of a yellow duvet cover, in his own bed, in his own house, in his own world, a little boy of nothing more than eleven, taken, somehow, from his own regular childhood life, November 22, 2002.

THAT NIGHT, ELIOT'S FAMILY was more or less arranged for dinner when the doorbell rang. Ben, father, at the end of the table nearest the window. A window that wasn't a window yet, but instead a triple-casing of semi-clear plastic nail-gunned tight-as-hell to the cedar window frame. Around the window the exposed fibreglass insulation resembled an apron of veined fat. He sat in front of all this unfinished business at the end of the table and fooled with his knife and fork, back and forth from hand to hand. Molly, mother, at the other end of the table, her back to the living room, where the recently laid hardwood floor still couldn't be walked on for another two or three hours. While, with a wooden spoon, Molly dug her way through a deep bowl of mashed potatoes and then passed them on to Susan, daughter, who sat facing the kitchen, her back to a wall that was nothing but a series of raw beams that gave the skeletal impression of what was to come. Behind the beams there was a room and the room was empty. The floor in there was made of unsanded half-dry concrete, the walls were more of that cellulitic insulation. Someday soon this would be Molly's office where she would maybe, finally, get some drawing done. And then Eliot, their son, sat facing this empty room.

Okay, listen to this, Susan said. She licked her lips and somehow prepared her mouth for the oddity of another of her enigmatic impersonations, this one a high helpless sound that went, *Tiu tiu—tiu tiu.*

That's what, Ben said, some kind of bird? A birdsong? It sounds familiar whatever it is.

It's a walk signal.

A what?

A walk signal. You know, like for when you get a walk light.

Do it again.

She made the sound again.

That's pretty good.

I never have any clue why they make that sound, Molly said without looking up from her plate. More noise, do we need more noise?

It's for blind people, Mom, Susan said. So they know when to cross the road.

Really? Is that really why? Well, I suppose I can live with that.

Blind people getting run over by cars, Eliot cackled.

That's not funny, Ben said.

That's not a joke, Susan snapped. That's the stupidest thing I've ever heard.

No it isn't, Eliot said.

Shut up, Susan said. Don't burn off too many brain cells, ya retard.

The doorbell rang.

Ben looked up at his daughter. Was that you?

No, that was the door, duh.

If you're going to make me go and answer the door and it's another trick, I'm going to be furious.

It wasn't me.

Ben looked at his daughter. The doorbell didn't ring again.

Eliot, his father said, go and see who's at the door.

I don't want to.

Go.

No, please, Eliot said. He held his toy marmot closer to his chest.

What did I just say? Did I just ask you to do something or not?

The doorbell rang again. This time it was definitely the door.

Go. I'm not going to let you continue to be scared of silly things like answering the damn door.

Make Susan answer the door.

Make Susan answer the door, Susan crybabied.

Eliot, Ben said.

Let's go together, Eliot, the marmot said.

Eliot took a deep breath and, with his marmot, fell from his chair and scrambled along the floor, over the new kitchen tiles, towards the front door, where a man was waiting on the other side in the mirror-sparkle of fading rain.

He won't listen to me, but he'll listen to that goddamn marmot.

What difference does it make, Dad? The marmot knew you wanted him to answer the door.

How does the marmot know? Molly said, a fiddlehead coiled on her fork, raised to her mouth. How does that marmot know anything is what I don't get. It's just a toy.

THE MAN AT THE DOOR looked exactly like Eliot's father. Eliot stepped back from the entrance, from his father, and let out a faint squeak. He hugged the marmot to his chest.

Dad, he choked.

This man isn't your dad, the marmot said.

No, the man answered, and smiled but didn't move. He didn't move forward or backward though the door was wide open. The rain gobbed down the side of the awning and landed on the man's shoulder. He smiled like Eliot's father but made no move. I'm definitely not your dad, the man said, but do I ever want to meet him.

Suddenly the man was laughing. Hold on, the man said. Who said that? Just now. Who said that?

I'm Eliot's friend, the marmot replied. What's your name?

Now it was the man's turn to step back. He raised a hand and pointed a finger from it. That's some incredible whatever you call it, kid. Throwing your voice like that. Ha ha. Had me going there for a minute.

Who is it? Ben called from the dining room.

Is that your dad? Oh, kid, tell him to come here. I can't wait for this.

Dad, Eliot said.

This man isn't your dad, the marmot said.

No, Eliot told the marmot, I'm yelling for my dad to come here.

Oh, the marmot said. My mistake, the marmot said, shifted its weight in Eliot's arms.

The man fell silent, eyes all dilated and confused staring at the marmot. His frowzy blue jacket was dappled with rain. Wind blew through the trees and took leaves from their branches and spun them away through the air until the trees were bare.

Yes? Ben said, coming up behind his son and addressing the man. Can I help you?

Pardon me, the man hooted. But do I ever want to let out a curse word.

Eliot looked to his father.

Ben kept his eyes on the man. Can I help you? We're in the middle of dinner.

Don't you see it?

See what?

The man raised his arms like this gesture might help. Come on, come on. I can't believe this. Take a good look.

Ben finished an irritated breath. Take a look at what, exactly?

The man pointed down at Eliot as if Eliot and the man had already been through this whole thing. As if they were somehow in *cahoots*. The man said, We look exactly the same, buddy. Can't you see it? Me and you?

Look. We're in the middle of eating.

You don't see it?

See what? That we look exactly the same? No. And I don't find this funny.

Kid. Tell your dad.

Don't talk to my son that way.

Kid.

It's true. Eliot shrank away.

Susan came down the hall towards the front door, chewing, and when she saw the man she started to scream and choked on the food in her mouth and began to cough and scream simultaneously. She doubled over and waved an arm in the air. She dropped to the floor and spat out a mouthful of chewed carrot.

What's going on? She spluttered a final pile of orange mush. What is going on?

Ben stood there at the door. The man proudly grinning in front of him waiting on the front step looked nothing like him as far as he was concerned. And the joke wasn't in the least bit funny. *I didn't want him in my house.*

SO, THE MAN SAID, I'M JUST PASSING THROUGH, okay, on my way through town. La-dee-da, I'm hungry, a bit tired. A lot of driving. A *lot*. So. And so I'm stopping down at the donut shop then to grab a coffee and maybe a sandwich. Have a cigarette even though I'm trying to quit kind of thing. Sit down for thirty minutes and have a coffee, a cigarette, and probably a tuna sandwich. And the one right near here is the first place I see. The donut shop right near where you live. It's on the Number One, right? And I guess you're friends or something because when I walk in the lady behind the counter says, Hi Ben—, to *me*.

She's an old high school friend of my wife's.

Your friend too, Ben.

She mentioned something like that. Anyway, of course she thinks I'm you, but I have no idea of that. So I say, Who me? My name's not Ben, I tell her. So she all laughs like, yeah right, and touches my arm and says, Same as always for ya then? Same as always? I say. I'm a bit confused now at this point. So I tell her, I think you have me confused with someone else. I'm not from around here, I say. I'm from a hell of a long way from here and I've never been here before in my life, I tell her, or something to that effect. I tell her I'm not from here.

Would you like some beans? Molly offered.

Sure, thanks. Hey, this is really great of you all. Whips the hell out of a tuna sandwich you know, pardon me. Which is what I've eaten now for, god, too many days in a row to count. I haven't had a home-cooked meal in wow, a long time. Oh, these are good beans. Anyway. Yada yada, the lady at the donut shop is saying, Well you look exactly like this guy Ben a friend of mine who always comes in here. Yeah, and I'm thinking that this isn't so strange. People always think you look like someone else they know. But no, she's insisting. No really, she says like insisting that I come see you. Exactly like him, she says.

I just don't see the resemblance.

That's a gas. That you don't see it and everyone else does. That's the funniest thing, isn't it? About this whole deal? I think that's the best.

How is that the best?

You know what I mean. That you don't see we look exactly the same.

Appearances aren't everything.

No, that's true. But still.

It frightens me, Molly said.

What, that there's another man walking around that looks like your husband? Afraid of getting us mixed up one day? The man smiled. He ate a long bean.

No. She rubbed her face. No. Lots of people figure someone else in the world looks exactly like them. That's not too unusual. I just don't think it's right that the two should ever meet. It's seems unfair.

Eliot, I'm hungry.

Eliot turned the marmot on its back and pressed a few hidden buttons in the fur on the marmot's belly.

This creature you have here amazes me, the man said to Eliot. I came here because the lady at the donut shop was so sure about us looking alike and because she was yabbering on and on about it until I couldn't very well not at least check it out, her story. But even though I'm sitting across from my very own doubleganger, I am more freakin' weirded out by this toy here. I mean, what is it? It's not alive somehow is it?

No, Ben said. It's a new line of robotic toys. There's a microchip in there.

There's *three* microchips, Dad, Eliot said.

It's a computer then.

Sort of, Ben said. But it learns and, I don't know. It seems to have—there's infrared sensors and voice recognition and a bunch of technology in there that makes it seem alive.

There's object recognition, Eliot said. And there's voice recognition. It also knows your sentences. Marmot teaches me songs. Also it knows when it's hungry and I have to feed it the way only I know how. Nobody else knows. So that way it knows it's being cared for. It collects data on you and then it can answer things like questions you ask it.

So it can answer.

It also asks, Ben nodded. Hey, Marmot, ask the man something.

The marmot's head turned to face the man. Are you enjoying dinner?

Incredible. Yeah, I'm loving dinner.

Try the ham.

Jesus. That's a bit scary.

Wanna hear a song? Eliot asked.

Sure, the man said. I love a good song.

The marmot sang:

I can learn a little bit,
all I ask is for a bit of food,
I can teach a little bit,
and maybe I can lighten the mood.

Yikes. So how much does a toy like that run you?

More than I'll ever spend on a Christmas present again if I can help it.

Jesus, I'll bet. The man took a couple of slices of ham, a knifing of butter. Hey. Ever asked it why it cost so much?

Why it cost so much? Oh sure, we've asked the marmot. The marmot's got an answer for everything. It just whistles a few bars of How Much is That Doggie in the Window and leaves it at that.

It can joke, the man said.

Some cruel programmer's idea of a joke more like.

Eliot lost the marmot's remote control, Molly said.

It doesn't have a remote control, Mom.

It doesn't?

No.

Oh, she said and stared blankly at the marmot. I thought it did.

FOR AN UNEXPECTED GUEST HE WASN'T TOO BAD. He charmed them through dessert with anecdotes from his days on the road. Like his car radiator being ulcerated and gummed up with grasshoppers after a hot drive through Manitoba, so bad that his car overheated and he had to pull over at a gas station and throw cold water on his engine, the hissing volcanic mofettes rising above his car the instant the water made contact, and the sludge-fall of all those bugs breaking off the grill onto the asphalt; or a story about losing his hat in one town and finding it in another two provinces over, same hat, with his name written in felt pen on the inside rim; another story about being chased off a camp-ground by a flock of goats, in the middle of the night, under the curve of a starburst sky, the goats storming past like a freaky low, low-level meteor shower, hooves pummelling the ground, their black coiling horns, the earth-whistle of their bodies across the field—a *flock* of goats, he said, if that's what you'd call them—, it seemed as unlikely a thing as he'd ever encountered, and all running who-knows-where as if life depended on it. Ben kept his distance, made coffee, filled the dishwasher, while the man ate his dessert—Deep & Delicious marble cake—and asked for seconds. His fork sliding cleanly from his mouth to lie back on his frosting-streaked plate.

HOURS HAD GONE BY and the furniture could go back in the living room now, so they enlisted his help. Every room had extra furniture strewn haphazardly through it, a brass lamp with a corrugated-cloth shade standing in the kitchen sink, an upright coffee table in the spare bedroom next to a set of iron fireplace tools—the house was unfinished but it was also in unlivable disarray. They wanted to have the living room set up so they'd at least have a space to sit down, if not the walls and windows to make it a complete picture.

There were a couple of side tables in Eliot's room. They let the man go up to Eliot's room and carry the tables down. *He was in Eliot's room that night.* He was just as strong as Ben, too, and seemed to get a kick out of doing the work.

When they were done and everyone was ready to sit down and take a load off, the man said, Hey, come outside and I'll show you all a trick I know. It'll only take a minute. And we can get a breath of fresh air. How 'bout it?

Just about to sit down, Ben said.

Oh, come on. A minute.

Susan sprang up. A trick? I love tricks.

He's going to fool us, the marmot said.

Oh, no, the man said. Not that kind of a trick. I can't believe I'm here defending myself to a toy. Does anyone have a hat? Ben, you must have a hat. Something like a fedora or a Panama.

What are those? Eliot asked.

Hats, Eliot, the man said. Like the kind detectives wear or whatever.

Oh, I know about detectives. Have you ever read *The Thin Man*?

I think I might've seen the movie.

The book is better.

Sure, Dad's got a hat. Susan ran for the closet by the front door and retrieved a felt fedora and gave it to the man.

Not— That's a good hat, so—

Temper temper, Dad, Susan said and wagged her finger at him.

The man flipped the hat between his fingers and inspected it. Dusted the brim. This'll do perfect. I won't damage it one aorta, Ben. Don't worry.

THEY STOOD ON THE LAWN. The sky was bleary-eyed and blue where the wind had taken the clouds away. Wind was the reason the man had them all come outside.

I learned this with my lucky hat I was telling you about.

He arced a hand through the air to test it and then readied the hat like it was a Frisbee.

What—? Ben started.

But the man had already thrown the hat into the air. He launched it off and it spun through the wind, gone, as good as ruined. Until it suddenly turned around and started coming back.

The man stepped to the left and picked the hat from the air as casually as he'd thrown it.

Pretty good, Susan said.

He threw it again into the wind and caught it again as it returned. The fedora made a very clean curve as it left his arm and jettisoned off across the lawn, only to bend back with the wind to recover its distance.

It looks easy, right? But you have to read the direction and, what you call it, velocity.

Can I try? Eliot said.

Hold on. Watch this. The man waited in position, hat extended. Finally he threw it, and when it returned this time, it landed perfectly on his head.

Ta-da.

He gave the hat another toss and again it came back to rest on his head, as if that's what it had meant to do all along. He did the trick one more time before handing the hat over to Eliot.

That's so cool, Susan said.

Now be careful, Eliot. This is your dad's good hat. I'm an expert, remember. I've had years of training. I'm practically a meteorologist. I've stolen many hours practising this trick in all kinds of winds in all different places. I've given up my life in order to pursue this trick. I don't want you falling under the same spell, okay?

It was a joke, but Eliot looked at him without even a flinching smile.

Don't be scared, Eliot, the marmot said.

Oh. The man looked to the family. Oh, no. Don't be scared, Eliot. I was only having you. I was kidding around.

Be careful, Eliot, Ben said, crossed his arms, quickly checked his watch.

The man stepped back and turned in towards Ben. How the hell did the marmot know Eliot was scared?

I don't know. It's either an educated guess, or maybe the marmot senses trembles. I'm not entirely sure.

I could use a toy like that, the man laughed.

After this, Ben said lowly, I think it's time you moved along. I should put Eliot to sleep.

Sure, the man nodded. Hey, look. I didn't want to—all I wanted was to say hello. I thought it would be neat.

That's fine. I think everyone had a good time.

Sure.

Eliot gave the hat a good chuck and it blew off in a crude, waggling arc right out into the road, where it landed in a puddle. He jerked around when he saw what he'd done and made a sorry face to his father. He didn't see the car run over it, but he saw everyone's expression go from bad to worse. His dad was furious. That was the end of the evening.

2

THE NEXT DAY ELIOT WAS GONE.

His bed was rumpled but empty, the marmot was tossed on the floor; right away the family knew something was wrong. Molly was the first. She went to his room and saw he wasn't there. She put an open hand to her mouth, a screen. Looking through the room she knew already. Evaginated sport socks lay in gutted clusters on the wall-to-wall carpet. The shelves of his dresser had been dragged to the floor, some of them ransacked and nearly empty, others hardly touched. Damage had been done. Molly saw that the window in his room was open, a rimy breeze trembled at the curtains—but the window was too small for anyone, even Eliot, to have climbed out of. The room was cold. As the chilled air poured by, Molly's legs felt weak, and she leaned against the doorframe and backed out into the hall with a stumble, calling, Ben . . . Ben . . . Ben.

They telephoned the police. They wailed. Molly's sobbing turned dangerous, her hyperventilation led her close to a faint. She squirmed and attacked while Ben paced and bellowed. Susan seemed to retreat. She was farther away somehow. Everything but her eyes, which remained animate and sadly lucid. Everything else had gone insane. Look: there were no walls, no real windows, barely a kitchen, hardly any living room. The house was empty and unfinished and now it had been invaded too. Someone had come in the night and kidnapped their son and brother.

What are we going to do? Molly cried.

Ben closed his eyes and took a deep breath. His jaw was at work.

What are we going to do?

Stop, fucking—just shut up. Just shut the fuck up.

Oh god. Molly crept from the couch to the floor. Oh god, she said.

I can't believe we let that man into our house. I can't believe how stupid—

You told him to get the door, Susan accused.

Ben turned and grabbed his daughter. His face was red. His hands fell across her and tore at her shirt.

Don't you fucking— Don't even say that. Go to your room. He shook her until her head rattled. A teenage girl, she was as light as a marionette. He could break her. He lifted a hand for a slap, but stopped.

She fell to the floor when he let go and she didn't say another word.

I should go up and close the window in his room, Molly said and ran her arm across her eyes. Her face was a ruined blur.

I should go up and close the window in his room. But she didn't move.

How long does it take? Ben said, looked to his watch. It had been three minutes since he'd called the police.

Should I go up and close the window in his room?

No. No, don't go in there. Don't do anything, don't touch anything. It's the scene of a— Don't go in there, anyhow, whatever you do.

Susan switched on the TV.

Turn that down will you, Molly said.

Ben left his family and went into the kitchen, where he tried to ignore the half chaos of stalled carpentry. The counters surrounding the sink were nothing but hollow frames that looked down at the pipes below. He rested his hands on the sink sides and broke out in the shakes.

THE POLICE CAME IN SETS OF THREES. The first three were dressed in policeman blue and they stood at the doorway and graciously refused to do anything, even step inside. They stood on the porch and didn't speak, aside from the occasional answer to a negative churn of static on a walkie-talkie. One of them scratched his face and finally went back to his car and sat in there. He rolled down the window and put an arm out.

The next three were dressed somewhat like civilians, like regular people. They were dressed the way average people often dress but really never do. These were detectives. They came inside without much of an introduction and all made quick scans of the house as they sat down in the living room, each on a separate piece of furniture: one on the sofa, one on a chair, one on a footrest. For a moment they were distracted by a game of beach volleyball on the television, but when an advertisement came on they were all business again. And they all had guns. All six of the policemen carried guns.

So you say you had a visitor last night that looked like you, sir?

That's right.

In what way did he look like you? When you say that—?

Well, he didn't actually remind me of myself.

Okay then.

Everyone else thought so, but I didn't see the resemblance.

So he didn't look so much like you but reminded people of you?

Fair enough.

No, no, Molly corrected. He looked exactly like Ben.

Really?

Yes.

Mom's right. Identical.

Sir?

What?

Ben had to keep turning his head to answer each detective.

But he was as, say, as big in weight-wise as you, obviously then.

I think so.

Now but really how much did he look like you?

He looked exactly like Ben.

Are we talking here about a man that looked exactly like this man here, is that what you're saying, miss?

That's right.

A detective rolled his eyes and appeared to dully contemplate his notepad before jotting something down on the page.

He's the man who took my son. It's obvious, isn't it? I knew it as soon as I found out Eliot was gone, I—

Sir, it's certainly safe to say he could be a suspect. After that— after that, it would not be wise to jump to anything.

But who else would do this?

What I'm wondering, for the sake of wondering . . .

Does your son have any friends in the neighbourhood?

Did your son have a best friend, someone he had, has, sleepovers with, on an often-type basis?

Maybe we should back up, is what I'm thinking.

Let's start from the beginning. Or at least a place far enough back that we can, if you see what I'm saying, get a picture. A whole picture.

No, I don't understand. The longer—all I can see is that the longer we sit here pretending like we're shooting the shit, or whatever this is, the harder it's going to be to find him. We know who took him.

See, sir, no, I really know what you're driving at. This is an absolutely stressful-type time. It's very hard. I can believe how troubling this must be. These first few hours. But listen. Let's be rational here.

What we're saying is this. For example, what we're saying is that it is entirely possible your son was not kidnapped. Of course—, no don't stand up, please, let me explain . . . Thanks. What I'm saying is that in all likelihood your son has just skipped out. This happens. It's a good thing to know.

Skipped out.

Exactly.

He's fucking eleven years old.

Understood. But. Okay. But. Listen. In 1999, we had in Canada something like sixty thousand missing children. That's a statistic. Now of that statistic, forty-seven thousand or there-abouts children were runaways. Not kidnapped.

That's a good majority, sir. Runaways are much easier to find.

And then you know how many went missing because of a veri-fied abductor? I won't make you guess. Fifty-two. In 1999, that's how many. Only fifty-two. In all of Canada, with a population of what, and how many of them children? So you see what we're driving at.

Yes but—

Some kids just wander off. They get some idea in their head and they just off and go. Not even realizing how freaked out their parents are. Sooner or later they wander on home again. Especially the little ones like your son. Now it's best to just not make the kid feel too bad about this, but to also let the kid know how important it is, if you see, to let someone know where they're off and wandering to.

Less than one percent of kids gone missing have been abducted. We're not going to rule it out. We're not going to rule anything out. But the statistics, I'm saying, are in your favour.

I see.

Now, but you mention that you had a stranger in the house the night previous. Last night, correct?

That's right.

Did he see the house? All through it?

He helped us move our furniture back into the living room like it is.

So yes is what you're saying?

Yes. Some things from the kitchen.

Did he see Eliot's room?

He was up in Eliot's room he— He—

Sir, it's okay. We're in no hurry. Take your time. Take your time.

A blue policeman came in the house with a cardboard tray with six coffees wedged in it. He passed around coffees to everyone in the room.

You didn't want anything right, Ms.?

No, Molly whispered. Thanks, I'm fine.

Your daughter, she—?

No, she's fine.

The blue policeman stood and stared at the TV for a moment, and then nodded and left the room to wait on the front step.

Yes. He saw the house. The furniture was in a lot of different rooms.

Some of it was by the back door.

Yes.

Okay.

We'll do a check for fingerprints. We'll need all yours, then, too.

A detective stretched his shoulders, said, You didn't hear any noises, sounds kind of thing, last night? You're in bed, you're sleeping or almost, and do you remember hearing anything?

No. I didn't hear anything.

Neither did I.

You said your son's room. He was in your son's room?

Yes.

Okay. Just for the sake of, has anyone been in the room since—? Touched anything, moved-anything-type situation, since—?

No. No, I told everyone to not go in there. I'm so fucking stupid.

Sir, no. No, sir. That you are not.

Here's a question.

Sorry, before you . . .

No, go ahead.

Thanks. I'm sorry, but the man's name. You know the name? First? First and last?

His name. Oh god, what was it. Oh, I'm drawing a blank here. Sweetie, can you remember?

I'm sorry, what? I wasn't listening.

The man's name.

Molly looked up at the ceiling, Uhm, she said, then her eyes closed. If a man's name was in there, she wasn't able to wrench it out. There were no names in there, just some kind of sallow fog. *She can't even remember his voice.* She had already forgotten the question. Her concentration had collapsed. She shook her head and curled up and began to bawl.

Sorry, my wife, she— I don't think I can remember right now either.

That's fine, sir. It'll probably come to you in a little while.

Maybe so.

Ben touched the tips of his fingers together and looked at the prison there, between his palms.

A detective turned his coffee to his lips and after a drink said, So here's my question. My question is, what I'm wondering is. Is there any reason why your son might have wanted to leave the house last night?

No. Ben shook his head.

Now there're lots of reasons.

No.

Any number of reasons. Nothing he wanted from the toy store for instance?

The *toy* store?

No place he likes to go at night?

Nope.

No fights?

No.

Well, you yelled at him, Molly said, when he ruined your hat.

Molly, no.

Sorry? What do you mean, ruined your hat?

He ruined Ben's hat, Molly said, and explained the trick the man showed them and what had happened when Eliot had tried. The wind, the puddle, the car, Ben's sudden outburst, the whole thing. She told them the whole embarrassing story. While Molly talked the detectives all took notes, and Ben's leg shook as if he was keeping pace with some furious beat, staring at the new hardwood floor, waxed and striped blond and hazel.

He completely flipped, Susan said. With the forehead veins and all that stuff.

Susan. It wasn't that bad. He turned to the detectives, She's exaggerating. I raised my voice. It wasn't that bad.

Hey, sir. It's okay. Dads and sons get into fights. No biggie. Look. Listen. Why I'm asking this is because this is the better, more-likely-possibility-type situation.

Better that he's mad at you for getting all mad at him than for somebody, a stranger, abduction scenario. If he's upset, he'll come back on his own, likely, or he's not far away. Like a pal's house.

Right.

I understand your hesitation. But really, in this, right now. For once, being a mean dad is better. He's pissed maybe at you. He's gone off probably to test your authority.

A school buddy, maybe.

Ben nodded.

IT WAS TIME TO PHONE THE WOMAN at the donut shop. Her name was Colleen. Ben called her up while the police listened from a discreet distance. They leaned on things, chairs and counters, and didn't say a word. No, she told Ben, she hadn't seen Eliot. The police asked Ben to ask if she could come by the house, and when she appeared at the door she was already rattled by the three policemen outside.

She took off her shoes to walk with naked feet into the living room. Someone on the TV groaned. Is something the matter or something? Colleen said.

Ben didn't look at her. We can't find Eliot.

Oh my god. She put both her hands in her hair. Her toes curled up on the bare floor. Well, where is he, where could he be?

The detectives introduced themselves, took her hand and gently shook it one after the other, and found her a chair. A blue policeman came in with a brown bag full of deli sandwiches. It was already noon. He passed the food around to anybody who wanted some.

Molly, Colleen said. Are you okay?

No, I'm fine.

Colleen stared at her, stuck for something else to say.

The detectives leaned forward. They leaned back. They asked more questions. They peeled over the pages of their steno pads and wrote casually. Their leather shoes bristled against the throw rug as they leaned forward or back.

No, Colleen said, I don't think he mentioned his name.

And he looked like this man here? Exactly like him, would you agree with that?

Yes, she wiped her eyes. Oh, Ben, I'm so sorry. I don't know what to say. I didn't think he—

On the television nothing of any consequence was happening.

Meanwhile Eliot didn't come home. There wasn't much else to ask at this point so the detectives introduced the next three policemen. The camera policeman, the evidence policeman, the calmest policeman ever.

The calm policeman stood in the living room and made a gentle circle, sort of sussing the place out. But unlike the detectives, he showed no signs of awkward professional zeal.

This will be a good house soon, the calm policeman told Ben and Molly while the other two new men tramped upstairs, chunky with gear.

I hope so, Ben said.

He looked through the living room with a graceful turn of his head. His pointed mouth smiled. The light in here is marvellous, he said.

A panel of sun came across the couch and up the wall. A lot of slow dust motes hovered in there. Sure it was marvellous, but now was not the time, as far as Ben was concerned.

I'm Colleen. She gave the calm policeman her hand.

That's right, Ben said. She's Colleen.

A series of white flashes and smoky pops broke across the stairs and banister as a camera shot off a roll or two of film in Eliot's room.

I mean, my name is Colleen.

Hello, Colleen. He shook her hand and bowed his head for a moment. I think I've seen you before.

I work at the donut shop.

Of course.

You get a bagel with jam and a medium coffee.

Good memory. He nodded graciously and then turned his attention to Molly. You look very tired, he said.

Molly squinted. Yes, she said. I am. I'm so tired.

He took her hands. Why don't you go get some rest. If you don't fall asleep that's okay, but it might do you good to lie down at least.

Maybe you're right.

I'll make sure my men explain everything very clearly to your husband, and I'll write you a note myself when I leave.

Molly agreed and went upstairs.

A policeman in the kitchen whisked for fingerprints, muttered, There's sawdust all over every damn thing.

Ben stood next to the window and watched a series of new
policemen, nine in total, walk carefully through his yard with their
heads down, all deep in contemplation. Either that or totally stupid.
It was too sunny for this late in the year, with long ribbons of tree
shadows cast all the way from across the street. The police looked
like inmates of an asylum out in the yard for fresh air and disorderly
calisthenics. Slowly they made their way over the grass and forever
circled the flower beds, never glancing up to see where they were.
Ben waited for a collision of skulls. All this apparent incompetence
made him feel ill. They were looking for clues, he knew that, but it
didn't appear to be the best way of going about it. Shouldn't they
have state-of-the-art equipment? Some kind of electronics? What
good was the human eye these days? he wondered.

Weird to watch them work like that, the calm detective said,
and looked out the window with Ben. It doesn't look like much,
does it?

No.

No. But if there's something out there, we'll find it.

AFTER SO MANY PEOPLE POKING, prodding, and muscling through
their house, it seemed deathly uninhabited when they all went
away. Sometime in the afternoon the police finally completed
their professional ambages and Ben and Colleen were left alone
in the living room together. Molly was upstairs asleep and Susan
was in her room checking her e-mail. Colleen was on the couch
with her legs crossed knee over knee. He sat facing her, sunk low
in a chair. The orbits of his eyes had become hollowed out,
exhausted grey pits. He had a roaring headache.

Boy oh boy, she said, could I use a cigarette right now.

He concentrated, if that was the word, on Colleen's feet. Like trying to come off a high fever, or a lousy drug, he just had to keep looking at her feet and everything would be fine. If he looked away from her feet he might be in trouble. If he started to think he would definitely be in trouble. Thinking was an impossibility. All he could do was sit there and look at those long toes, the private arc of her heel, or the slender vein along the top of her right foot, and try not to break down.

Ben, she said, after a while. And he wondered how long they'd been sitting together, silently.

I'm sorry, he said.

This is all my fault, isn't it?

No, no.

Her feet walked towards him. He felt her hand in his hair, run through his hair. Against the ear she stopped. He looked to her and that was that.

Do you think you'll be all right?

I'll be fine.

Well, if you think you'll be okay, she said. I should probably go, she said.

Going to meet your new policeman friend?

She stood there with her finger in the puzzle of his ear. Then she moved away. If you need anything, call me.

He nodded. She left. He closed his eyes and then her feet came back, only to eventually fade again, and when he woke up it was dark out and the phone was ringing.

THE SOUND ON THE OTHER END WAS ALL NUMB, full of ill-weather-cackle. His little voice seemed like a scribble of thin dust ready to be blown away.

Dad.

Eliot. Eliot, where are you?

In a tongue's click the line went dead.

NO ONE SLEPT THROUGH THE NIGHT. Susan made coffee and they sat at the dining-room table with a detective and wondered if the phone would ring again, now that it was tapped, even though they all knew it probably wouldn't make another sound.

Do you wanna play blackjack? the detective asked, halving a deck of cards.

No, Susan said, and stood up and walked to the couch, lay down there but didn't even shut her eyes.

I think I'll read, Molly said but didn't move.

Hit me, Ben said.

There was a sound but it wasn't the phone. Something quiet, maybe the voice of someone walking by on the sidewalk. Ben stood up to look out the window.

Did anybody hear that?

I heard something.

Like a baby or what?

I thought it was a voice.

When Ben looked out the window he took a startled breath: the man was there.

What's wrong? Susan said and jumped off the couch, ran up beside him, and suddenly screamed. She grabbed her father's arm.

Oh, she said. Sit down, Dad. That's terrible. You scared me.

Now he could see the resemblance. Now that he was exhausted, scared, and practically sick with anger, now he recognized the man who came to dinner. Now that Ben looked like him and not the other way around. He turned away from his reflection in the window and looked at his daughter.

Don't tell me what to do.

Don't yell at her, Molly said.

What am I, what is this?

I'm sick of you yelling all the time.

I'm yelling? *You're* yelling.

I'm yelling because you're yelling.

Just shut the fuck up. Both of you. I'm sick of all this useless talk. I'm sick of it.

You've got no right, Molly said. You think *you're* sick and tired. Listen to yourself for a minute. See what *we* have to put up with.

I don't have to take this shit from you two.

Why don't you just complain about it? Go ahead, Molly waved her hands in the air, we're listening.

Ben ignored her, curled back down into his chair, muted.

The detective shuffled his cards.

ONCE, LONG AGO, MOLLY FOUND A BLACK STEEL COMB beside the tire of a pickup truck. She put it in her pocket, and when she got home cleaned it off in the sink with hot water, and from then on that was the only comb she used. Nothing weird, she just liked the weight of it and the way the tines ran clean through her hair. Since Eliot had disappeared, that comb had been going through her mind a lot, and she knew why. Because she hadn't seen that comb in almost a month, and it had been nagging at her a bit since she'd noticed it was gone; and then when Eliot disappeared, the thought of this great comb of hers, that she'd found and brought home and had used now for what was probably close to twenty years, was really digging at her, unwilling to let her have a moment without thinking, even in the back of her mind, about the fact that she'd lost it. She tried not to think about the comb at all as she stood against the frame of what would be the wall to her little office. She wondered about her office, as a way of pushing aside thoughts of the comb, but she wondered nothing in particular. She had no thoughts, certainly none to do with hard work or pleasurable work, the things she might someday accomplish in this space off the dining room. No, she just stood there and wondered about it. The floors so unquestionably grey. No room for argument there. Maybe Ben or Susan knew where the comb was, but she wasn't ready to ask any questions quite yet. Something kept her from asking. She didn't want to start a fight, and part of her suspected one of them had wrecked the comb, or thrown it out, or lost it, or stolen it, and she wasn't ready or willing to get into a fight about it. So where did that put her now?

HOW LONG HAD HE BEEN SITTING IN THE CHAIR? His chin touched his chest. There was a depressing taste in his mouth of the dry leftovers of a bad sleep. How long had his arms been bent at the elbow? Long enough to have grown so stiff he shrieked with pain when he moved them. He had to practically pry his fingers off the ends of the armrests. His gut was folded and nauseated and plugged with gas. How long could two legs stay bent at the knee? Two feet touching the same few panels of hardwood? His joints popped so loudly when he stood up that his wife came into the room to find out what had made the noise. He looked through the windows and saw that it was sunny. The sun was out in a shitty way.

They're sending a doctor around.

Who?

The police.

Ben rubbed his face and squeezed his neck. What did you say?

He saw she was tired, when he finally paid attention to her. He wondered if he looked even half as bad as she did. Something about the police are sending a doctor around, she said. That's what the message says.

What message?

The message Susan left.

Where's Susan?

She went to buy some groceries.

She went to buy—why did you let her leave the house? Why'd you do that?

I didn't.

Why the fuck did you?

I didn't. I wouldn't ever. And listen to yourself. You instantly raise your voice at me. Look. She went out while we were asleep. There's a note.

Ben took a step and he took a breath and pinched the bridge of his nose. Oh my god, he said. Now both their kids were gone. Molly came towards him on hesitant feet. In front of him she paused. He did nothing. He stood there. *A terrible parent*. She put her head down and leaned into him. She was trembling. Her arms, her body, her head. She was nothing but shakes. He put his arms around her.

She's going to come home, sweetie. Don't worry.

Ben, she said.

What? he said. She had her head up, looking above the slope of his forehead. She let him hold her like that; the ceiling only half stippled.

All day Molly kept inadvertently summoning up memories of Eliot. If it wasn't the comb, it was sure to be Eliot that was on her mind. But when it was Eliot, all her thoughts were nightmares. The times when he'd been an awful child, or worse, when she'd been an awful mother. Or the just plain scary times. Molly looked around their living room. Nothing seemed too small to hide behind any more. She saw a flint of light and then a teasing shadow behind the claw foot of her antique sewing machine box and for all she knew it was Eliot playing hide-and-seek with her. Each fold in the drapes was a possible ambush. She had the sudden and crazy compulsion to lift the lids off all her glass candy jars, to see if he was in there with the jelly beans.

Sometimes when you were away, Molly said, like on business or when your mother was in the hospital, I'd let him sleep in bed with me at night. And whenever he woke up in the morning, he'd look up at me with these freaked-out eyes and he'd say, Who are you? And he really looked like he had no idea who I was. And I'd say to him, Honey, it's just me: Mom. And he'd look at me like very skeptical.

Hey now, Ben said, touching her face. It's okay. It's okay.

And he'd say, Molly said. And he'd say to me, I thought you were somebody else who just looked like my mom.

SO MANY SIDEWALKS, AVOIDING ALL THE CRACKS, like a child. Susan wondered if he'd come home while she was gone. She'd

gone on a very long walk, and as she made her way up the steps
to the house, not knowing if there was new information, or if he'd
appeared on his own like the police seemed to think, or if he'd
just been hiding in the basement under one of the myriad cardboard boxes—; she could practically feel that he was home.
Somehow she'd made up her mind that by going for a super-long
walk it would ensure his safe return. That all she needed to do
was to get out of the house and he'd come back. She'd been a
merciless sister who'd told him on numerous occasions that she
thought he was totally and unadulteratedly retarded. If he wasn't
coming home, maybe it because she was there, the sister who
called him a retard. Maybe he expected her to berate him and cut
him down for disappearing like he did. And so that was why he
hadn't come home yet. She was mean: it was best that she went
away for a couple of hours.

WHEN SUSAN CAME HOME WITH A FEW BAGS of groceries, Ben was
lying on the couch and Molly was running a cloth along the wood
furniture to pick up whatever dust might have landed since she'd
last made the rounds about an hour ago.

Susan, Ben said as she walked in the door. We're all under a lot
of stress right now.

She didn't reply.

Let me back up. I'm sorry, I should've started differently. All
I'm saying is that if you want to go out—

Susy-susy, what your dad is saying is that we would have liked
it better if you'd woken one of us up to tell us. Instead of just what
you did.

I'm sorry, Susan said. You were sleeping.

That's okay, Susy-susy, Molly said. Why was she calling her Susy-susy? (She hadn't used that name in years, but all of a sudden—) You know, we were worried.

We were worried is all, Ben said.

I'm sorry.

That's okay, no, that's okay. So what did you buy?

I got some fruit and some chocolate bars and a loaf of bread.

Here, Molly said. Let me help put some of it away.

No, Susan said. No, I'll do it. Did the doctor come yet?

No. What's that all about anyway?

I don't know.

I can't figure out a doctor, Ben said. What else was the message from the police?

Nothing. Just that a doctor would be by the house.

I can't figure that out.

She didn't want to ask, she didn't need to ask. Susan already knew that Eliot hadn't come home. She'd walked out the door, she'd walked for over three hours, nearly half of the time with plastic bags heavy with groceries in each hand, and even after all that, when she'd got back home he was still gone.

She put away the groceries and went upstairs.

SHE FELT STUPID DOING IT. Maybe it was the dumbest thing she'd ever done. Practically retarded, and she knew it. Susan sat on her bed in her room with the door locked and peeled open wrappers to half a dozen Twix bars. She lifted the individual bars out of their copper-tinted envelopes and she lined them all up along her dresser. Very orderly, tip to tip, a sweet trail. She opened another half-dozen Twix bars and set those bars along her windowsills. The windows looked out over their backyard. If he was out there, if he ever was, he could maybe see the Twix bars waiting for him. But she didn't see Eliot, all she saw was the cheap yard landscaping that followed precisely the paid advice of a twenty-eight-year-old at a nursery and greenhouse in the suburbs who'd suggested stuff like a dumpy hedgerow, a flowerless deutzia, and a starved elm. The firepit was already full of dog crap even though they'd only been living there a few months and they didn't have a dog. She could still see the grid of their phone-ordered lawn. And the compost heap had damaged the sod grass and now sat on an angle oozing the juice of decayed leftovers out into the alley. This was what homes were now. When people talked about owning their own home, this is what they thought of. She hated this place. At fifteen she already wanted to die.

She said, Fuck you.

She said, Fuck *you*.

Susan said, Fuck you, you stupid little asshole.

She said, You fucking retard.

AND THEN IT WAS DARK. Everything was dark. The three of them had all definitely heard crying, and now they were trying to figure out where it had come from. It was the middle of the night. The sky above their house was an oily orange from the street lamps reflecting back off the sidewalks and the roads and all the strip mall rooftops, and there were no stars up there at all. Maybe it wasn't crying. They had heard a series of wails then, if it wasn't so much crying. Like the lowing of a pained cow, or a cat crawling back home after being half run-over. But it wasn't exactly an animal sound either. Toes were stubbed as they tried to locate light switches. There was no moon out beyond any of the windows. At about 3:00 a.m. they heard the wails. It had an animal quality, the noise, but it wasn't an animal. *He's calling out for help.* The sky was empty. Ben had passed out only an hour earlier. That was no animal noise. He was stumbling around in the semi-dark calling out Eliot's name, frantic but worn out. It felt as if, even though they'd all heard it, the crying or wailing or whatever it was, it still could have been a dream. It was definitely in the house. Outside not a star had appeared. The sound had come from inside the house. Susan swore it had come from upstairs, even though that seemed crazy, and they hadn't found anything. They searched every room. They opened Eliot's room and looked inside and saw nothing. The closet was wide open and he wasn't in there. And there was nowhere else to hide. So he wasn't in his room. With flashlights and knives they tore apart the basement, sawing apart cardboard boxes and opening the freezer. They checked the freezer over and over. The terror of having not thought of the freezer earlier made them check it many, many times. They didn't hear any more crying. They called out his name but there was no answer.

They went outside. The temperature had fallen to zero but there wasn't any snow. The grass snapped under their feet as flashlights swerved through the yard. Everything was black.

If once all three remaining members of the family had left the house there could still have been a set of ears left inside, to listen to their voices muffled by windows and doors and night and snow, those ears would have heard the family calling out to each other.

I'm sure I heard something.

I heard crying.

I did too.

I thought it was crying I heard but I wasn't sure.

Not like crying crying.

No.

More like . . .

I thought it was a dream.

So did I.

We can't all have dreamed about it.

It's possible.

All at the same time?

We're under a lot of stress.

Yeah, but still.

Eliot.

Eliot.

Eliot.

Goddamn it, I'm freezing cold.

He's not out here.

Maybe he's in the alley.

Go look.

Will you come with me?

There was a moment of silence when all that could be heard was the mindless humming exhalation of the central heating and also the drone of the fridge, until they discovered there was nothing in the alley.

This is horrible.

I can't cry any more. My eyes. My whole head is empty.

They came back inside, locked the door, wound shut the aluminum venetian blinds, and sat around the kitchen table.

You stupid fucking bitches, Ben said.

Pardon me, Molly said without much real conviction. What did you say?

I said, Ben rubbed his face. You know what I—you heard me. We should go out and look for him.

We just did.

No, we didn't.

Don't be stupid.

There was some silence. The night was a drag.

Someone left a burner on, Susan finally said. She'd been looking towards the kitchen for who knows how long, had been watching the burner for some time now.

Molly and Ben both turned their heads, where in the dark they could plainly see a single red coil atop the stove. No one moved to turn it off quite yet, so it continued to kindle there for a while, sedulous and predatory.

Molly put her head in her hands. I think I've slept two hours in the last two days.

Look, Ben said, raised his arms. I've got some kind of a rash.

I'm not feeling so well either.

No, me neither.

BEN WOKE UP TO THE PHONE RINGING. He stared at it for a second, let it ring. He was terrified to pick it up. What if it was Eliot, what was he supposed to do? What had the detectives said?

Hello?

Like before, there was static, and silences, and other interference. His heart stumbled.

Who is this? Ben said.

Hi-uh, this is the doctor that—

Oh, god.

I'm sorry.

Oh, god.

Sorry. Did I catch you at a bad time? I'm sorry. I was supposed to come by yesterday.

Ben felt his violent heart beat. He'd broken out in a sweat.

I'm the doctor who was supposed to visit yesterday.

Okay. Yeah. Right. We got the note.

The note, yes. Unfortunately I didn't. They failed to tell me, so I'm very sorry about that.

That's fine. What's this about anyway?

Actually, I'm in my car just about to turn on to your block so maybe we can talk about that when I arrive.

He hung up the phone and it instantly rang again. He answered, somewhat bewildered, and heard a woman's voice.

Ben, I've been thinking and I need to see you.

Colleen, look.

No, listen. Will you just listen?

Not right now.

Ben.

I have to go. I'll call you.

Will you? No, you won't.

I can't right now, okay?

Okay.

The doctor parked his car beside the driveway and came to the front door. As he walked away from his car it made a noise Ben had heard his daughter imitate. The doctor walked in a simple way. He looked endlessly composed. His face had no expression,

the way a ball has no edges. After they'd all shaken hands at the
door and led him to the living room they sat down and strained
to smile at one another. They were used to strangers now, people
who came to their house and seemed to distract them from the
absence, and already they'd formed clenched little habits for
these visitors. They asked if he'd like something to drink and
Susan served him a Crush.

So. I don't think anyone is sure what this is about. Is it about
Eliot?

Yes and no. Yes, but no, not directly related to him, specifically.
Unfortunately. I'm a doctor paid by the city. Thank you for the
drink by the way. See, in situations such as this, people often
don't realize they might need some help, assistance, etc.—, so the
police routinely send out someone like me to let you know that
we're here. A doctor who can help you. You don't have to accept
it, of course, and some don't, but obviously some do. It can be
beneficial. Might only be for a brief while, a couple days, a few
weeks, but there are often a number of things, events, that you
don't anticipate. Or see the need—the use of the events not antici-
pated, right? If need be, I can be here for advice in coping with
these new things.

For instance?

For instance, well, good question. With a missing child, one
of the best support systems is actually the media. In assisting
with the locating of the child. A short news segment, with a
photo, can often help tremendously with the investigation. The
police are working hard right now on this, but out of a unit, only
a few men can be spared full time. The eyes of the public can be
incredibly—, are an important resource in locating a child.

Okay.

Now what happens is that the police call me up and I come here and I can, for instance, suggest these recourses to you, that probably hadn't occurred to you. Stress and the uniqueness of the situation make it hard to think. So then, as well, I can give you advice on how to handle all this. You want to do something to help, of course.

Absolutely. This is what we're thinking. But they haven't given us any—

No suggestions, no tasks.

Nothing, that's right. We just sit on our asses.

Well, exactly. But the difficulty, one of the difficulties in a situation such as this, is that the mind wants to shut down.

Yes.

It wants to stop thinking, because thinking leads to memory. Memories . . .

Yes.

And so, even though you feel you want to help the police, that every moment at home is precious time wasted—on your asses, like you said—the body and mind are unwilling to cooperate with your desire to go out and find your son.

Ben nodded.

Find your boy yourself instead of leaving it up to people who've never even met Eliot. Don't know him from Adam, right? Love him . . .

That's right. This is how I'm feeling right now, goddamn it.

You're the ones this matters to the most.

Yes.

And for them it's just their job.

Ben nodded.

It's a tremendously overpowering feeling. But, well, first of all, the reason it's their job and not so much yours is because they know from experience what and how to look for a missing child. Whereas what you know is that you love him and want him back. Because of this, it ends up that the police are better equipped, i.e., mentally, because they aren't as outright affected. Whereas right now, for you, trying to sleep and eat are major accomplishments. I'm guessing.

The doctor smiled at Susan and took a sip of his Crush. Still, there are things you can do to help. A family's love can often be what brings a boy home.

They sat with the doctor and discussed their options. There was something very lonely and defeatist about the doctor and their list of options. The doctor was there to help them deal with the fact that Eliot was gone, but up until then it had been sort of possible to think he was just not around. Somehow it was different to see it that way. He might come back any minute now kind of thing. He might walk through the door. But with the arrival of the doctor, it began to sink in that, in fact, Eliot might not come home. A new possibility arose. He might never come home.

If you would like to, the doctor said. If any of you would like to, I often, what I do is speak with each member of the family one on one. We can sit in this room, or your own bedroom. Whatever makes you comfortable. It often helps to have a moment to think privately about what has occurred. Talk privately with someone. Clear the head a bit.

I'd like that, Susan said.

Molly nodded. I could really use something like that, I suppose.

Okay. And you, Ben?

Ben nodded. I saw my brother go through some kind of therapy for drug rehabilitation.

The doctor sat silently.

It seemed to help.

The doctor finished his drink. He didn't glance at his wristwatch. All right. If it's okay with everybody, I'd like to meet with Susan first. About an hour. Where would you like to talk, Susan?

My room is okay.

SHE LAY ON HER BED WITH TWO PILLOWS crushed under her head, looking up at the ceiling, where she'd stuck a constellation of glow-in-the-dark stars and planets. Even in regular light their milky nuclear colour fascinated her. She never saw these things in the sky. It was too bright in the city to actually see stars.

Something about a doctor in her room made her incredibly sad not to be in love. She stared at her ceiling, and her bed felt half empty, and she worried she'd done something wrong because the doctor wasn't talking.

So that's my story, she said, waiting to be prompted.

She heard the noise of his pants crease as he shifted a leg. She heard the sound of her own blinks. More times than she could count, she checked the clock. He never once checked the clock.

I'm not sure what else to say.

What else do you want to say?

That's what I'm not sure about.

How has it affected you?

What, Eliot?

Yes. He folded over a page of his notepad.

There was something about his silence that was giving her time to hear herself, rather than the steady echo of inquiry and police radios that up until now she hadn't been able to shake.

She finished a gluey swallow and said, I'm either going crazy or I'm not sure, but it's like I don't even care because it's happening to someone else. For all I know I'm dead and just watching me do all this from above my body.

What do you see your body doing when you look down at it?

Well, I see my body not being predictable. She nodded and paused, but he didn't say anything. Like ignoring my parents or not talking for hours and hours, she continued. Like all these stupid Twix bars I've got here for him. Like looking up at myself floating up there, dead, and wishing we could switch places. My body wants to be up here where I am. But that sounds retarded, doesn't it?

Of course not.

She saw the doctor write a few notes and imagined them to be kind of like her diary, only from someone else's point of view.

MOLLY STOOD BY THE WINDOW in her bedroom while the doctor sat by the door, and she expected a question or advice, but instead the doctor remained silent, and suddenly she began to really bawl. Up until then she thought she'd been bawling, but now she knew that all that had just been preparation for the real thing. Just a lot of heavy weeping, a big long rehearsal cry. But this was bawling. She could barely breathe. The volume of it scared her, the uncontrollable nature of it. This was an ache so big she got lost inside it.

I'm so sick of crying, she told the doctor. I think it's the stupidest thing. And I'm tired. You know, this is just—I'm not happy. With myself. Like this. You see?

She had moved into a series of shudders that pinched and inflated her throat, staggered her voice, and seized her lungs. Donkey-sobs, she'd called them when her kids used to make these noises—now she was the *big baby*.

Take a couple deep breaths, the doctor suggested.

She stopped talking and did as he told her to.

When the crying finally levelled off, she asked, What should I do? She rubbed a Kleenex against her nose.

He didn't say anything.

I mean, I don't want to just sit here bawling like this. I can't. I have to do something. I have to get out of this house or I don't know what. What should I do?

He gave her some suggestions.

AFTER BEN AND THE DOCTOR TALKED for a while, the doctor leaned forward and, while scratching his ear, said, I can suggest a number of medications, some of which will work to curb the anger impulse and might help keep you more stable. Another would be better for what you're saying about bursts of anxiety, heart palpitations, and shortness of breath. Of course, most of these will counteract the depression, but some might actually make it worse.

I think if I'm going to help Molly with the television and what you said, then I'm going to need something for the anger. The anger impulse you mentioned.

It's a temporary medication, and there's no reason to maintain a prescription. There are a couple side effects, of course. You'll have some short-term memory losses, sort of like being back in your pot-smoking days, ha ha. That kind of thing.

I already have a terrible memory.

Well then, I would expect that to continue. But it should help you with an evenness of mind while your wife handles the more complicated issues.

I'm glad one of us is doing fine.

Fine might be a strong word in this case. But her processes, emotional processes, are a bit more advanced, yes. See how she handles. See how she does, but it's fair to say, at this point, that she'll be the most comfortable with the more complex situations.

No, I got you. I understand.

Ben felt like a big fucking idiot. He couldn't handle this. He needed drugs now, while Molly took control. He sat there and didn't say a word, crossed his arms against his chest and bit the inside of his cheek.

Ben, the doctor said after a moment. I understand how this might bother you. But everyone has a different reaction to this. No reaction is better, no one is any more equipped to handle the disappearance of a child. Certain people need to do certain things to survive the ordeal, that's all. Right now Molly needs to keep occupied. And you need to concern yourself with the moment to moment, not get bound up in too many guilt traps. Your daughter especially needs you to be level-headed, you understand?

Okay.

3

ONE OF THE FIRST DETECTIVES THEY'D MET came back to ask if
he could see a shoe. He had with him a high-resolution photocopy of an X-ray taken of a footprint found in their yard, which
he laid out on the dining-room table. Susan was first to come for
a look; an involuntary twitch had been making her head kick to
the left all morning. Until her body accepted certain chemicals in
the drug he'd prescribed, the doctor had predicted that this might
happen for a while. A minor and short-term side effect, he'd told
her. But overall she felt more alert, after just a day or two of pills,
and that was encouraging.

The picture on the table was black and white, and at first
glance it looked like a mistake.

Ben stared at the picture for a long time before he began to see
any kind of shape that looked to him like it could be a foot. No
way that was a foot. It looked more like the impression of a
banana or a bird's head.

There's a lot of reasons why we think this footprint was made
the night your son disappeared.

How is that even a footprint?

Good question. Let me explain our theory. The popular
theory is this. First of all, I think that if what we can tell from the
footprint is true, then your son has definitely been abducted.

Ben said nothing.

I'm sorry to tell you that.

Go on, Molly said.

Okay. The detective took a breath. What we have here is a
single footprint. He pulled a pen from his jacket and with the

end of it he traced the outline of the foot. The reason it seems a little out of whack is that probably what happened is that the abductor was carrying your son. He himself was smart to stay on the grass, since there are no other verifiable footprints. But at some point we think our abductor here lost his grip, or what have you, and for whatever reason, your son slipped almost from his— Enough to land a single foot on the ground. The detective pointed to the bottom of the picture. Your son landed with the heel first, at an angle, causing the earth to shovel in that direction like so. Then, why we have the top of the foot, the toes, all folded like that on the upper right, is likely because the abductor twisted back to regain his grip. So the two predominant impressions are of the toes, seen here, and the heel, way over here.

Here's a shoe, Molly said.

Ben felt drowsy. He said, I think I'll sit down.

That's fine. He took the shoe. Perfect. I'll probably need to take this with me.

Of course, Molly said.

Susan's head flicked to one side.

Sorry? Ben said.

What? the detective said.

I didn't hear you.

Did I say something?

Yes.

Oh. Oh, I think all I said was that I need to take the shoe with me down to the lab.

Right, I heard that.

Okay.

Molly put a hand on Ben's shoulder. Susy-susy, she said, could you get your dad a soda or something from the fridge?

Susan began to nod, but the nod ended abruptly, and she walked to the kitchen.

The detective laid the shoe on top of the photocopy. Yeah, it's hard to tell because of the bend, but I'd say that it's the same size. Wouldn't you?

I'm not the expert, but I think I see why you'd say that.

Yeah. The other reasons we think it was your son's foot, and on that night, was because of the moisture content of the soil. And then, I thought this was interesting, but the traces of dew in the footprint were a fraction less than in any other portion of the rest of the dirt in the garden. Pretty interesting.

Science.

That's exactly right. Science. It's my favourite part of the job, learning all about science.

What about solving crimes? Molly said.

The detective stared at her. Yes, he said, and solving crimes.

THE HOUSE WAS SILENT except for the crinkle of snow landing on the roof and windowsills. Inside, Ben sat in his chair and stared at a wall. I can stare at a wall for a long time, Ben thought. I can sit here without moving and stare at this wall and all I'm thinking about is the fact that when I finally blink it feels good. The moist lick of the eyelid dropping, it feels good. I don't even know what's on the wall, if there's something on the wall. Because I'm not really looking at the wall, as I sit here.

She said his name and at first he didn't respond. She kneeled down beside him, barefoot as usual, quietly, and watched him stare at the wall. On the wall she saw nothing special to look at. It was one of the few finished walls in the house, but other than that—

Ben, she said. Yo, Ben.

He didn't respond, or maybe wouldn't. He didn't even blink. So she clucked her tongue.

Hey, Ben, she said and put a hand on his lap. He startled to life and looked at her with a buzzy expression.

Colleen. What are you doing here? How'd you—?

Are you—? she said. Well, what are you looking at?

Hm, oh. Nothing, nothing.

Okay.

Yeah.

Ben, I can't sleep at night.

You and me both.

I even made a map to show him how to get here.

She turned and walked to the coffee table and pinched a nut from a glass jar and put it in her mouth. I saw Molly and Susan down at the shop.

What were they doing?

Buying donuts.

I didn't know they'd left the house.

They said they'd asked if you if you wanted to come but you said no.

Yeah, I probably didn't.

They were putting up posters.

What for?

Pictures of Eliot and you.

Oh.

They put a picture of you on the cash register.

Oh.

He really looked like you, didn't he? The guy.

Everyone thought he did.

Did you?

No. Not at first, no.

She picked at her teeth and sucked the salt off her finger.

How are you? she asked. Do you need something?

I'm fine. No.

Do you want to come to my place for a while? Get out of the house?

Yeah, I haven't thought about it, no.

She walked over and put her hand on his ear. She brushed his hair.

What do you want?

I want my boy back.

Well, what're you doing about it?

As much as I can.

His hair fingered, she moved to his cheek.

You know how I feel, she said.

The wall. He wasn't looking at the wall. She kneeled and opened her mouth and kissed him.

Please, Ben. I know you're not happy. She kissed him again, her hand gripped to his chin.

Happy has nothing to do with it, he said.

You know what I mean. She made a trembling attempt to find a way through the buttons of his shirt, somehow she was sitting on him, how did he let this happen?

You're my wife's friend.

I'm more your friend. I don't talk to Molly as much—, not like we talk.

We don't talk.

We don't do anything.

We don't do anything, Ben said, that's right.

I have to stare at your picture every day now. You're on my register.

Don't think of it as me.

Every time I sell someone a donut I have to look at you.

It's not meant to be me, he said after her tongue had left his mouth, while she bit his neck.

I'm going to have to look at you all damn day now.

What he was doing was kissing her, why was he kissing her? and he could feel her body relax against his hands. She made a special kind of noise, something unmistakable.

Don't think about me.

She said, How can I not think about you?

She said, I have to stare at your picture every day until they find Eliot.

He stood up suddenly as if in pain and she had to stumble backwards to keep her balance as he threw her from his lap.

I'm sorry, she said. I shouldn't have said—

That's fine. No. It's good, it's better.

Ben, you know how I feel.

I know and I want to but I can't.

Why not?

I just can't.

They stood there, facing each other, breathing heavily, calming down.

I'm very attracted to you, Ben said. It drives me mad sometimes.

Well, then? Why not?

It's nothing to do with you.

Nothing to do with me, no, of course not. She sat down on the couch and rubbed her hair. Goddamn, you know. I'm thirty—in my mid-thirties, I'm a fucking—I'm working in a donut shop, and I'm single. Ben, I didn't know what to do when that guy came into the shop, I wasn't even thinking. Am I pretty?

You're very pretty. Absolutely.

Then why won't you—? Like I said. You tease me, you let me kiss you like that but nothing comes of it. Why? I mean, what's *up* with me?

Nothing.

Is there something the matter with me?

There's nothing the matter with you.

No, you're wrong. I have troubles. I'm very nervous around men.

He stood in the middle of the room and watched her fuss with her hair in an awkward way, while neither of them would speak and both were waiting for the other to say something. A wedge of cloud had pushed itself over the city and it could have been hail on the roof but it was just a few birds pecking at the old berries fallen from the big tree in the next yard over. When Ben looked at Colleen his head rattled.

Finally Ben said, You want to stay for dinner?

Colleen said, You won't ever sleep with me? Not ever?

I'm married. I'm happily married.

Are you? Are you really?

Yes, Ben said. I am.

She stepped forward, and when he didn't back away, she kissed him again, one last time. And then they watched TV and waited for Molly and Susan to get home so they could have dinner.

LATER THAT EVENING, the detective came back to the house and asked for another shoe. He looked tired, flushed, as if he'd been running.

. . . bothering you like this.

Not a problem, Molly said.

I had the shoe at my duck-carving class, and then I'm sure I had it in the car, but when I got to the precinct—

It's just a shoe. I'll go get the other.

Thanks.

WHEN THE CALM DETECTIVE CALLED just before bed, Molly had all but forgotten that they were waiting for another, more important call. (Whereas Ben couldn't get it out of his mind; in fact, it was the only thing he consistently remembered: the sound of his son's voice.)

I'm sorry to scare you, the detective said to Molly. I'm driving around. Actually, I'm parked. I'm in my car, but I'm parked.

Why would you have scared me?

I know you're waiting for a call. I'm sorry.

Oh. Suddenly she was frightened to be on the phone. Oh, she repeated.

I'm calling about two things. Hey, were you outside today?

You called to tell me this?

No. Sorry, I was just thinking that all that warm weather is gone.

I haven't given it much thought.

No, he said. She waited for him to continue. He said, I think we're going to need the other shoe.

The other shoe. Another shoe, you mean?

It's nothing. It's not a problem. Everything is fine. She heard a car drive by on his end of the phone and someone yelled, Fucking pig.

Ha ha, the detective said. Anyway. We're going to need the other shoe. Thought I might come pick it up, maybe in the next day or so.

You've already taken two.

You mean one.

No, she said. The detective came back for a second one this evening.

Oh. Well, that saves me a trip. Ha ha.

I guess so.

Oh my. The detective paused and all Molly could hear was the keen of traffic. She waited for him to continue but he didn't.

Anyway, Molly suggested.

Yes, anyway, ha ha. You strike me as a brave woman, Molly.

The calm detective was beginning to get on her nerves. My son is missing, she reminded him.

No, yes. I'm sorry. Molly, I want to let you know that this is getting a lot of focus from our men. Your son means a lot to all of us, I hope that doesn't sound too trite. But I wanted to mention that just in case you were wondering. I don't want you to be worried because of this. But it is unusual for us not to have received some sort of ransom note by this point.

A ransom note. My god. It hadn't even occurred—

Of course this can mean a number of things.

Like what?

Exactly, good question. I don't want to worry you.

There's nothing you can do in that department.

No. Well, okay, it can mean a few things. It means the reasons for the abduction might not be related to money, obviously. Or that the abductor hasn't settled down yet, still feels the threat of a police search. I'm thinking it's only fair to also let you know that it can mean a few darker possibilities.

Yes.

No one is making dark assumptions yet, obviously. Nonetheless.

No, I understand. I suppose you mean we have to prepare ourselves.

If you—

Psychologically.

Psychologically, yes. The doctor—

I have to go now.

Okay.

The phone clattered down to the cradle and Molly went for a walk, going nowhere. It wouldn't have mattered anyway. Where could she go?

WHAT DAY WAS IT, YES, GOOD QUESTION. When late into the night Ben finally came downstairs he looked a mess. Half his hair went straight out the side and the back was firing off in all directions. He belched and smacked his lips.

God, I'm so hungry. When's dinner?

I called you, I don't know, umpteen times, Ben.

No, you didn't.

Ben, I went up and told you right to your face.

No, you didn't.

I'm not going to have this argument, because I called you over and over.

I was asleep.

Sure, I can tell. But not when I told you. I distinctly remember you said, Okay, I'll be down in a minute.

Well, Ben said and absently scanned the room. I don't remember this at all.

Susy-susy, did I go up and tell your dad it was dinner?

I don't care, Susan said and walked out of the room.

What's wrong with this daughter of ours? Ben said.

It's not funny. She's depressed or upset. She's been quick-tempered all evening, and you've been no help, conked out like that.

I must've been tired.

Ben sat down beside Molly and together they watched the television, relentlessly. The remote control in her hand, Molly blinked through channels with no discretion. He made no complaints. It was dark and it was late and cop shows turned to paid programming; a lonely-looking man sold vacuum cleaners with HEPA filters. Molly had a sustained desire to buy one and charge it, to gladden the salesman, but she was too lethargic to dial the number on the screen.

The warm front had passed. It started to snow again.

IN HER ROOM, SUSAN FILLED OUT an online form at a website devoted to abducted children. She'd already built her own website for Eliot, and she was in the process of setting up links to her page and adding new ones at related sites. She scanned a picture of Eliot and put it up on her page of the website.

Age: 11. Date of birth . . .

Build: slight frame. Eyes . . .

Hair: dusty blond . . .

Last seen . . .

She decided to scan in a picture of her dad, and wrote a brief description of the man who had come for dinner.

She added, If you have any information, please e-mail shysusan@llink.net

Waiting for the page to load, she leaned back in her chair and stared at the constellation on her ceiling and noticed a ring of glue where one of her planets was missing. She looked to the carpet where it would've fallen and saw nothing there, wondered where it was, and, for a faint moment, thought she might have a panic attack.

She made a search for his name on the website and found her page up and running. There, in pixels, was the picture she'd posted, and the statistics of her brother's life. Now he was cruelly famous. Another jpeg on monitors the world over. The picture was his school photo, smiling on demand, in front of a sky backdrop with white laser-like bands airbrushed over the blue. Eliot was wearing a Nintendo T-shirt in the picture, and his hair was an embarrassment of cowlicks. She looked at the eyes of her brother, wondered if there was anything in them that might tell her something. Could she tell from his eyes that he was the kind of boy who goes missing, gets abducted?

The Twix bars had begun to turn a dry white.

She sent a test e-mail to herself from the webpage to make sure the link worked. Re: re: re: re: re:, she typed, and then received.

She made a cursory scan of the other pages on the website, the other missing children. A lot of the kids had been abducted by a parent. Some had been gone for a long, long time, birthdays close to her own. She looked at their pictures for telltale signs but saw few similarities aside from smiles. It occurred to her that kids in pictures were always smiling. That's the thing, that's why it's impossible to tell who these kids were. The homogeneity of the say-cheese happy face made all kids looked doomed to misery.

She went to her bed and lay there with her prescription bottle in her hand, looking up at the apsides of certain glow-in-the-dark moons.

MOLLY MADE LISTS, MEANWHILE, in her sleep, on pads of paper, mental tallies, whatever worked, at night and during the day. She could sit at the kitchen table with the television on in the background and stare at it without any attempt to concentrate, and when an item came to her that related to the one or two lists she was at work on, she wrote it down. Laundry detergent, for example. Her purse was full of such lists. The Home Repairs List. The Grocery List. The Abducted Child List. The latter was a long one, over four pages, itemized and in order of importance. An unusual list only because of the topic. The list was essential. There was no way she could handle this whole thing without a list. Every day she rewrote it, checking items off, with the date next to each checked-off item, and revised the order. An item, Xerox posters for lampposts, was at the top today. It needed to be

done. She had a photo chosen, and she had worked out a short bit
of text. Phone the local news. She had to do that today as well.
She had so many things to do. She put the pen at the top of the
page of the list and aligned the pen with the left corner. It was
time for a nap.

BEN, IN THE MIRROR, WAS A CRIMINAL. He stood there, face to
face with the criminal. The skin of his face, the flesh of a criminal. Sunken, blackened eyes. The criminal venation around the
irises, a shattering of red. Thick tongue, thick paste on it. The
voice of a criminal. He didn't just look like the man. *Wake up, it's
your dad.* Entice him from bed, gag him quickly with a sock or
two. Take the boy under an arm and drag him across the
midnight lawn, away through cul-de-sacs and treeless parks. He's
too afraid to put up much of a fight, trembling like a bird against
my chest. Smells like Sesame Street shampoo—eleven years old
and he still wants to use Sesame Street shampoo. Freight him
across an unlit street. An empty parkade near the Superstore
where I'll throw him in the back of a waiting van, tinted windows
and rusty latch waiting, stained mattress waiting, duct tape his
mouth shut and bind his wrists and ankles with plastic cord. Beat
the fuck out of him a little. Hurt him a little. Do I cut him? Do I
draw blood on him? Do I rape him? Will I kill him? he wondered,
unable to breathe, hating himself for what, for how, holding
himself from collapsing. Will I kill him?

MOLLY, HE SAID WHEN SHE ENTERED the bedroom to fall on the
bed. He walked through the wall between the master bathroom
and the bedroom since it didn't make any difference. The

doorframe and the wall sections were virtually identical holes. He stood over the bed and waited for her to respond. When she didn't, he continued. I'm going nuts, he said. I can't look at myself.

She didn't open her eyes.

Molly, he said. I can't look at myself in the mirror.

He watched her inhale, and let it out, but her eyes still didn't open. She couldn't have fallen asleep that quickly, he thought.

Why aren't you answering me? Listen. When I look in the mirror— Molly, you don't understand. I can't even look at my own reflection.

Honey, she said finally, I can't look at you either.

I look like the man who—

This is all Colleen's fault, she said.

What?

And I don't like the way she looks at you.

Like what? What do you mean?

Don't do this to me, Ben. I can't lose you, too. Don't try and ruin me. That's not what you want is it?

No.

Is something going on I'd be better off not knowing about?

No, honey, no.

You're not who I think you are, is what Molly said next.

And what was he supposed to say to that? He almost wanted to agree with her. She was lying there, eyes shut, her mouth a wet slit across her tired face. He wanted to hate her, but whatever anger he had in him soon mutated into something like desire. He sat down on the edge of the bed, undid his pants. Let's do this fast, he said, slouching, if we're going to do it at all. She yawned, came across the mattress on her hands and knees, still with her eyes closed. All right, she said, and felt for him with an extended arm, as if she'd lost her glasses in the dark. She fingered his shirt until the buttons came loose and pulled the sleeves away from his arms.

I'm not even thinking about sex these days, he said.

You think I am? Blindly, she drew her hand across his open jeans, lowered her head.

She'd barely started when he said, Actually, maybe don't, and pushed her back on the bed.

Why not?

I feel sick. These stupid drugs I'm on or something.

Kiss me, she said.

She lay there.

We need to take our minds off this, even just for a few minutes, she said.

He was looking at the socks on his feet, or maybe the floor.

Did I ever hit him?

What? Molly said.

I can't remember if I ever hit him.

Well, did you?

I don't think so. No.

Good.

He watched as that terrible draft in the house made the curtains lift and sway, a little bit.

You're a smart man, Ben.

Ah, he said. My erudition is really coming in handy now, finally.

Don't talk that way. You never used to talk that way.

How did I used to talk?

I don't know. We used to *discuss* things. Back in university we would've been discussing this problem.

It's not fair to call this a problem.

You're right.

He listened to the whistle of her breath pass between her front teeth.

He said, Open your eyes why don't you.

No.

She turned her head away from him and gathered some of the bedsheet in her fist and peeled it off the mattress.

What are you going to do? she asked.

I'm going to fuck you.

Don't use that word.

You're always whining. You whine too much.

You're mean to me. You don't talk to me and then you're mean to me.

I'm honest.

Above her now, he kissed the slope of her eyelids. The thatch of hair beneath his collarbone, she clawed it.

You still love me?

Of course I do.

Say it.

I love you. Molly, I love you.

Do you think I'm fat?

No.

Oh, so honest.

Be quiet.

Oh.

Uh.

Grunt grunt.

He laughed. Moan moan.

Grunt moan.

He laughed. Look at me.

No, honey.

Is it because—?

Just—

Maybe it *was* me.

Don't joke like that.

They both heard a sound like the phone ringing or like crying.

What's that?

He slipped out of her.

Wait, she said. It was probably the phone or the TV. Come on.

He went to the door and opened it a crack, listened. There was no more sound.

Come back here.

No. He started to yank on some clothes. I think I've had enough anyway.

You're incredibly selfish sometimes, you know?

He dragged open a dresser drawer and pushed through a pile of balled socks and looked for a fresh pair of underwear.

I need to talk to that doctor about getting me another prescription, I'm almost out.

Have you seen my comb? she said, before he could leave the room.

Your what? No, I haven't.

I lost my comb. The black metal one.

I know the one.

Are you sure?

I know the one.

No, I mean, have you seen it?

I can't believe you're asking me this.

Well, I am. Have you seen my comb? It's a pretty simple question.

Ben looked at a corner of the room while he made a show of giving her fucking comb some thought. No, he said. I haven't seen your comb.

I'm serious.

Serious about your comb? I thought you were supposed to be the balanced one. The one to have all the responsibility. And this is the way you talk?

I've had that comb for twenty years.

So what? Twenty years gives it first priority, is this what you're implying here?

No, I—

This conversation is disgusting. I can't believe you're actually thinking about a lost comb right now.

He stood there waiting for his wife to respond, but she didn't; she lay in bed with her eyes closed. So he walked out of the room.

OPENING DOORS AND ANSWERING THE PHONE. Walk through the doorway and hear the phone ring. There was a noise and he thought it was the telephone. He thought, All I do these days is walk through doors and wait for the phone to ring. My bedroom door, my kitchen door, my front door, waiting for the phone to ring. A call from Eliot, who I haven't seen in I-don't-know-how-long, what day is it anyway? That's what his life amounted to nowadays. Why hadn't he heard more? Where was his son, as he waited for the phone to ring, as he walked through doorways, as he waited, as he walked, where was his son, Eliot, where? Waiting and walking. So when he heard the noise he assumed it was the phone (he hoped it was the phone). But then he realized Eliot didn't have a phone in his room.

Hello? he said, leaning through the doorway to Eliot's room. Is anyone there? he said.

Alert, said a voice.

Who's there? Ben wavered, he felt weak.

Alert, the voice said again.

Ben squinted. His mouth was dry. He couldn't see a damn thing. Eliot, he barely said.

Where's Eliot? I'm quickly hungry.

It was the marmot.

4

THEY WERE ALL SETTLED IN THE LIVING ROOM, the family and the police, the calm detective with his detectives, including the detective with the shoes (he'd brought both shoes back with him, I found the first one under the seat of my car, ha ha), the doctor, and Colleen (the calm detective had received the call while he was at the donut shop, and suggested she come along), all of them patiently waiting for something to happen, an exclamation mark of some sort, a warning window of evidence from the hard drive of an animal, a creature showing all the worrisome signs of priva-tion—marked lack of memory, disorientation, hallucinations, weakness, lack of concentration, long sleeps, depression—which

was slowly being plied for clues leading to the whereabouts of
Eliot. So far, the marmot was their best chance at a witness, but
no one could find the owner's manual.

The marmot sat on the coffee table, shifting its weight now
and then. Everyone studied it as it moved, listening for a critical
burp of data.

Someone needs to feed it.

That's the problem, it's a pass code Eliot invented.

So you're saying is, what you're saying is that we can't feed it?
I think so.

And then what happens when you can't feed it?
I think it dies.

This marmot really spooks me, Colleen said, and put her hand
on the calm detective's arm.

Well someone do something, Ben said.

What's he call the thing, this whatever, rodent, your son?

Marmot.

Is that what it's supposed to be, a marmot?

That's right, it's a marmot.

And he calls it Marmot?

He calls it Marmot, yes.

Okay then. Marmot? Hey, Marmot?

Please feed me.

Okay, good. How can we feed you?

It goes much faster.

What does that mean, what goes much faster? Someone tell
me what the fuck that means.

I'm hungry.

We know you're hungry. How do we feed you?

Eliot feeds me.

The calm detective picked the marmot off the table, turned it over on its back, and rubbed through its fur, examining the buttons. Oh, crap, he said, there's twenty-six buttons here. That's quite a few permutations. Is the code a certain length, say, like any variation of three buttons, or could it be a string of any length of button combinations?

I haven't a clue, Ben said.

We're wasting our time here, a detective said. Someone call up the manufacturer and get a specialist or programmer or what-the-fuck on the line. If this thing witnessed the abduction we don't have time to fiddle with its belly buttons.

Marmot. Do you remember what happened the night Eliot went away?

I forget but the question is too fast.

Okay. Call somebody.

Help, the marmot cried. I wanna take— Everyone leaned in close, waiting for more, but the marmot's eyes closed, put itself to sleep.

That was Eliot, Molly said faintly.

NO, THE WOMAN ON THE OTHER END OF THE LINE told them, no you can't do anything about that. The point of the animal is that it *can die*. If you try and open it up and dismantle the hard drive you'll damage the thing anyway; part of its wiring is connected to the actual tegument, and you might rupture a major circuit if you perform any kind of surgery. You can restart the marmot, but that would clean its memory bank, so it wouldn't do any good anyhow. See, if the marmot is neglected, or if the original guardian is absent, the marmot will die. It's not a flaw, it's part of the conceit of the design. The point of the animal is that it *can die*.

Yeah, you already mentioned that, a detective said. How long does it take for the thing to do that?

Do what?

Die.

Oh. We make sure it takes a while. A month or so, depends on the level of care given to the marmot before the, uh—

Yeah. Okay. He hung the phone up and pinched the bridge of his nose. Fuck, he said. Fuck me with a ten-foot fucking pole.

The police ransacked Eliot's room for any kind of information on the feeding code. They scrutinized every scrap of paper for discernible symbols, turning over his bulletin board after untacking every postcard and every doodle, fingering along the floorboards and so forth for anything loose where a secret hiding place might be. The carpet Ben had nailed down just a few weeks ago was painstakingly removed, but there were no clues underneath. In the end, they found nothing, and destroyed Eliot's room in the process.

His bed had been knifed open; gory foam viscera spilled out from the mattress and lay in deposits on the floor. Of course there was nothing inside his bed, but they wanted to be thorough.

Every stuffed animal was routinely gouged and emptied.

Eliot's own clothes were stripped from their hangers and left indecently in the mess.

Dejected and tired, the police stumbled down the stairs and left the house, going back to their cars, to continue solving other crimes and protecting other people. While back at this home, a family was still missing one little boy, whose abduction was becoming old news, whose name was no longer the focus of an energetic investigation but rather the dim reminder of a failing case, whose room was now a sign of their pessimism, a mutilated horror.

I can't believe they didn't get anything from the marmot, Ben said.

What did you expect, it's a toy. Molly watched the last of the useless police drive off down the street with no sirens, no lights, with excellent tires, men, every one of them.

No, but— Ben picked the marmot up. Hey, Marmot?

Its eyelids opened, one after the other, the silent blink of double cursors. Yes? the marmot said.

Ben took a breath. Where is Eliot?

I was remembering . . .

What, yes?

I wish he were here.

Me too.

I have a song for Eliot.

Sing it for me.

I quickly couldn't.

No, please do.

Molly kneeled down to listen, while Ben hunched forward, anticipating the most unlikely of events. They waited to find out where their boy was.

The head of the marmot lolled back and forth, very slowly, with a somewhat jagged quality, the unpleasant hint of machinery at work, and remained tilted towards the window.

Marmot, hello?

When did it start to snow?

A few days ago, Ben said eagerly.

I didn't notice.

That's okay.

You didn't notice.

I did.

They why didn't you come . . . ?

Come where, what do you mean, Marmot?

When I was crying.

I'm sorry, what?

Did you hear me crying?

Hear you crying . . . Oh, but it came to him, and Ben could've died right then and there. A sharp pain seized his neck, a sudden headache of fucking realization. All that time, all those noises, all those nights wondering if it was a dream or whatever, a sick hallucination, and all that time, all of the noises had been the marmot crying out to be fed.

I'm so sorry, Marmot, Ben said finally, when he had composed himself. I am so sorry.

Too late now, the marmot said, and put itself back to sleep.

Re: Abduction

Hey I thought I saw the man who took your brother but then I realized it was just yr. dad. Im' sorry.

Re: Eliot

I'm so sorry to hear that Eliot is gone. If you are interested we are meeting every week at the community centre room 11A if you would like. We're a support group for people with missing children. Please attend, there will be coffee and juice served and muffins most weeks.

Re: Website

This is an automatic message, please do not reply. Your webpage has received 242 hits since it was created.

Re: School

Susan: As you requested I've kept your homework, but really, it's okay. I'm glad to see you want to attend class, yet please don't feel guilty over absences. I want you to know that you have my most sincere sympathies (your other teachers feel the same) and would rather you do only the amount of work you feel comfortable with, and to not feel any added pressure to keep up with the pace of the class.

Re: Eliot

my son was also taken by a man, but he turned out to be my ex-husband. are you sure that it wasn't actually your husband who took eliot and not some other guy??? i'm so so sorry to read that he was missing (i still check the websites out of habit) and hope hell be back soon.

AND SOMEHOW WHOLE DAYS WERE TRASHED and it was time for another meal. At the dinner table, mother and daughter passing bowls of corn and beans back and forth as if their lives were somehow beginning to accommodate the lack. It was five in the afternoon but the sun had gone down a long time ago. Outside the snow fell in a dead flutter. An obdurate crust of ice had formed at the corners of the windows while they tried to eat boiled hot dogs. The floor of the house was freezing cold from the competing drafts that had taken over the house the past couple days. They sat cross-legged in their chairs and wore moccasins with bead patterns and fur lining. Despite the roar of the heater only their heads were warm. They wore sweaters. Life was not busy. Ben hadn't had the time or the brain for building and no one wanted to nag him. Molly had had a bit of a cold but now she was back on track. Susan was trying to make it to school again, at least one or two days a week.

The marmot lay on an ottoman nearby and made noises of a slow and terminal sort.

Ben, dinner. Your dinner is getting cold.

Where is he?

He's upstairs, I think. I went up and told him that dinner was ready.

Yeah, that sounds familiar.

Otherwise he seems good though, don't you think?

What do you mean?

Not as upset. His temper.

I guess so.

Yeah, oh well. Molly dangled a fork in a jar of relish and without much interest spread some across the inside of her hot dog bun.

I have a new noise, do you want to hear it?

I suppose I have no choice.

Susan made a familiar and horrible sound that Molly always likened to the *scree* a magpie would make if under a rolling pin.

Don't do that again. You see me owning a fax machine? That kind of noise causes brain cancer.

It's good, isn't it?

It's accurate.

Molly and Susan ate their dogs.

Susy-susy, will you go and tell your dad that dinner is ready?

Could you stop calling me that?

What?

What you said. That's not my name.

What isn't your name?

I'm not going to say it because it's fucking retarded.

What did you just say?

I said it's fucking retarded.

Go to your room. Using language like that. Go.

Fuck you.

What has got into you?

Susan tore open the milk carton and poured herself a glass of milk.

Are you listening to me?

Don't call me that again.

What did I say?

You called me Susy-susy.

I did?

Yes.

Molly looked at her plate. She moved a kernel of corn away from the pile of potato chips. I didn't even know I was calling you that.

Well you were.

It just came back to me. That's what I used to call you when you were—

Yeah, Mom. And I'm not a little kid any more, okay?

Okay. Fine. But I don't want to hear you swearing like that.

Mom. I'm sorry, but I don't care what you think.

Go to your room.

Mom. No. Listen to me. Did you hear what I just said? I said, I don't care what you think. Okay? I'm not your baby or something.

Oh my god, Molly said, and rested her hands on the table as the dishwasher in the kitchen sighed. She took a moment to calm down, thinking she might not be able to speak properly, then said, Please, Susan, don't do this to me. Her hands rattled loose-hinged at the wristbone. No matter how much she might have wanted to be calm, it wasn't possible. She made sure her daughter could see her hands, the involuntary shaking of them. Susan, she confided, I need you to be nice right now. You understand what I mean?

Susan twisted her head to avoid her mother's eyes. The potato chips on her plate, salted, curled, and not very moon-like, still reminded her of the lost planet from the ceiling in her room, and she wondered, somehow guiltily (because it had nothing to do with her mother, who right now looked on the verge of weeping), if someday she might ever walk into a room expecting to be kissed.

Honey, she said to Susan, honey, I just need your help.

I'm sorry.

I know. But there's only three of us who know how this feels, right? It's hard. And your dad and all, but, I just think it's unfair that—

I'm sorry. Susan bit her lip, the way she used to when she was a little girl, with her head bowed low. Mom, I am sorry.

You know how I hate that kind of language. It's violent.

It's just words.

No, it isn't.

Come on, don't be so serious about everything.

I'm not serious.

You're serious all the time.

I am?

Yeah, you are.

Hm. Molly wiped her eyes and pecked at her corn. Well, fuck you too.

Susan laughed.

When they were done eating they cleaned their dishes and put them back in the cupboard and went to the living room to watch the news.

When Ben finally came downstairs he looked a mess. His shirt was on inside-out and one of his pant legs was tucked into his sock. He belched and smacked his lips.

God, I'm so hungry. When's dinner?

I called you, over and over, Ben.

No, you didn't.

Ben, I went up and told you right to your face.

No, you didn't.

I'm not going to have this argument, because I called you over and over.

I was asleep.

Jesus, Susan said, this all sounds really fucking familiar.

What the hell did I just hear you just say? Ben stared at her.

Oh, give it a break, Ben, Molly said as she put the commercials on mute.

Ben couldn't blink when he looked at his wife. He said, What the hell is going on around here?

Sit down, watch the news.

I don't want to watch the news, I'm hungry.

The local news logo swam across the screen, as it always did, becoming a fractal, a digression of specks, an organic swarm, logo particles colliding to invent new and even smaller logos. Finally, as all the minutiae joined to recreate the logo large again, the accompanying soundtrack became deadly ominous, as was the convention with news music.

The anchor spoke in a deliberate way, while in the top left corner above her shoulder there was inserted a photograph of Eliot.

Ben sat down.

The picture, Eliot's face, his smile, grew to encompass the whole screen. That untidy haircut of his. Something was being said, what was it, something about the fact that he was missing, but how did the news know what was going on? Someone said his name (Ben), the name of his wife (and his wife, Molly). And then suddenly they were both on the television.

If anyone has seen him—, Molly was saying.

Geez, do I look terrible. Molly shook her head.

What the hell is this? Ben screamed.

We miss him so much, Ben was saying. We just want to see him home safely.

With some amount of awkwardness and apologies, Molly held up a picture of Ben and told viewers that this was a good representation of who they suspected was Eliot's abductor, a picture of an unshaven Ben in a dirty fishing jacket that he wore on vacations to the lake.

He looks exactly like my husband here, Molly was saying.

Ben and Molly were standing next to the river, a striped wind-sock visible in the distance, turning a bit on its pole. An electrical line shot across the sky above them. The reporter's microphone was a long black thing that rose obtrusively to their mouths when they opened them.

When the fuck—?

Today, Ben.

Today. The word made him gasp.

He looked at the man on the screen who was apparently him and couldn't believe it. The man on the screen looked nothing like how he remembered himself, not the same man at all. This man looked caved in, a haunted thing, a degraded echo.

It suddenly seemed possible that it wasn't him at all, that it was the man who'd taken Eliot. Here he was standing right next to Molly and pretending to be Ben, while she pined to the camera for help, assistance, in finding the man who'd abducted her child—what a bastard. The malicious bastard had them fooled.

Are you sure—?

Yes, Ben, Molly said.

Please, Molly was saying while Ben (or the man—*it was the man, it had to be*) seemed distracted by something in the grass near his foot. If you have any information, Molly continued, please call the police.

Again, Eliot's face appeared on the screen, along with the number to call, and then the news anchor returned and offered a brief analysis of the various wars before going to another commercial break.

Ben put his face in his hands and massaged his eyes. I'm losing my memory.

It's stress. You went straight to bed when we got home.

I did?

Yes.

I can't believe it. He shook his fists, No matter how hard I try I can't remember a goddamn thing.

Oh, the marmot said.

What is it? Susan replied without much interest.

Did I hear Eliot?

No.

Can I tell you quickly a joke?

Go ahead.

They waited, but the marmot said nothing.

NO, HE COULDN'T REMEMBER the day of the week. Or the month. No, he didn't know what time it was, and it worried him that the doctor said he'd given him the time only a minute ago. All he had was the excruciating comprehension of the emptiness. In bed he imagined how many weeks might have gone by that he'd forgotten about. And then it scared him to think that maybe only an hour had passed, that he was only imagining lost weeks, when in actuality only an hour had gone by. That he didn't know the difference. How long had he been lying in bed? He had no idea. It wasn't funny; it was like the cartoon coyote walking off the cliff and *then* remembering to check below his feet—that's where Ben was forever fixed, in that suspended instant of vertiginous and terrible knowing before the plunge to the canyon floor. Always about to fall. It occurred to him that he was having a heart attack and he tried to scream for help and then he felt the prick of a screwy rush and maybe he fell asleep, he couldn't remember. What time is it? He didn't know.

Ben, a voice said. It's me. Colleen.

Colleen.

Do you remember me?

Yes.

What do you remember about me?

She watched him stare at the ceiling as if it were rushing towards him. When he didn't answer she asked him the same question again. She waited, but he didn't say anything. With a sigh she stood up and said, I guess I couldn't help, I'm sorry, detective.

It was worth a shot, the calm detective said, and they both left the room.

In the hallway she held the calm detective, while he petted her hair and kissed her forehead, and she said, I love him, you know, don't you know that?

Yes, the calm detective said. Yes, I know that, he said.

WELL, THE DOCTOR SAID, I think what's happened here is an extreme reaction to the drug, very rare. He looked up for a moment before his eyes fell down again, as he turned a few sheets back on his notepad and seemed to read them over, maybe for answers, maybe to kill time, maybe just out of some analytical reflex, Molly didn't know, but she wanted better answers than the ones he was giving.

He's off the medication now, the doctor mentioned.

I should hope so.

Yes.

And his memory will come back?

Oh, I think so. A percentage of drug residue will probably remain in his system for a while, and a small percentage will, naturally, remain for some time. But not enough to cause this memory malfunction to continue on much longer, okay?

Okay.

And Susan, she's not having difficulties with her medication?

Susan is on medication?

She didn't tell you?

No.

Oh. The doctor tapped his finger on his notepad. Well, he said, she's definitely a private girl, and felt probably ashamed. You know teenagers.

Didn't we need to approve medication or—?

Well, your husband signed—

Ah. Molly blinked.

Oh, that reminds me, the doctor said, and he twisted in his seat as he stuffed a hand into the briefcase on his lap, to inexplicably pull a circle out and put it on the table.

A circle, Molly said, looking at it.

I found it stuck to my pants after I left your house that day. I think it belongs on Susan's ceiling.

Molly picked the circle up, noticed it was a bit sticky on the bottom. It's a moon or something, she muttered. Glow-in-the-dark, is that what this is?

Hm. I remember she has them on her ceiling.

She does?

Yes. All over.

Molly examined the circle.

Anyway, we won't continue with Ben's medication, obviously, but I'll write you a note for Susan, since the situation has, uh, remained—

They were seated in the dining room with a glass chandelier above them that didn't yet have functional wiring, and she held a moon meant to stick to the ceiling. Between them, the table, which had come into the room as smooth and polished as wood can get, was, thanks to myriad police officers and their requisite notepads and stabbing pencils, a mess of scratches and fine troughs. Shattered pieces of her name had been imprinted on the wood by some note-taker. And she could see very clearly the accidental engraving of a doodled chicken.

Sorry, Molly said. What did you say? I got distracted.

Oh, I uh, I said—, the doctor put his hands to his face. I said my wife is ill. I was just explaining why I won't be able to continue as the doctor for your case. I'm sorry.

Oh.

Yes. No, it's treatable, thank god, ha ha, but she'll be in and out of the hospital for the next year or so while the therapy—

The doctor choked and so stopped talking. He bowed his head and squeezed his eyes in his fingers. Oh, damn, he said. Damn damn damn.

It took Molly a moment to make sense of what had just occurred. She stared at the doctor, his wife a sick woman. Then she reached across the table and took his wrist gently in her hand. Thank you, she said. I want you to know. Really, thank you for everything you've done.

The doctor nodded and smiled and nodded, then he decided he should go, yes, okay, wiping his eyes, he would leave now.

They shook hands at the door and Molly gave him a hug, he held her, and then she waved goodbye as his car skidded down the driveway and out along the black ice and white snow towards all the green lights and stop signs.

WHILE THROUGH HER BEDROOM WINDOW, still laid out with desiccated Twix bars, Susan watched the doctor leave in his car, unaware that he wouldn't be coming back, or that eventually his wife would die. She didn't even know the doctor was married; in fact, she imagined she was in the car with him, holding his hand, the wedding ring on his finger the companion to her own. Would they go for dinner tonight, or would they make something? What do doctors like to eat? I bet doctors like fish, but she didn't know how you cooked fish, so she would have to learn. Her mother came and knocked on the door and interrupted her.

Are you busy?

I guess not.

Molly produced the circle and held it out for Susan to take.

Here. The doctor said he found it stuck on him when he left the other day. She looked up at the ceiling, studying the constellation for the first time. Wow, she said. That's interesting.

Susan came forward and took the circle. He had it? she said.

Yeah. It was stuck to him, on him, or something.

The circle in her hands. Oh. She looked at it, the missing moon, and imagined all the places it had been since it had left her room.

Hey, by the way, Molly said. Have you seen my comb?

Your comb?

My black steel comb, you know?

Oh, Susan said, a bit dazed by the circle. Yeah, I have it. She opened a drawer of her desk and shuffled over a pile of lipsticks and found the comb.

Here you go. She passed her mother the comb.

Oh. Why, why, I mean, why did you have it?

I don't know. I borrowed it. Sorry.

That's okay. Molly looked at the comb. I was looking for it is all.

Sorry.

Molly half turned as if to walk out the door, and then turned back and said with a funny face on, Thanks.

Okay.

I'm going to go start dinner now.

Okay.

Molly shuffled out the door staring at the comb.

The door shut, Susan sat down on her bed and put the circle in her lap, looked at this moon. Now lying on the bed, the circle found itself on her chest as she gazed up at her own stars for what seemed like the very first time. The glow-in-the-dark universe, so close she could peel it away and cover her body with it if she wanted to. With the lights off, though, the only thing that really mattered was the moon returned to her by the doctor. The phosphorescent hole in her.

5

AND THE VIEW FROM A STAR LOOKING DOWN on the neighbourhood of a family missing one brother, one son, wouldn't be of a

straight line or a grid, no, it would be more like looking at a
drawing of smoke. Or, more accurately, a kind of root, a cement
rhizome of sidewalks lined against yards and houses, a system
cluttered with two-car garages and unused chimneys, fiddlehead-
like roads curling up into cul-de-sacs and freshly sodded parks, a
grey coil of slush-washed asphalt, unfinished houses on each
block, the beam skeletons exposing the dirt and scrub of an imagined neighourhood beyond this new neighbourhood. (She hates
this place, she wishes she were old enough to go away, the house
down the block exactly like your own house, exactly like the
house diagonally across the alley, exactly like . . .) Look down at
the system of houses, roads, adolescent trees, and convenience
stores. Look down at dirt alleys stabbed by wire-dangling telephone poles. Look down at a neighbourhood where there's no
beginning and no visible exit. No one living here can see beyond
here, when they're at home, in the dark, towards the world.
There's a high school being built, and there's already an elementary school. The two will eventually share a park. Look down at
the way the roads weave and knot. (Where could Eliot have been
taken, Ben is forced to wonder, remembering little of his life—
there's nowhere else possible for his son to be.) A system repeating itself into the infinity of the available real estate beyond itself,
poor farmers on one end and a dilapidated industrial district on
the other. The suburban recursion, a root with no flower. Look
down at the pattern which is not a pattern. Here is a thin spread
of houses creeping into the terrestrial emptiness around it.
Looking down and wondering where the boy is, where and how
he could ever have been taken out of this world, all-inclusive as it
is, a shelter cruelly planted with grocery stores and discount

clothing outlets and everything a person could want, supposedly, so that you never have to venture outside the walls meant to keep the noise of traffic from bothering those living next door to it. The safety of a place like this, smothered in sameness and snow. (Molly has tried to draw this neighbourhood so many times, from so many angles, but she's never seen it from above, has always wanted to, but she doesn't have the energy to lift a pencil any more, so what's the point.) Look at how the wind comes unexpectedly and steals away the lovely things, the leaves off trees and the fluttering torn pages of catalogues from department stores—; the children who play with wood and long knotted-together shoelaces have their hats blown down the street and they run after them as their parents scream for them to come home this very instant, this very instant, this very instant.

BEN SUDDENLY REMEMBERED THE MARMOT, who, at the moment Ben remembered it, was convulsing as programmed and more than two-thirds dead. It cried out Eliot's name many times without variation. On its ottoman, Molly watched it, then held it, talked to it.

Who am I? the marmot eventually asked.

You're a toy, Molly said, brushing back hair from its eyes.

I did not know that.

You used to know that.

Let's stay the alphabet.

Okay, Molly said, you begin.

One, two, three, four . . . The marmot's voice was beginning to break off now and then, as if bits were being extracted from the sine wave of its speech. Wa-n, t-o, th-ee, f-r.

Oh, Marmot, Molly cried, holding it up to her cheek, rocking it in her arms. That's not the alphabet.

She carried it up the stairs and into her bedroom and lay down next to Ben, who had thankfully stopped shivering and seemed to be asleep. With the marmot in her arms she softly hummed a children's bedtime song.

Go to sleep, go to sleep . . .

Please try again, the marmot said.

Shh, Molly pet it, go to sleep . . .

The marmot's body expanded as it took in what seemed to be a deep breath. It held the breath for a moment, then let out a whistling exhalation, closed its eyes, and relaxed. She could tell it was gone; the toy had died. She held it next to her in the warm bed and quickly fell into a dream.

WHEN BEN WOKE UP HE SAW HIS WIFE beside him with the marmot huddled against her and the marmot sounded like a bell. No, the telephone sounded like a bell. He turned and looked at the telephone but it didn't move. It rang again without moving. But then, telephones don't move at all, it was the marmot that moved. He looked towards the marmot, but it wasn't moving either. Now he was confused so he answered the phone.

Hello?

Your son is missing.

I know that.

I don't have him.

Neither do I. Who is this?

I took him, but I don't have him.

Ben thought for a moment and considered the marmot and his wife beside him in bed, and still nothing moved. Why did he want the marmot or the telephone to move? He was beginning to properly wake up and this dialectic was starting to show its flaws.

What did you say?

I said—Jesus. Jesus fucking Christ will you listen for fuck's sake?

Okay, okay. What is it?

I said, I said I took your son, your boy Eliot. I took him, fuck.

You. Finally he understood and it made him hunch forward like he might be sick, struggling to regain his mind. What do you mean you don't have him?

I don't have him. That's all.

Where are you?

Don't be stupid.

I'm sorry. I'm scared.

No, no. I'm sorry.

You're apologizing?

No, that's not what I meant. Fuck. Your stupid fucking kid is gone.

What do you mean he's gone, where'd he go?

How the fuck should I know? Think I'd call you if I knew where he was?

Ben wondered if the man sounded like him, if the voice on the other end of the telephone was the same voice as his own. How will that sound, he wondered, when the detectives play it back?

He tried to concentrate on not interrupting the man, so that their voices wouldn't be confused later.

What do you want me to do? Ben asked.

What do you want me to do. This is really fucking annoying. Don't talk down at me like that. I'm not so stupid. I'm not your fucking whatever, you can't manipulate me.

No, I didn't mean it that way.

I'm the one who took your boy. I'm the one who had him. So don't try and manipulate me, my mind.

Okay. I just want to know what you mean when you say you don't have him any more. Is he—I mean, is Eliot—?

What? Is he what? Say it.

Is he, is Eliot alive?

How the fuck should I know? It's cold out, it's cold where I am, is it cold where you are?

There's snow, yes.

Yeah, so who knows. He's probably dead. He's probably frozen to death, the little goddamn fucker.

You have to understand something, okay?

What? Ben listened as the man sniffed and coughed. What is it? the man said, his voice strangled and upset in a familiar way.

You have to understand that this is good news for me.

You think I don't know that?

That's all I'm saying.

Well, here I am.

Okay. So then, what you're saying is that Eliot got away?

He got away. Don't you fucking ask me where I am or some shit like that, or where he got away from or—

No, no. I probably wouldn't know where you meant anyhow.

No you wouldn't, that's right. That's exactly right, goddamn it. And the stupid kid, I'm sorry, but big mistake.

Tell me why you took him.

Eat shit.

Why, what's the difference now anyway?

I would not have killed your kid, understand that that's the difference now, okay, and probably he's dead in some field, frozen like a whatever. Like a bird.

I just don't understand.

Whoop-dee-do, okay. Big whoop what you think.

It's just that— I don't understand.

What don't you understand? What?

Did you always plan to take him or—?

He heard the man sigh. No, he said.

Then why'd you do it?

There was no reply, all Ben could hear was the ambient wind of the connection, probably long-distance, a pay phone somewhere using a phone card probably bought at a nondescript gas station somewhere else. Suddenly he heard the man was crying.

What's wrong?

I love him, I take care of him, I make sure he's fed three times a day and goes to bed exactly on time. I'm his father.

What?

That's right.

What are you saying?

You heard me.

You're wrong.

Shut up.

No, listen to me.

You're wrong.

Shut the fuck up.

I'm his father.

I'm his father and you know that.

You just think you're his father.

Will you just listen?

Don't do this.

Don't do this, I can't believe you.

I should fucking kill you.

I can't believe you talk like this.

I should find you and kill you.

It's too late. He's gone.

Haven't you figured out how much he means to me?

You took my kid. That's all you did. Anybody can do that.

He's my kid, I didn't take him.

I'm not having this argument.

You're the one who's wrong.

You're not his father, he doesn't know you.

He knows me.

And yet you don't know where he is.

No, he said, I don't know where he is. Now the man was blubbering and it made Ben angry. Later the police would have trouble separating their voices, but for Ben it was no different right now than it had ever been before. It was very clear to him who was who.

I don't know where he is, the man cried.

Ben looked to his wife and said into the phone, Goodbye then, and hung up.

Finally the phone call he'd been waiting for had come. He was fully awake now, two months after Eliot had disappeared.

7

FOR THE FIRST TIME IN MONTHS he was fully aware of the fact that he was stepping out of the house. The sensation of having been in his yard was his closest thing to a memory of being outside, but that hardly counted. Now he was about to get into a police car with his family and go to the hospital where Intensive Care reportedly had their son Eliot.

Pulled over his arms his winter coat, now zipped up, then a pair of leather gloves, a toque, and some waterproof shoes; he stepped out and locked the front door and followed his wife and his daughter into the back of an unmarked police car, while a detective rounded the hood, opened the car door, and sat down in the driver's seat.

I left the car running to keep it warm, the detective said, unzipping his jacket. It's a cold day, he said.

It's winter, Molly said.

It sure is, the detective said, levered the car into drive and waited for two other cars to pull out before he edged away from the curb and down the road.

Susan sat in the front with the detective, quiet, with her head down, the dead marmot in her lap. I'm scared, she said.

The detective nodded, It's going to be okay. It's going to be good.

In the back seat, with her fingernail, Molly scratched a man into the ice formed on the window. She drew a man running, while signposts and fenceposts and mailboxes scrolled past the car—; Ben looked away and down at his gloves. He pulled off the gloves and examined his hands. Turning to his own window in the back of the car, he too scratched something in the ice with his fingernail.

Molly, he said and touched her shoulder.

What is it? she said.

He pointed to the window.

On the glass he'd written, Hi Sweetie.

THE HOSPITAL STAFF WAS RESPECTFUL, giving them a wide berth as they made their way down the glassy tiled floors, escorted by detectives past doors with circular windows, guardrails and wheelchair accessible inclines, doors that opened at the push of a large, square steel button, the typical smell of antiseptics that was no less acrid than the fluids they absorbed and masked, the various threatening gurneys and mechanical beds in the hallways, the black-bagged garbage pails—, they walked past it all, terribly nervous.

A doctor said, I should prepare you by saying that your son is in critical condition.

Another doctor said, Ben? Is that you?

Todd?

I thought it was you. I haven't seen you since—

It must be second year.

That long? Holy smoke.

You look good.

Well, you—

You're a doctor now.

Yeah, yeah.

That's good, Ben said. Look, it's nice to see you but, I—

The doctor nodded and waved goodbye and politely disappeared through a doorway.

They stopped in front of a door and the doctor took a breath.

You don't know how relieved our staff was. We're very happy for you.

The doctor whispered that he'd wait outside while the family went in.

MOLLY PRESSED THE DOOR OPEN and they all slowly crept in, one after the other, towards the bed and the machines surrounding it, and their son and brother, lying under green sheets, poked with tubes and sensors. He was there in front of Molly, sleeping.

Oh, she said and fell to the bed and wept and stroked his hair and kissed him mercilessly. Oh, she said. She felt at his arms and removed a hand from beneath the sheets and held it and kissed it. He was so thin and pale he was nearly blue with veins, and his eyes were both bruised, his glasses nowhere to be found. A long cut starting on his neck ran below his nightie, gross with new black stitching. A slender tube ran up one nostril.

Susan ran to the other side of the bed. She cried and laughed and told her brother how much she loved him, how much she loved him. She loved him so much.

He opened his eyes finally, and they swirled for a moment before becoming lucid. He studied his mother and sister, and his father behind. A little smile they all recognized broke out on his face.

We're so happy to see you, Molly said.

I escaped, Eliot said.

That's right, honey, Molly said. You did.

Ben walked towards his son, kneeled down and brushed his hair.

How are you? he asked.

I escaped.

I know, Ben said, and I couldn't be happier, you little nut.

I brought you some Twix bars, Susan said, rummaging in her pockets. But they're kind of old. She started to cry again.

Marmot, Eliot said when he saw what else his sister had with her, his lip trembling.

I'm so sorry, Eliot, she said and passed him the toy. We tried everything but he died a few days ago.

Eliot gently turned the marmot on its back and for a few seconds pressed down a button on its stomach. Finally the marmot began to move again, eyes opening, head twisting.

Hello, what's your name? the marmot said.

Eliot.

Hello, Eliot. You look like a nice boy. Would you like to sing a song?

ACKNOWLEDGEMENTS

Jon Sawatsky & Laura St. Pierre;[1] Jessica Johnson;[2] Zsuzsi Gartner;[3] Rick Maddocks;[4] Charlotte Gill, Nancy Lee, Laisha Rosnau & Chris Tenove;[5] Madeleine Thien;[6] Kevin Chong & Steven Galloway;[7] Keith Maillard & Peggy Thompson & Al Forrie & Caroline Adderson & George McWhirter & Shannon Stewart[8] & (classmates); Marita Dachsel & Sioux Browning;[9] two Michaels;[10] Denise Ryan;[11] Josh Fullan;[12] Ken Roux, Jeffrey Allport, Nicole Obadia, Tara Malinowski & Tom Scholte;[13] Liz Philips;[14] Mark Jarman;[15] Marcel Dzama & Martin Gould;[16] Barbara Berson;[17] Anne McDermid (& Co.);[18] Heather Frechette.[19]

1. Inestimable friends, first & foremost.

2. For being there when I wrote the great bulk of these stories—I'm indebted to her intelligence & honesty.

3. Hardcore inspiration & generous advice—the apical Anxious Girl, god bless.

4. For the simple art of living.

5. For, among other things, good company—our steadfast little Groop.

6. Dinners of endangered species, etc.

7. All that obscene amount of time spent at Helen's Grill talking obscenely.

8. Teachers, exceptionally so.

9. Grateful for your help on more than one of these stories.

10. Schultz & Kennedy.

11. For insane amounts of support in the strange world of Saturday journalism.

12. Known in e-mails.

13. For many small personal things I won't mention.

14. Who was first to publish, in *Grain Magazine*, my fiction, "Sheep Dub," which went on to appear in *The Journey Prize Anthology*, no. 12.

15. Second published story, "Attempts at a Great Relationship" in *The Fiddlehead*.

16. Deluxe interior & exterior art & design.

17. My esteemed & awesome editor.

18. My inimitable & cherished agent.

19. Love of my life.

marcel DEAMA